"We need to get something clear right now, Tara."

Brad's words were very matter-of-fact, his attitude all business. "I expect to have my instructions obeyed without hesitation or questions. Your life could depend on your immediate response to my orders."

Tara glared angrily at him, but he stood his ground and refused to back down. Brad Harrison had her confused. He was a virtual stranger who had burst uninvited into her world, tried to take control of her life and demanded that she trust him. Yet his unwavering gaze sent a ripple of desire through her body unlike anything she had ever experienced. There was a lot more at stake here than a question of control.

Every time he touched her, a sensual rush coursed through her body. It was totally inappropriate for the situation and equally out of character for her. But for reasons she could not clearly fathom, she had made the decision to tentatively trust this very sexy and desirable man. Hopefully it would not be the biggest mistake of her life…or worse yet, the last decision she would ever make.

Dear Harlequin Intrigue Reader,

Harlequin Intrigue has four new stories to blast you out of the winter doldrums. Look what we've got heating up for you this month.

Sylvie Kurtz brings you the first in her two-book miniseries FLESH AND BLOOD. Fifteen years ago, a burst of anger by the banks of the raging Red Thunder River changed the lives of two brothers forever. In *Remembering Red Thunder*, Sheriff Chance Conover struggles to regain the memory of his life, his wife and their unborn baby before a man out for revenge silences him permanently.

You can also look for the second book in the four-book continuity series MORIAH'S LANDING— *Howling in the Darkness* by B.J. Daniels. Jonah Ries has always sensed something was wrong in Moriah's Landing, but when he accidentally crashes Kat Ridgemont's online blind date, he realizes the tough yet fragile beauty has more to fear than even the town's superstitions.

In *Operation: Reunited* by Linda O. Johnston, Alexa Kenner is on the verge of marriage when she meets John O'Rourke, a man who eerily resembles her dead lover, Cole Rappaport, who died in a terrible explosion. Could they be one and the same?

And finally this month, one by one government witnesses who put away a mob associate have been killed, with only Tara Ford remaining. U.S. Deputy Marshal Brad Harrison vows to protect Tara by placing her *In His Safekeeping*— by Shawna Delacorte.

We hope you enjoy these books, and remember to come back next month for more selections from MORIAH'S LANDING and FLESH AND BLOOD!

Sincerely,

Denise O'Sullivan
Associate Senior Editor
Harlequin Intrigue

IN HIS SAFEKEEPING

SHAWNA DELACORTE

HARLEQUIN®

TORONTO • NEW YORK • LONDON
AMSTERDAM • PARIS • SYDNEY • HAMBURG
STOCKHOLM • ATHENS • TOKYO • MILAN • MADRID
PRAGUE • WARSAW • BUDAPEST • AUCKLAND

ISBN 0-373-22656-X

IN HIS SAFEKEEPING

This edition published by arrangement with Harlequin Books S.A.

® and TM are trademarks of the publisher. Trademarks indicated with
® are registered in the United States Patent and Trademark Office, the
Canadian Trade Marks Office and in other countries.

Visit us at www.eHarlequin.com

Printed in U.S.A.

ABOUT THE AUTHOR

Shawna Delacorte has delayed her move to Washington State, staying in the Midwest in order to spend some additional time with family. She still travels as often as time permits, and is looking forward to visiting several new places during the upcoming year while continuing to devote herself to writing full-time. Shawna would appreciate hearing from her readers. She can be reached at 6505 E. Central #300, Wichita, KS 67206-1924.

Books by Shawna Delacorte

HARLEQUIN INTRIGUE
412—LOVER UNKNOWN
520—SECRET LOVER
656—IN HIS SAFEKEEPING

Don't miss any of our special offers. Write to us at the following address for information on our newest releases.

Harlequin Reader Service
U.S.: 3010 Walden Ave., P.O. Box 1325, Buffalo, NY 14269
Canadian: P.O. Box 609, Fort Erie, Ont. L2A 5X3

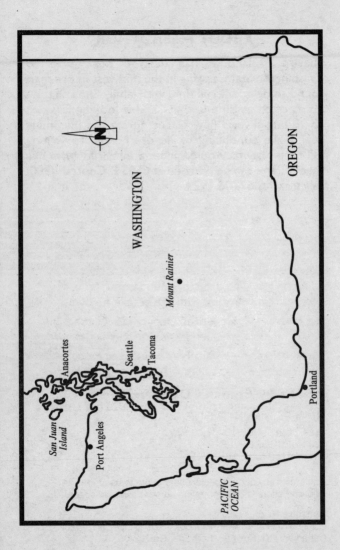

CAST OF CHARACTERS

Brad Harrison—Has this Deputy U.S. Marshal uncovered a diabolical plot or is it just a series of odd coincidences?

Tara Ford—Is she really in danger, and if so, can she trust her life to this handsome stranger?

Shirley Bennett—Is she really the efficient employee she seems to be, or does she have a separate agenda?

Judy Lameroux—Is Tara's new co-worker the friend she pretends to be, or does she have an ulterior motive for her kindness?

Thom Satterly—Has his stalled career with the Marshals Service pushed him into a life of crime?

Ralph Newman—Has this Deputy U.S. Marshal's mounting gambling debts put him into a compromising position with the people he owes?

Ken Walsh—Is this retired Deputy U.S. Marshal the friend and mentor Brad Harrison thinks he is?

Danny Vincent—Is Tara Ford's ex-fiancé responsible for the strange happenings that have plagued her?

Doreen Vincent—Is John Vincent's only child following the same crime-strewn path as her father?

**To Marilee
We'll all miss you**

Chapter One

A car pulled into the driveway, drawing Brad Harrison's attention back to the house he had been watching. The woman climbing out of the car matched his photograph of Tara Ford and then some. The photo definitely did not do her justice. For one thing, it was only a head shot and didn't reveal the fantastic body that went along with that gorgeous face. He scanned her personal information in his file—twenty-nine years old, five foot seven, auburn hair, hazel eyes and not married.

He watched as she bent over to retrieve the sack of groceries from the trunk of her car. Her tailored slacks hugged the curve of her hip without being obvious and the soft knit of her sweater rested gently against her breasts. He took a deep breath to break the tightness that pulled across his chest, but it didn't help much.

She was certainly beautiful, but that didn't tell him how she got involved with John Vincent. Was she really the innocent bystander she *claimed* to be or was she...

He snapped to attention, quickly dismissing his personal thoughts and becoming all business when he saw her nervously glance up and down the street. He unzipped his jacket for easy access to the 9mm semiautomatic handgun, but did not remove it from the clip-on belt holster. Her gaze fell on him for a second or two, causing him to crease his forehead in concentration. She appeared to be searching for something, her apprehension marring her delicately sculpted features. It was not the type of thing he would expect from someone who didn't have any worries.

The tension knotted in his stomach as he continued to watch her house. The uncertainty of how to proceed weighed heavily on him. The last remnants of daylight faded. He had seen everything he could. He started his car and slowly pulled away from the curb with his headlights off.

TARA FORD CAUTIOUSLY peeked out from behind the mini-blinds at the kitchen window. The man who had been sitting in the car parked across the street was gone. She wished she had gotten a better look at his face, but was afraid to stare for fear he would suspect she had noticed him. For the past few weeks she had been plagued by an uncomfortable sensation that someone was watching her, but this was the first time she had actually seen who it might be.

She wanted to believe it was her imagination, a residual effect from the turmoil of being one of the key witnesses at John Vincent's trial. Her portion of the testimony dealt with information she had discovered while employed by Green Valley Construction—the looting of his company's pension fund and the income he had hidden from the Internal Revenue Service. But the testimony of other witnesses showing his bookmaking operation, loan-sharking and ties to organized crime had come as a complete surprise to her. That had been six months ago. John Vincent had been convicted and sent to prison. For a while everything seemed to be okay. She thought she had put the nightmare behind her. A little tremor of anxiety rippled across her skin. She wasn't so sure anymore.

The ringing phone startled her out of her thoughts. She placed her hand on the receiver, then froze as a shiver of trepidation darted up her back. She was sure it was another of those calls where someone was there but no one said anything. She had been plagued with a rash of them over the past few weeks. On the fifth ring she finally picked up the receiver. The apprehension churned in her stomach before she could even say anything.

"Hello." She heard someone breathing. She spoke louder, trying to force a calm control to her voice. "Hello...is anyone there?"

"Tara...it's Danny."

The shock left her momentarily speechless. Danny Vincent. John Vincent's thirty-four-year-old nephew—and her ex-fiancé.

An odd combination of irritation and relief passed through her. It wasn't her anonymous caller, but it was the last person she wanted to hear from. Her displeasure forced its way into her voice. "How did you get my unlisted phone number?"

"Well, I have to admit that it took a little doing. First I had to find out where you had moved."

Her anxiety level increased. "Have you been following me and making anonymous phone calls?"

"Following you? Anonymous phone calls? What are you talking about? I only discovered where you were living a few days ago and just got your phone number yesterday."

Her exasperation traveled the phone line as she spoke. "What do you want, Danny?"

"I thought we might have dinner. Are you free tomorrow night?"

"No. I'm not free tomorrow night or any other night. It's over between us. I thought that should have been obvious when I broke off our engagement."

"Just a friendly little dinner. Surely that couldn't hurt anything."

A new wariness rose inside her. Why now? Why after all this time should he suddenly have the urge to track her down and want to have dinner? Especially when her testimony at his uncle's trial helped get him convicted.

"No…no dinner, friendly or otherwise. Please don't call me again." She hung up without waiting for a response. Even though she had broken off the engagement three years ago, she and Danny had still come in contact periodically due to the fact that they both worked for his uncle, although Danny wasn't in the office very often. But she hadn't seen or talked to him since the day she quit her job at Green Valley Construction and agreed to testify against John Vincent.

A sick feeling welled inside her, one laced with trepidation. Could Danny possibly be the person responsible for harassing her? An attempt to get back at her for testifying against his uncle? Perhaps combined with some residual anger over her having broken their engagement? A show of anger certainly wasn't anything unusual for Danny Vincent. Nor was there anything new about his desire to control everything—including her. It had been bad enough to have to put up with her mother's manipulations for so many years, but when Danny started doing the same type of thing to her she knew she needed to get out of the relationship.

She had refused to put up with his outbursts when she objected to him making decisions for her. The final straw had been when he canceled hotel and flight reservations she had made for her vacation without even consulting her. She had been angry with him and he had responded by actually threatening her. Five minutes later their relationship was finished and she had told him she wanted nothing to do with him again.

Then her mother had started in with her incessant nagging and criticism, this time about how Tara should have forgiven Danny. After all, one day he would probably own Green Valley Construction and Tara would have a comfortable life. That had been a pivotal downturning point in her rapidly declining relationship with her mother and the impetus for her vow never to allow anyone to have any control over her life again.

So, what had prompted Danny to call her? And why now after so much time had passed? The headache throbbed at her temples. Her hand trembled as she turned on the water and reached for a glass. She took two aspirin, then leaned back against the counter and closed her eyes.

Every day of late had become a new experience in the bizarre and stressful. Her personal life had been a tangled mess ever since the day she had agreed to testify at John Vincent's trial. She had become leery of strangers and fearful about going out alone at night. She had started to feel as if she was a prisoner in her own home.

All six of the primary witnesses against John Vincent had been threatened and were put under the protection of the U.S. Marshals Service for the duration of the trial. A couple of weeks ago she had thought about contacting the marshals to ask for protection again, but decided against it. What could she say to them? She didn't have any proof, only an unsubstantiated feeling that something was very wrong. Were her concerns real or only her imagination? It was a frightening place to be, caught in the middle between her unconfirmed fears on one side and what might be real danger on the other.

She took a deep breath, held it for several seconds, then slowly exhaled in an attempt to bring a calm to her inner turmoil. She had survived the threats before the trial and taken charge of her life. She certainly wasn't going to let this get the better of her. Then the phone rang again. Apprehension surged through her body followed by a sinking feeling. Her throat started to close off. She took another swallow of water and quickly switched on the answering machine. Anonymous caller or Danny Vincent—either way she didn't want to answer it.

She nervously paced back and forth between the living room and kitchen. She needed a security system for the house…she needed a large watchdog…she needed a gun. She stopped pacing. A *gun?* Had she totally lost her mind? A gun meant violence and said that someone could be hurt…or worse yet, killed. That was definitely not what she needed and certainly the last thing she wanted in her house or in her life.

She gathered her determination. What she really needed was to get her anxieties under control and stop making more out of the circumstances than they deserved. She had let her imagination run away with her common sense. She took a calming breath in an attempt to settle the jittery sensation churning inside her, then opened the refrigerator and took out some lettuce and a tomato to make a salad.

After eating dinner, she watched television for a bit then took a book to bed and read for a while until she became drowsy. But sleep eluded her. Troubled thoughts kept taking her to the car that had been parked across the street and the man who seemed to be watching her house. An uneasiness burrowed its way into her consciousness. The more she tried to ignore it, the stronger it pushed at her. Had he returned? Was he watching her house again?

The uncertainty forced her out of bed. She made her way through the darkened house and peeked out the living-room window. Everything looked normal, yet her concern refused to leave. She finally managed a few hours of troubled sleep.

BRAD SPENT a restless night. He had tossed and turned, his mind refusing to relinquish the onslaught of thoughts, foremost of which was what to do about Tara Ford. It continued to plague him as he drove to work. He had a busy morning, lots of details to take care of that had nothing to do with the immediacy of his Tara Ford problem. But even though he stayed physically busy, his thoughts were never very far from her and the mental image that had burned into his mind.

At lunchtime he drove to Tara's place of employment,

parked his car, then continued on foot. There were several places to have lunch within a two-block area of her office and he intended to check them all, hoping she hadn't elected to have lunch at her desk. The third place he tried proved successful. He peered in the window of the deli and spotted her seated at a table with an attractive blond woman in her early thirties. He took in Tara's sleek form and beautiful face.

His throat tightened and his mouth went dry, causing him to bristle with irritation. It had been a long time since he had come up against this type of involuntary physical reaction to any woman. He didn't seem to have any control over it, something inexcusable for a man whose very life depended on maintaining control not only of himself, but everything that went on around him.

He collected his composure and entered the deli. He ordered a sandwich, then made his way across the room, smiling politely when she looked up at him. He selected a booth far enough away that he wasn't right next to her but close enough to hear her conversation.

While eating his lunch he eavesdropped on the two women, their conversation telling him that they worked together. They discussed a work situation that had occurred at the office that morning, talked about a movie they had seen and discussed the latest best-selling book. The choice of topics was ordinary. The women appeared to be nothing more than two friends having lunch together. The only thing contradicting the outward appearance was the way Tara nervously eyed everyone who entered the deli. She seemed every bit as edgy as when she'd carried in her sack of groceries from her car. He had nothing to compare her actions with, no knowledge of how she behaved before the John Vincent case, but she did seem anxiety ridden.

He also found her much more beautiful up close than at a distance, so much so that she nearly knocked him for a loop. The physical attraction was immediate. He tried to shrug it off as being the understandable allure of a beautiful woman. Probably nothing more than the fact that it had been several months since he'd had a date. At least he wanted to believe that was all there was to it.

The two women left the deli. He noted that the blond woman was about the same height as Tara, maybe an inch shorter. His gaze became riveted to Tara's retreating form. He studied the way she moved as she walked toward the door, a smooth graceful walk almost reminiscent of a dancer. He lingered on the way her clothes fit her body and the glossy highlights of her auburn hair. The heat of desire settled low in his body in defiance of his controlled outer calm. After taking a steadying breath, Brad followed her out the door and watched as the two women walked back toward their office.

Over the next two days he made sure he was on hand when she arrived at work, went to lunch and got off work. Then he kept her house under surveillance for a couple of hours in the evening. And each time Brad saw her he became more fascinated by her, with who she was, how she became involved with all of this, what she wanted out of life. And underlying that was the very distinct effect her voice had on his senses. It possessed a low throaty quality without being forced or artificial. A little ripple of excitement made its way through his body just as when he'd first heard her speak at the deli.

Uncertainty and doubts swirled in his head. His original plan had been to keep her under surveillance until he could gather more information and collect enough facts to prove his theory of a conspiracy in which it seemed that Tara Ford figured prominently. He needed to confirm his suspicions before he could act. But the more Brad thought about it, he was not at all sure he was following the best procedure by continuing to watch her from a distance. He needed to initiate a face-to-face meeting with her, something that would appear accidental and not alert her to anything being wrong...and the sooner the better.

THE NEXT DAY Brad spotted Tara having lunch at the deli with the same woman as before. He entered and ordered a sandwich. He carried his food toward a table against the back wall. As he passed Tara's chair he purposely bumped it, jarring her arm and causing her to spill a glass of water.

A startled Tara jumped up from her seat. "Oh, no..."

He immediately grabbed her arm as if steadying her so she wouldn't fall. "Are you all right? I didn't hurt you, did I?" Her felt her muscles tighten under his touch and the tension course through her body, something far more than a response to a simple accident.

"I'm fine."

He tried to hold on to her arm, but she eased it out of his grasp as quickly as possible without jerking it away. "Are you sure you're okay? That was very clumsy of me. I'm sorry..."

His gaze locked on her for a moment, just long enough to drink in the luminescent quality of her hazel eyes. But he found something else there, too...something that disturbed him. She radiated a certain level of wariness, an underlying layer of fear marring her beautiful features. Again, something far more than what should have been caused by a simple bumping of a chair. At that precise moment he wanted to do everything in his power to protect her, rather than suspect her of being part of a conspiracy...to keep her from becoming victim number five in what he believed was a conspiracy of very clever murders of the witnesses in the John Vincent trial.

She shot a quick look of displeasure in his direction as she picked up a napkin from the table and dabbed at the water spot on her cream-colored blouse. He grabbed another napkin and mopped up the water from the edge of the table where it dripped to the floor. He noticed the blond woman hadn't made any move to help. Her blue eyes seemed to be taking in everything, almost as if she were studying the situation. He needed to find out who she was.

Brad tried not to stare but couldn't keep his gaze from gravitating to the wet spot on Tara's blouse and the way it revealed the delicate lacy bra underneath. He sucked in a steadying breath and tried to pull together his rapidly disintegrating composure. It was the first time he had been this close to her—close enough to reach out and touch the creamy texture of her skin, to clearly see her eyes…and the uneasiness they held. He shook off the unwelcome pull on his senses and his inappropriate response. Purposely bumping her chair to create a face-to-face connection had produced far more than he had bargained for. He had to pull his composure together. He couldn't afford the personal distraction. Lives were at stake.

"Are you sure you're okay?"

"I'm fine, except for this…" The heat of embarrassment spread across her cheeks when she looked down and saw the way the water spot had made her blouse nearly transparent. She pulled the fabric away from her body, then glanced up at this tall stranger.

She had noticed him on several occasions over the past couple of days, but this was the first time she had gotten a close look at him. Her breath caught in her lungs—a combination of panic and surprise. The gash on his chin, the split lip and the faint remains of abrasions across his cheek gave him the appearance of a violent man, someone to be wary of, while in no way detracting from his handsome features. In direct contrast his crystal-blue eyes revealed warmth, yet held a hidden mystery. His dark hair was styled in a casual manner.

"This was all my fault. I insist on paying to have your blouse cleaned." The tantalizing fragrance of her perfume captured his attention, causing his nostrils to flare as the scent wafted past him. It was light, spicy and sexy without being overwhelming or obvious.

"Thank you…but that won't be necessary. It's just a little water. It'll be fine."

He reached for his wallet and pulled out a twenty-dollar bill. "I'd feel better if you'd let me pay to have it dry-cleaned." He suddenly felt like a total incompetent, falling all over himself and offering her money. Beyond purposely bumping her, all his carefully prepared maneuvers failed to materialize. The moment he looked into her eyes a shortness of breath hit him, nearly driving away his purpose in being there.

He quickly pulled himself together, smiled and extended the money toward her. "Here, take this…please. It will make me feel better about being so clumsy."

"No, really, I couldn't." Something was wrong. He seemed to be trying too hard. Or was it just her imagination again? She wrinkled her forehead in concentration. There was something about him that left her uneasy. And at the same time there was an unidentifiable quality that she found incredibly exciting.

The angle of his head, the definition of his features—a sudden jolt of panic grabbed at her. This was the same man she had seen parked in front of her house that night. She was positive…well, she was sort of sure. The fear pushed at her until she couldn't control it any longer. She had to get away from this very disconcerting man and quickly. She gestured toward her friend. "We were just about to leave. So, if you'll excuse me…"

"The least I can do is introduce myself. I'm Brad Harrison." He stuck out his hand, clearly expecting her to accept it. He cocked his head, raised an eyebrow and stared at her as if waiting for her to do or say something.

She nervously cleared her throat. "My name is Tara." She hesitated a moment, then accepted his handshake. The moment their hands clasped…skin against skin…a surge of sensual heat raced up her arm and through her body. She saw the look of surprise on his face that said she wasn't alone in the experience. She quickly withdrew from his touch and took a step back. A shortness of breath told her something significant had happened, but she wasn't sure exactly what.

"It's a pleasure to meet you, Tara." He glanced at the blond woman, nodding his head to include her while reinforcing his need to find out who she was. "Maybe we'll bump into each other again sometime." He forced an upbeat laugh. "But hopefully without such disastrous results."

Brad watched as Tara and her friend left the deli. The warmth of her touch lingered, giving impetus to his loosely constructed plan to protect her. It was odd the way she hurried off, as if she had suddenly been frightened by something. Had he blown it? A little ripple of disgust told him it had been a perfect example of amateur time in the way he had handled the entire incident. No one had ever thrown him off track the way she just had. There was something very special about her, but he wasn't sure exactly what. She gave off vulnerability, yet she did not come across as helpless.

He had orchestrated the physical contact but hadn't been prepared for the surge of lust that jolted his reality. If this wasn't a *business* matter—and a very serious one—he would definitely have asked her out with one objective in mind. But it *was* business. Serious business. Life-and-death business—literally.

He tried to force his libido aside and concentrate on what had to be done, but thoughts of a much more personal nature continued to circulate in the back of his mind. A very desirable woman and a very serious business…a dangerous combination for sure.

BRAD HARRISON…Tara kept turning the name over in her mind as she sat at her desk. She knew he was the man she had caught glimpses of the past few days, but she wasn't sure whether he was the man she had seen parked in front of her house that night. And there was something very strange about their meeting in the deli at lunchtime. The entire incident left her decidedly unsettled and on edge. She had noticed him as soon as he entered, just as she had the previous time when he was at the deli while she was having lunch. It was almost as if he had gone out of his way to pass by her chair. There were plenty of other routes to the tables against the back wall without passing by the table where she and Judy Lameroux were having lunch.

Equally distressing was the wave of desire that had swept through her the moment they shook hands. Her immediate attraction to this mysterious stranger was confusing yet undeniable. But with the strange feelings and odd incidents that had been happening to her lately she knew she needed to be very cautious around strangers. Should she trust her fears or her desires? She shook her head. There was nothing that dictated that she had to make a decision between the two. It was a onetime accidental meeting—nothing more.

She couldn't afford the luxury of dwelling on the thought any longer. She had to get her life straightened out, not complicate it. Whether Brad Harrison was nothing more than a man who simply worked in the same neighborhood she did or a mysterious stranger with an ulterior motive who had been following her, she had to keep her wits about her and maintain a distance from him.

"Are you okay?"

"What?" A startled Tara jumped at the sound of Judy's voice. "Oh…yes, I'm fine."

"Are you sure? You looked like you were a million miles away."

"It's nothing, just a few things that I was trying to sort out in my mind. Nothing important."

A teasing grin came to Judy's lips. "I don't suppose it had anything to do with that Brad Harrison person who bumped into your chair at lunch. The sexual magnetism practically oozed from his pores and he was obviously interested in you.''

"I…uh…hadn't noticed." A twinge of apprehension poked at Tara's consciousness. Brad Harrison had been dominating her thoughts all afternoon, and regardless of her level of anxiety she had to admit Judy was right…the man oozed a lot of magnetic sex appeal.

"It's way past quitting time. Do you have any plans for tonight?"

Tara forced a laugh, an upbeat attitude she didn't really feel. "My only plans are to go home and do some laundry, otherwise I won't have any clean clothes to wear tomorrow."

Judy emitted a soft chuckle. "That sure sounds like an exciting evening. I'll see you in the morning. Good night."

"Good night, Judy." Tara cleaned off her desk, then left the building. She walked the half block to the company parking lot.

"Miss Ford…Tara…wait a moment." Brad stepped out from behind his car and approached her.

Total panic gripped her the second she saw Brad and heard him call to her. She stopped in her tracks, a nearly uncontrollable urge to run tempered with a curiosity about what he wanted. She took a step back, trying to put some distance between them without showing the fear that pumped through her body. Was this the culmination of her feelings that someone had been watching her? Was this man really a deranged stalker who meant to do her harm? She tried to swallow the lump in her throat without much success.

"How did you know my name?" Tara barely got the words out as her throat tightened and her mouth went dry.

Brad extended a friendly smile. "We met at the deli, remember? I introduced myself and you told me your name."

"I never told you my last name." She took another step

back while desperately scanning the area for anyone who could help her. She fumbled with her keys, but was all thumbs as she tried to set off her car alarm and use the automatic car starter, ending up by dropping the remote on the ground. To her dismay, they seemed to be the only two people in the parking lot. She had never felt so alone, as if the entire world had deserted her. She mustered as much courage as she could find and stuck her hand inside her purse.

"Don't come any closer. I...I have a gun and I'm not afraid to use it." Her fingers touched everything she could find, but the only item that even remotely resembled a weapon was a nail file. Her heart pounded so hard she was sure he could hear it. Her stomach churned to the point where she feared she would become physically ill.

Brad held up his hands, showing her they were empty. "I'm not here to hurt you, Miss Ford." He took another step toward her.

Total blind panic gripped her insides and twisted them into knots. She wrapped the shoulder strap of her purse around her hand and swung it at him. Her improvised weapon made solid contact with the side of his head. He staggered backward a couple of steps. She turned to run, but not in time. His strong grip caught her arm, then his hand clamped over her mouth before she could scream.

Chapter Two

"Don't be afraid. I'm not going to hurt you." He shouldn't have waited so long to make contact with her. He had wanted to wait until he had more information, could present a more reliable scenario to her, but he couldn't put it off any longer. "Listen to me. I'm a deputy U.S. marshal. I believe you're in danger and I'm here to help you. We need to talk."

She felt her eyes widen in shock as she stared at him in stunned disbelief. Her adrenaline surge began to subside and she stopped struggling. He finally removed his hand.

"You're what?" She had trouble making sense of what he'd said, but then so many things didn't make sense of late.

He released her arm, then slowly reached into his pocket and withdrew his identification. "I'm a deputy U.S. marshal. I believe your life is in danger. Can we go someplace where we can talk in private, rather than stand out in the open in the middle of this parking lot?"

"I…uh…" She wasn't sure what to think or say. A deputy U.S. marshal—it was the last thing she expected to hear. But could she believe him? Anyone could flash a badge and claim to be a deputy marshal. She took a step back, enough to remove herself from his immediate reach. "I think I should call my attorney."

He took a step toward her but the panic that immediately blanketed her features stopped him. "That's your privilege, but there really isn't any need to do that. You aren't being accused of any wrongdoing. I'd prefer that you didn't call your lawyer, at least not until you've heard me out. You don't need to say anything, all you need to do is listen."

"Well..." She shoved down her anxiety, making a bold attempt to regain control of her galloping pulse rate and pounding heartbeat.

He indicated his car and opened the passenger door for her. "Shall we go?"

"Uh...no...I'd rather drive my own car, maybe meet you in a public place...a restaurant perhaps."

"Okay. Any particular one?"

She gave him the name of a restaurant she frequented. They each took their respective cars and left the parking lot.

THE ANGRY WORDS traveled over the phone line. "I thought you told me you'd have everything handled by now. Why the delay? I don't like surprises. Is there some problem you haven't told me about?"

"No...no problems. I've already contacted Pat and said I wanted the job finished tonight. Winthrope has already been taken care of and I was assured that things would be wrapped up very quickly."

"You waited too long. I think there may be a deputy marshal involved now."

"You mean she's been put under the protection of the Marshals Service?" The quaver in his voice conveyed his apprehension at the unexpected news.

"No, I don't think so. I think it's just one man who has made contact with her. He seems to be working on his own."

"Then it shouldn't be a problem."

"You'd better be right."

BRAD ARRIVED at the restaurant first, made arrangements for a table, then waited just inside the door. A few minutes passed and still no Tara Ford. She had been right behind him when they had left the parking lot. A moment of alarm pushed at him. Had she changed her mind? Was she out there alone and vulnerable, not knowing that someone wanted her dead? Again he mentally kicked himself for not contacting her sooner, even though he still didn't have anything more to go on than strong suspicions and too much coincidence without any solid proof.

He wondered if she had decided to skip out on him. A hint of panic pushed at him as he reached for the door, but it opened before he touched it and she entered the restaurant. He quickly pulled her aside. "I have a table for us in a nice quiet corner."

Her anxiety level increased as soon as they were seated. She had started to turn around and go home rather than drive to the restaurant. But then her common sense told her that he knew where she lived, so she might as well meet him. "You claim to be a deputy U.S. marshal. I don't recall seeing you before or during the Vincent trial when I seemed to be surrounded by deputy marshals."

"I have Special Operations Group training and I'm occasionally assigned to them for specific jobs. I was on a fugitive-apprehension mission out of state at the time deputies were assigned to protect the witnesses, so I never became involved with the John Vincent case."

She frowned in confusion as she studied him for a moment. "Then why are you involved with it now, rather than one of the deputies who protected us during the trial?"

"Well…that's kind of a convoluted story. I was wounded during my last mission with the Special Operations Group and was placed on recuperative leave then came back to work on light restricted duty until the doctor releases me for active duty again. Part of that light duty has been updating case files. One of those files is the John Vincent case."

She looked at him questioningly. "There's something new with the case since the trial ended?"

"Yes. Two weeks after John Vincent started serving his prison term, he died of a heart attack. I've been notifying the witnesses and others involved in the case of his death."

"Uh...do you mind if I see your credentials again? You flashed them rather quickly and I'd like a better look."

Certainly a reasonable request along with her valid questions, but one that only confirmed his assessment of the situation. Tara Ford was afraid of something and being very cautious. Perhaps it was that caution that had protected her from harm so far. Brad took his identification from his pocket and handed it to her. He watched as she studied the identification card, the badge, then glanced several times back and forth between his photograph and him.

He tried to make light of the situation. "I should look more like that picture in a few days when this gash on my chin and my cuts and scrapes finish healing. I was on courthouse duty last week and got into a little scuffle with a very large man who took exception to the judge's ruling."

She handed his identification back to him without responding to his comment.

"Good evening." The waiter handed them menus. "It's nice to see you again, Tara."

"Thank you, George."

"May I bring you something to drink?"

Brad noted that the waiter addressed the question to him, but gave an appreciative glance in Tara's direction. An inner smile of approval confirmed his assessment of her being very resourceful. Not only had she chosen a restaurant she knew, she had chosen one where they knew her by name and would take more notice of the person she was with. But on the downside, if someone was stalking her they would also know this was a place she apparently frequented.

They placed their dinner order and as soon as the waiter left, Brad turned to the problem at hand.

"A week and a half ago, while doing follow-up on the Vincent case, I discovered that over the past six months four of the six witnesses who testified against John Vincent have met with strange *accidental* deaths.

"I found the coincidence of this having happened four times over just a few months to be too great to accept it so casually. After I started checking into these accidents they seemed to me to be more and more like connected crimes. Then four days ago the fifth witness met with a similar type of strange *accidental* death. The five deaths occurred in five different parts of the country under the jurisdiction of five different law enforcement agencies."

He took a sip of his water, then continued. "On the surface there didn't seem to be any connection between the victims. There wasn't any reason for the local authorities in the individual cases to be suspicious of what appeared to be an unfortunate accident or think that it would have any connection with anything else. Each one seemed to be an isolated incident—just an unfortunate accident. What makes it particularly compelling is that two of those witnesses were in the Witness Security Program and had been given new identities and relocated. The fifth *accident* happened in Portland, Oregon, and was the only one thoroughly investigated beyond what appeared obvious."

"The fifth one? What happened to make that the exception that it would be handled differently?"

"I have a friend on the Portland police force. He's a homicide detective. I contacted him unofficially just two days after the death happened and asked him to go over everything very carefully, to not be too anxious to write it off as an accident. I heard back from him this afternoon. It was a carefully and expertly disguised murder."

Tara's eyes narrowed as she stared at him. "The way you describe this...I have a friend on the Portland police force...contacted him unofficially...makes it sound as if you're doing this investigation on your own rather than it being an official position of the Marshals Service.''

Tara Ford was definitely a smart and perceptive woman. Brad drew in a deep breath and slowly expelled it while trying to determine how best to express himself. ''I won't lie to you. Yes, I'm doing this investigation on my own. I took the information I had to the head of the Seattle office after I discovered the fourth death and he said it was speculation on my part that the victims hadn't died as the result of accidents and without anything more there wasn't a case. It was a couple of days later that the fifth…accident occurred. I've kept that information to myself for the time being because I don't have any evidence showing that this murder had any connection to the other deaths, even though it was another of the witnesses in the Vincent case who had been murdered.''

He paused for a moment before continuing. ''From what I've observed about you the past few days, I think you're the type of person who would rather have the information straight out rather than have half truths. So—''

''The past *few days?*'' Her eyes widened in shock. ''You haven't been watching me for a few weeks rather than a few days?''

He saw the fear return to her eyes and the wariness that blanketed her features. ''No, only a few days. It was only a little over a week that I started pulling information together about the first four deaths and formulated a theory about someone systematically killing off the witnesses from the John Vincent trial—a theory reinforced when the fifth death occurred.''

Tara stared down at the table. The anxiety twisted her insides into knots. If he was telling her the truth, then things were worse than she thought. But *was* he telling her the truth? What reason would he have to lie to her? She was no longer sure of anything or anyone. She didn't know what else to do, but she had to do something. She couldn't just sit here staring at her water glass. She decided to go along with what he told her, at least for the time being.

She recaptured his gaze. Again, as in the deli when he bumped her chair, his eyes held concern rather than hardness or danger. "For the past several weeks I've had the feeling that I was being watched. Nothing I could put my finger on, just a bothersome sensation. Then suddenly a few days ago there you were every time I went anywhere. At first I thought you worked in the same neighborhood where I do, then I wondered if you were the person who had been watching me."

Brad glanced around, making sure their conversation was private. "Did you have any impressions about who it would have been?" He allowed a soft chuckle. "Other than me, of course."

"No. I never really saw anyone. It was just an uncomfortable sensation…you know, like when someone is staring at you and you can feel their gaze on the back of your neck even though you don't see who it is."

They both stopped talking when the waiter approached with their food. As soon as he left, they resumed their discussion.

Apprehension filled her voice. "Do you…do you know who killed the other witnesses? Who would be watching me?"

"No, unfortunately I don't have any idea. As I said, I just recently got involved with this case. My first thought was that the deaths had to do with Vincent's organized-crime connections, since the first four witnesses who were killed had testified specifically about his criminal activities. The two who were in the Witness Security Program testified to his organized-crime connections, helping to convict John Vincent under the federal Racketeer Influenced and Corrupt Organizations statute. RICO has been used with great success in obtaining organized-crime convictions. But neither you nor the man in Portland were involved in that aspect of the testimony. Both of you testified to his company pension fund and income manipulations.''

Her words came out as a mere whisper. ''And with the man in Portland dead that leaves only me?''

''I can't officially offer you the protection of the U.S. Marshals Service at this point. My theory has already been shot down by the head of the Seattle office. I can't take it over his head or go directly to the FBI without proof to back up my speculations.''

''Wouldn't the Portland death being declared a murder be enough to start an investigation?''

''There's nothing that links his death with the others. He could have had enemies of his own with no connection to John Vincent or the trial. There's not a scrap of proof at this time that shows any connection between his murder and the other deaths or that the other deaths were really murder. What I can do is work personally to protect you, but I need your help if I'm going to find out who's behind this and gather evidence to warrant an official investigation.''

What he didn't tell her was his suspicion that there was a leak within the Marshals Service, something possibly originating from the Seattle office, concerning the protected witnesses. There shouldn't have been any way for someone to have found the two people in the Witness Security Program—one of the facts thrown up to him by his boss as reason for him to forget his crazy theory. It was also the reason he knew he couldn't trust anyone else until he had some solid facts to work with. Any information he put into an official report could easily be accessed by whoever was responsible for the leak.

Tara noted the hint of apprehension that crossed his face. Her concerns about who she could and could not trust, what was true and what wasn't, kept her at a cautious distance from him. She nervously cleared her throat. ''I need to think about this, consider the pros and cons, go over all my options.''

He leveled a purposeful look at her, his voice adding emphasis to his words. "I don't want to frighten you unnecessarily, but please don't take too long to think about it."

Her anxieties jumped into high gear. His words of warning said it all. They silently ate their food. He seemed as absorbed in his own thoughts as she was in hers. Following dinner they left the restaurant.

Brad walked her across the restaurant parking lot toward her car. "You've had some time to think about what I've said. I'm afraid I need an answer from you now. This is a very serious matter."

As they approached her vehicle, she took the lock and ignition remote from her purse. She pressed the button to unlock the doors and start the engine.

The sound of a horrendous explosion ripped through the air. Tara's entire body jerked around, then she stood frozen to the spot. She stared in the direction of the conflagration with her eyes wide and her features contorted into a mask of shock and fear. She heard a loud scream, then realized it came from her. A moment later strong hands grabbed her shoulders and shoved her to the ground behind a van. The next thing she knew Brad had protectively covered her body with his.

A few seconds later, Brad stood up. He raked his gaze efficiently across the scene, taking everything in.

Tara struggled to her feet and started toward the charred mangle of metal that just seconds earlier had been her brand-new car. Waves of fear washed through her, something nearly akin to stark terror. Her body shook uncontrollably. Her legs turned wobbly. She tried to run but was brought up short when someone grabbed her arm and held it in a strong grip.

"Stay put!" Brad's no-nonsense voice barked out an order as he took control of the situation. "Don't you dare move from this spot."

"Let go of me!" She tried to jerk her arm free. Her heart pounded in her chest. She heard the blood rushing in her ears along with the echoing sound of the explosion playing over and over in her head. She had to do something even though she wasn't sure what. She started toward her car, but was again brought to an abrupt halt when Brad took hold of her arm.

"I told you to stay here!" He left her no room for argument.

"But..." She heard the quaver in her voice, the uncertainty that matched the panic building inside her.

"No buts! There's nothing you can do over there."

"My car—"

"Your car is history. There's nothing over there except twisted metal." The hard edge to his voice softened a bit. "There's nothing there that you need to see."

She went numb inside as she fought off the need to run in the opposite direction as fast and as far as she could. Everything Brad told her about the danger had come back to hit her in the face. She felt light-headed. Her knees started to buckle.

"Tara...Tara, answer me. Are you all right?"

"I...yes, I'm okay."

He held on to her, providing support while keeping her from walking off. A crowd gathered, any one of whom might have been the person who had planted the bomb. Brad scanned the faces, but no one jumped out at him as being suspicious or familiar. One thing was crystal clear. Someone had followed Tara, watched her park and go into the restaurant. There was no way anyone could have known she would be going there since it was a decision that had only been made moments before she left the parking lot at work.

And whoever saw her had most likely seen the two of them talking before that. Perhaps it was the presence of a deputy marshal that pushed the killer to abandon the use of *accidental* means and go the more direct route. But that only prompted another question. How would the perpetrator know he was a deputy marshal, since he wasn't connected with the original case? *If* that was what had happened.

Then another thought occurred to him, one he didn't like. What did he really know about Tara Ford? Out of the six witnesses at the John Vincent trial she was the only one who still lived in the Seattle area and, therefore, the easiest to locate. Yet she was the only one still alive. All the other murders had been very clever, but the attempt on her life had been clumsy and had failed. The perpetrator had made no attempt to have it appear to be an accident.

Could his having shown up and saying she was in danger have alerted her that someone was suspicious of the accidental deaths? Could she have rigged this herself to throw him off track? Maybe she had stopped to call someone while en route. It would explain her arriving at the restaurant several minutes later than he had when they'd both started out at the same time. If that was the case, then she must have a motive for the murders, and on the surface he didn't see what that motive would be. But one thing experience had taught him was not to ignore small details and not to dismiss seemingly insignificant events too quickly.

A quick jolt of irritation told him how distasteful he found his line of speculation. His assessment of her character said she was far too straightforward to be involved in that type of subterfuge. Was he merely grasping at straws in an attempt to put some much-needed logic to a confusing problem? Was he allowing a beautiful, enticing woman with a sultry voice to cloud his reasoning?

His thoughts drifted in another direction, this one a painful memory more than anything else. He had been with the Marshals Service for a year. Then one day while he was involved in a high-profile fugitive hunt someone planted a bomb in his car. The bomb had missed its target. Rather than him being killed, the victim had been his wife of six months.

He had carried the guilt of his wife's death with him ever since then, a guilt that came rushing back at him the moment Tara's car exploded. Here was another woman who had been put in danger with a car bomb. Was it because of him? If his original theory was correct, Tara was next on the list of victims, and if they hadn't tried a car bomb it would have been something else. He hadn't been able to keep his wife safe from danger and it had left a gaping wound that refused to heal even though he had closed off his heart to the possibility of any future relationship.

He saw the confusion and fear on Tara's face. It worked itself inside him until it touched a place of vulnerability buried so deep he had forgotten it even existed. She was so tempting, so enticing. She stirred a very primal desire in him. It had been a long time since he had been this instantly attracted to any woman. He had failed to protect his wife, but he would do his best to protect Tara Ford.

It took the sound of the approaching sirens to banish the ghosts of the past. He turned to Tara, his words emphatic as he exercised total authority. "I'll handle this. Respond directly to the questions you're asked with the shortest answers possible. Don't volunteer any information. Follow my lead."

He put his arm around her shoulder and guided her toward the arriving police car. He felt the tension running through her body. "Everything is going to be okay, just stay with me."

Brad's mind raced ahead to what he should say to the police. Identify himself as a deputy U.S. marshal and say she was under the marshals' protection and cut the local police out of the loop? That would *officially* throw the whole mess back into the lap of the Marshals Service and put his activities out in the open before he was ready to disclose that he was still working on his theory. Or maybe he should play ignorant of any and all reasons why the explosion had happened. Perhaps he should pretend that a freak malfunction, rather than a car bomb had caused the gas tank to explode. Whichever way he decided to go, he needed to make a decision and do it fast.

He watched two policemen climb out of the car, the older one going toward the fire engine at Tara's car and the younger one heading toward the restaurant. The young policeman looked as if he couldn't have been on the force very long, possibly still on probation from the police academy. He most likely didn't have any experience dealing with federal cases and interfacing with federal agencies. Brad decided that discretion would be the best avenue for the time being.

He approached the young officer. "My name is Don McMillan and this is my fiancée, Tara Ford. It was Miss Ford's car that just burst into flames." He used a phony name for which he had identification. Hopefully the inexperienced officer wouldn't think to take down the number on his car license tag. He purposely avoided using the word *exploded*, not wanting to put any ideas into the officer's head.

The policeman took out his notebook and began writing. He paused to glance at Tara's left hand, then directed his attention to Brad. "Your fiancée? I don't see any kind of ring."

He bristled at the officer's implication, in spite of the fact that the man was correct in his observation and more astute than Brad had given him credit for. "That's because I just asked Miss Ford to marry me while we were having dinner in the restaurant. We plan to shop for a ring tomorrow."

"I see." The policeman continued to make notes.

Tara took several deep breaths in an attempt to calm the nearly out-of-control panic rampaging through her body. Only the consistent strength radiating from Brad as he protectively kept his arm around her shoulder prevented her from falling prey to those fears.

The policeman looked at Tara. "You're the registered owner of the vehicle?"

"Uh..." She swallowed to break the dryness in her throat. "Yes, it's my car."

"I need the make, model and license number. I also need your address and phone number."

Tara provided the officer with the information, all the while drawing comfort from Brad's reassuring presence.

"And you, Mr. McMillan...I need your address and phone number." Brad gave the officer Tara's address and phone number, alluding to the fact that they were living together.

"Okay...now, what happened here?"

Brad immediately took control of the conversation. "I'm really not sure, Officer. We came out of the restaurant and started across the parking lot. I was walking Miss Ford to her car."

The young officer looked up from his notebook, addressing his question to Brad. "You arrived in different vehicles?"

"Yes, it was more convenient for us to meet here since we were coming from different directions."

"What happened then?"

"Miss Ford took her car remote from her purse and clicked it to unlock the door and start the engine. There was a loud noise and the car burst into flames."

The officer stopped writing again. "Burst into flames... are you saying there was an explosion?"

"I can't really say what happened, Officer. Miss Ford and I—" he placed a tender kiss on her forehead "—didn't actually see it. I assume it was caused by some sort of malfunction connected to the remote starter. Thank goodness no one was injured."

"I see. Wait here, please."

Brad and Tara watched as the officer crossed the parking lot and conferred with his partner. "How are you holding up?" He gave her shoulder a reassuring squeeze. Even though he spoke to her, his gaze never left the officers as they talked.

"Okay, I guess." There was no denying the tremor in her voice.

"Hang in there. We'll be out of here in a few minutes."

Another half hour passed before they were able to leave. One overriding thought kept circulating through Tara's mind. She had to keep her wits about her and pull up all the inner strength she could muster. It was not the time to let her fears get the better of her. After what she had been through with the trial and all the chaos it had introduced into her normally ordered life, getting through this should be just one more hurdle to jump. Unfortunately, no matter how hard she tried, her brave thoughts didn't do anything to calm her fears.

They drove away from the restaurant in Brad's car. He carefully measured his words as he spoke, not wanting to frighten her any more than she obviously already was, but not wanting her to misunderstand the seriousness of the situation, either. "You won't be going home tonight. We'll stop at a store and you can buy whatever you'll need for a day or two, then I'm checking you into a motel."

She jerked around in the seat until she faced him. "A motel?" She couldn't conceal her irritation. He had made the decisions for her back at the restaurant when he had restrained her and when dealing with the police, but this was different. "You're *telling* me I'm not allowed to go home? You're making this decision on your own without even doing the courtesy of consulting me?"

He snapped out an answer to her defensive attitude. "There's nothing to discuss. Anyone determined to do so could find out where you live in a matter of minutes. I'm sure whoever is behind the bombing already knows where you live in addition to where you work."

His words struck a chord with her. If it was that easy, then why had Danny Vincent claimed it had taken him so long to discover where she had moved? Or had it really taken him that long?

She glanced at Brad as they drove onto the interstate. Someone had just tried to kill her and now her life was in the hands of a total stranger who was driving her to an unknown place. She wasn't sure exactly what to think or feel anymore.

She had briefly thought about moving to another state and starting over after the trial in order to distance herself from the chaos that had been forced on her, but running away wasn't her life pattern. The trial was over, she had a new job and she was free to return to her normal routine of dull and predictable. She had thought the only change would be her move from Seattle across Lake Washington to Bellevue to be close to her new place of employment. How wrong she had been.

She had always done what was expected of her, gone along without making waves, which included agreeing to testify at the trial. She had information about John Vincent's activities. It was her duty to testify—it was expected of her.

Even taking the job at Green Valley Construction as soon as she graduated from college had been to please her mother. She had spent most of her life trying to be the daughter her mother wanted. As a child she had been subjected to constant fights between her mother and father. Finally her father walked out the door for good, leaving a ten-year-old girl to deal with her mother's demands. She felt as if she had been abandoned, leaving her to believe that she couldn't trust anyone. She had done her best to cope, but from that moment on her mother had leaned heavily on her for emotional support, draining her of a happy childhood. Her mother insisted that she was too frail and couldn't manage by herself. She needed Tara's help.

She could still hear her mother's words. *Being a dancer isn't any kind of respectable career for a young woman. Get yourself a nice secure office job where you can grow with the company, and if you don't find yourself a husband, at least you won't be washed up by forty and you'll have a nice pension when it comes time for you to retire.*

She had finally been able to break away from her mother's constant control when she had saved enough money from her job to move out and get her own apartment, but it didn't stop her mother's relentless attempts to interfere in her life. Getting married had not been on Tara's list of goals, and as it turned out an office job had ended up being anything but secure. The only true risk she had ever taken in her life was agreeing to testify at John Vincent's trial. That decision had turned her life upside down...and now, when she thought it was all over, it had come back to turn her life into a nightmare.

The one shining moment had been her new job. Finding it had been a real stroke of luck. She had been at her favorite bookstore and had reached for a book at the same time as Judy Lameroux. They struck up a conversation that quickly turned into a friendship. Judy told her about a job opening at the company where she was the office manager. It was almost as if fate had stepped in to help her in her time of need. She liked her new job, her co-workers and her new home. And two months ago she had bought a new car...her first car that was brand new rather than used. It had seemed as if everything was going to be okay in spite of her brief sojourn in a chaotic situation.

She glanced at Brad again. Trust hadn't been easy for her since the upheaval of her childhood. It had been even more fleeting since her disastrous engagement to Danny Vincent, then reinforced by the subsequent arrest of the man who had employed her, followed by his trial and her being thrust into the very awkward and uncomfortable situation of being a witness.

She took in Brad's handsome profile and strong determination. When he put his arm around her shoulder in the restaurant parking lot he had provided her with a silent strength while at the same time calming her fears. It had also sent a little tremor of excitement through her body, something totally inappropriate for the situation yet a very real sensation. He was as fascinating and dynamic as the danger surrounding her was traumatic and frightening.

And now she was all alone with this very appealing stranger in whom she was forced to place her trust. Her very life depended on whether that trust was valid. Another shiver of anxiety confirmed what she already knew. The danger was very real. A chapter of her life that she thought was over had come back to haunt her and throw her life into turmoil again. Could she trust this man to help her? She wanted to, but she wasn't sure she even knew how to trust anymore.

Chapter Three

Brad headed south from Seattle, exiting the interstate at Tacoma. He stopped at a discount store so Tara could buy the items she would need to stay overnight. They drove to a nearby motel. He checked into the room using the same fictitious name he had given the police officer, and paid cash in advance for two nights.

He unlocked the door. "It's not fancy, but it's clean and will be safe for the time being. I'll check with you in the morning."

She stood in the middle of the room, her gaze nervously darting from the bed to the television perched on the dresser, then to the small table and two chairs and finally the large stuffed chair in the corner without lingering on any one spot for more than a couple of seconds. Her words were soft and filled with the anxiety coursing through her body.

"It never occurred to me that testifying against John Vincent would continue to control my life after the trial was over."

She finally looked up at Brad, capturing his gaze and holding it. She attempted to put on a brave front. "I'm not the type of person who is accustomed to taking chances. I knew it was my duty to testify at John's trial—" a lump formed in her throat "—but I never dreamed my life would be turned upside down like this."

The words were difficult for her. Digging into her inner fears and expressing them did not come easily. "I thought when the trial was over everything would go back to normal with the only change being superficial…a new job and a different place to live. I had assumed my daily routine would return to what it had been before all this started." She forced the words while trying to keep her anxieties from creeping into her voice. "But that's not the way it turned out."

Tara glanced around the small room again. "I guess I'd better get settled in—" she focused her attention on the floor "—although all I have to unpack is the sack from the discount store." She looked up at him, her voice falling off to a frightened whisper. "Will I be here for very long?"

It had been quite a while since anything latched on to Brad and turned him inside out the way he was at that moment. Tara was obviously frightened and trying her best not to show it. He marshaled his composure. If nothing else, he needed to maintain a calm and in-control outer presence in order to instill a confidence in her that said he knew what he was doing. "Just tonight, maybe two nights at the most while I work out a plan to keep you safe until I gather enough new information to be able to convince my boss of the danger and get you some official protection."

"But doesn't someone's planting a bomb in my car qualify as proof?"

"It's proof that you, Tara Ford, are personally in danger, but it doesn't tie anything in with the John Vincent case or the deaths of the other witnesses. The culprit could be a disgruntled lover, a co-worker or even a relative. There's nothing there that takes this out of the realm of a local police investigation, or that makes it the concern of the U.S. Marshals Service. There's no evidence to connect the bombing with the protection of witnesses in the John Vincent case."

"Oh." She glanced down at the floor, the disappointment

ringing loud and clear in her voice. "I see. I didn't realize what the difference was."

He placed his fingertips beneath her chin and lifted until he could see her eyes. The physical contact sent a tingle of excitement through him that he tried to ignore.

It was much easier when someone was officially under the protection of the U.S. Marshals Service. She would have been allowed to pack a suitcase, then been taken to a known safe house or nice hotel room with deputy marshals on duty to protect her around the clock. All he had offered her was a sack of bare essentials from a discount store, an out-of-the-way motel and his promise that he would protect her even though he would be leaving her there alone. Again, his failure to protect his wife came back to haunt him. It was the day he had closed off his heart.

He quickly shook away the disturbing memories and returned his attention to the problem at hand. He wasn't sure how he was going to accomplish the task he had set for himself, but right now he had to do something to help her over the first of what he suspected would be many rough spots.

"I need to go back to my office for a little while. I have a few things to do that can't be done during normal hours." He saw the trepidation come into her eyes and it pulled at his senses. "I'll check back with you in a couple of hours. But first, there are a few things I need to go over with you before I leave. Come on...let's sit down."

He placed his hand at the small of her back and escorted her across the room to the large chair. He grabbed a straight-back chair and sat down facing her. He took the cell phone from his jacket pocket and handed it to her.

"Here...this is one of my personal cell phones. Keep this with you at all times. No one knows you're here. I registered at the front desk using the same name I gave the officer at the restaurant—Don McMillan. I've paid for two nights in advance. There's no reason for anyone to be calling you here, so I don't want you answering the motel phone. If I need to get in touch with you I'll call you on my cell phone. Don't answer it right away. I'll let it ring twice, hang up then call right back. Don't answer unless it's that signal.''

He took one of his business cards from his pocket and jotted a couple of phone numbers on the back, then handed it to her. ''Here's my phone number at the office and my Marshals Service cell phone number. I've written my home phone on the back and also the number of my other personal cell phone. If you need to get in touch with me, try my personal cell phone first, my home second, my Marshals cell phone third and the office as the last choice. Don't leave your name, just say you're my cousin from Los Angeles and I'll call you back.''

''Okay.'' She took the card, looked at it for a moment, then put it in her purse.

''I'll see you in a little while.'' He offered her a confident smile, reached out and squeezed her hand. ''In the meantime, try to get some rest.''

The last thing he wanted to do was leave her and it was as much personal as it was business. The feel of her hand in his sent a ripple of excitement through his body. He reluctantly let loose of her hand. He had to keep focused on business. He could not allow his newly awakened emotions to get the upper hand.

BRAD LEFT the motel and headed back toward Seattle. If nothing else, the bombing of Tara's car told him he was on the right track with his theory. What wasn't immediately obvious was what to do about it.

He arrived at his office, unlocked the door and let himself in. It was after hours and he looked forward to having the place to himself. As he made his way down the hallway, a sound from the file room brought him to an abrupt halt. Someone else was there. He quickly detoured toward the coffee room, plunked some coins into the slot and took the cup of coffee from the machine.

He rounded the door toward his cubicle and literally ran into the office's computer expert, Shirley Bennett. The hot coffee splashed over the top of the cup. He jerked his hand back, dropping the full cup to the floor in the process. Shirley tried to maintain a grasp on her purse and the two department-store sacks she held in her arms without any success. Everything fell to the floor.

"Damn…" Brad shook his hand, then pulled his wet shirt away from his body where the coffee had soaked through to his skin. "That's hot!"

"Are you all right?" Shirley's formal, all-business voice gave no hint of any irritation at the collision.

"Yeah, I'm fine." He glanced down at the contents that had spilled from her purse and the items of clothing that had tumbled from the shopping bags, what appeared to be gym workout clothes.

"I'm sorry about that. I didn't realize you were there. Let me help you with this." He kneeled down and began picking up the items—her wallet, a day planner, a comb, a small makeup pouch, a bottle of eyedrops and the case for her glasses. He stared at the eyeglass case for a moment, noting the name of the optometrist before handing everything to her.

"It seems we go to the same eye doctor. How do you like Dr. Keeson?" A slight grin tugged at the corners of his mouth. The bold pattern and bright colors of the case didn't go with the style of her glasses or fit in with her plain appearance.

"He's very nice." Shirley took the items from him and shoved them in her purse. "You're here late. I thought you were on light duty until your shoulder wound healed completely. And to that we can add your most recent abrasions." She gestured toward his face.

He chose to ignore her comments about his split lip, the

gash on his chin and the scrapes across his cheek. "I'm feeling fine. The doctor thinks I should give this shoulder another week or so to heal from the bullet wound before he releases me to field duty."

"Is there a problem of some sort that brings you back to the office after hours?"

"I'm catching up on a little paperwork. I thought I could get a lot of it done tonight when no one was around. I want all of it cleaned up so I can get back to field duty."

"Well, if there's nothing you need me for, I think I'll call it a day."

"I'll see you in the morning, Shirley."

Brad watched as she walked down the hall and disappeared around the corner. She had only been in the Seattle office of the U.S. Marshals Service for a couple of months. He didn't know her very well as she seemed to keep mostly to herself. She had been transferred from another district to fill the vacancy created when their computer expert retired.

She seemed very efficient at her job of being their software expert and maintaining the computer system. No matter what the problem, she had it fixed immediately. Any difficulty accessing files or finding information on the Internet and she was a whiz at handling it. In fact, she exactly fit his concept of a computer-nerd stereotype...straight brown hair worn short with bangs, medium-brown eyes, horn-rimmed glasses, about twenty pounds overweight, most of which seemed to be on her hips and around her waist probably due to lack of exercise, very little makeup, quiet and kept to herself. She was short compared to his six-one height. He guessed she topped out at five foot three.

He listened until he heard the front door close, then grabbed the John Vincent folder from the file room. He made copies of everything to take with him—something very definitely against the rules. Then he went to his cubicle to do some computer research. He needed information that he couldn't access from his computer at home, and during office hours there was too much of a chance that someone would see what he was doing. He worked quickly, finding and printing out what he wanted.

As soon as he finished he drove back to the motel to check on Tara. He knocked on the door, at the same time calling to her. "Tara…it's me."

She looked through the peephole in the door, then opened it to let Brad in. "Did you get everything done that you wanted to?"

"Yes, I think so. How are you doing? Is everything okay? Is there anything you need?"

She glanced around the small room. A little sigh escaped her throat. "I can't think of anything specific that I need."

He heard it in her voice and saw it in her eyes…the anxiety, the apprehension and the loneliness. Her despair tugged at his senses and pulled at his emotions. She was obviously scared and trying to put up a brave front. He was responsible for her being stuck away in a small motel room, but if he hadn't taken action when he did she would probably be dead by now. The thought helped lessen his guilt but didn't calm his own anxieties. He desperately wanted to do something to try to comfort her and ease her mind.

"There's a special on television tonight that I wanted to see, but it comes on in ten minutes and I can't be home by then. If you don't mind, I'd like to stay here for a while. I can watch the special and keep you company for a bit…" He offered his best confidence-inducing smile. "If that's okay with you." He took off his jacket and tossed it across the foot of the bed.

Her attention flew to the holster clipped to his belt, becoming fixated on the handgun. A shiver darted up her spine and anxiety churned in the pit of her stomach, confirming what she already knew—she was in serious danger. She closed her eyes. The sound of the explosion and the vivid image of the burning car assaulted her senses. She shook her head, trying to rid herself of the disturbing vision.

"Tara? Are you all right?"

His voice pulled her out of her thoughts. She opened her eyes, her attention again riveted on the weapon, her thoughts telling her of the danger it represented. "Do you...uh... always carry a gun?"

"Yes. We're issued a .357 magnum, but I prefer this 9mm semiautomatic. I find it more comfortable to carry and to use."

"To *use?*" A knot of anxiety pulled tight in her stomach. "Do you have to use it often?"

"Occasionally." A twinge in his shoulder gave a sharp reminder of the last time he'd needed to use it.

She pulled her attention away from the weapon, glancing around the room as she composed herself and tried to project a positive manner. "I didn't mean to get off the subject. What were you saying?"

"I was asking if you minded my staying to watch a program on television. Maybe keep you company for a little while until you're feeling more comfortable?"

"Uh...no, I don't mind if you want to watch something on television. Go ahead."

Tara retreated to the corner of the room, curling her legs under her as she sank into the large chair. Try as she might, she simply couldn't concentrate on his conversation. She kept hearing the explosion over and over, the horror of pieces of metal flying through the air. The churning in her stomach drove a sick feeling up her throat. She knew it was a memory that would continue to haunt her the rest of her life however long—or short—that life might be.

She watched Brad as he sat on the end of the bed staring at the television, although he didn't seem to really be watching the program. He appeared casual enough, as if he didn't have any concerns, but the tight set of his jaw belied that. She could almost feel the tension pulling his muscles into knots. But in spite of that he radiated a sense of confidence that surpassed his take-charge attitude. A quick dash of irritation flitted through her. Confidence or not, his was still a take-charge attitude in which he gave orders and expected to have them obeyed without question. Although it was something quite different from the way Danny Vincent had tried to control her life.

A little shiver darted across her skin. Things were too confusing…too many strange things had happened in the past few weeks, and her totally unexpected phone call from Danny after all this time was definitely one of them. Again the image of her bombed car popped into her mind followed by the way Brad had taken control without hesitation. He had taken charge, but it was not a domineering type of thing. He had known exactly what to do and how to properly handle the situation.

A warm feeling replaced the shiver as she thought of his arm around her shoulder while they talked to the policeman. She had felt safe, at least for that moment. She studied his handsome features. A ripple of excitement invaded her senses, a sensation that started with a tingle deep inside and quickly spread through her body. Her life was in danger and her world had been thrown into turmoil. The last thing she should be thinking about was an attraction to a very desirable man.

She straightened in her chair in an effort to pull herself together. She didn't want to show the depth of her fears to this very together—and extremely handsome—man. She certainly didn't want him thinking she was some silly little twit who fell apart at the first sign of an unpleasant situation. With everything she'd been through since agreeing to testify, she should be able to take this in stride without any problem.

Another sigh of despair tried to work its way into the open. Testifying at a trial was not the same thing as having someone try to kill you. Her brave intentions did nothing to calm her fears. She knew she was only lying to herself.

Brad seemed to be alert to everything going on. Every

time the sound of a car engine or car door invaded the room he was on his feet. He'd pretend he needed to stretch and would make his way to the window and peek out around the edge of the drapes. But in spite of his casual outer manner, it was obvious he was far from relaxed.

Then another memory flooded her consciousness—Brad's body protectively covering hers when he had shoved her down behind the van in the restaurant parking lot. And then the tender kiss he had placed on her forehead. It was more than his having put his life on the line for her. A totally unexpected sensual rush had hit her like a ton of bricks. Brad Harrison was a very desirable man—handsome, confident and extremely sexy. He exuded the strong presence of someone who knew what he was doing and could be depended on in a crisis. There was something very reassuring about a man who had the ability to take control of a precarious situation.

Then another dark thought clouded her perception. Was his take-charge manner just one small step away from the controlling efforts of Danny and the domineering manipulations of her mother?

"I guess I'm a little too restless to stay with the television program." Brad's words drew her attention back to what he was doing. She watched as he stood and stretched his arms above his head, then behind his back.

He cocked his head and raised a questioning eyebrow. "How about you? You look comfortable enough, but your expression seems more worried than at ease...although I can certainly understand why." He glanced down at the floor for a moment as if trying to collect his thoughts. "I know it's of little use for me to tell you not to worry, but I'll try it anyway. Please think positive, we'll get through this and everything will turn out okay."

Before she could respond, he grabbed the ice bucket from the table. "I noticed an ice maker and a vending machine a couple of doors down. I'll get us some ice and a couple of soft drinks. Be right back. I'll take the key so I can let myself in. Don't answer the door if anyone knocks.'' He opened the door and quickly scanned the parking lot before stepping outside.

The image of Tara curled up in the large chair had truly gotten to him. She looked too desirable. He wanted to pull her into his arms and move the few steps over to the bed. The urge needed to be dealt with, and walking out the door into the cool night air seemed to be the most expedient way of doing it. He took in a deep breath, then another. It helped clear his head a bit, but did not chase away the feelings. He filled the ice bucket, bought two soft drinks from the machine and quickly returned to the room.

When he stepped inside, he found her exactly where he had left her. ''I hope this is okay. I didn't think to ask you what kind you preferred.'' He set two cans on the table, put ice in two glasses and opened one of the cans for himself.

''This is fine. Thank you.'' Tara took the other can, poured the contents into the glass, but left it on the table without taking a drink.

He seated himself at the small table, maintaining a view of the door and window. ''Tell me, Tara Ford—'' he ran his fingertip around the rim of his glass, trying to project an easygoing manner that he hoped would calm her nerves ''—how did you get mixed up in all this?''

''Don't you have all that in your files?''

''We have some information, but not that much.'' He wanted to hear it from her, get an impression of what she was thinking and how she felt about things rather than go by some cold facts on a piece of paper in a file folder.

''Well...I, uh...'' She swallowed the discomfort that welled inside her. His intentions were obvious, the uneasiness in his eyes saying far more than his words. ''You really don't need to do this.''

"Do what?" A hint of surprise darted through his eyes, followed by curiosity.

"You don't need to sit here with me to ease my discomfort. I'm sure you have other things you'd prefer to be doing than this."

He leveled a steady gaze at her as if trying to read her mind. "Actually, I don't have anything else I'd rather be doing right now." He creased his forehead in a moment of concentration, then flashed a mischievous grin. "Other than maybe sailing in the South Pacific or skiing in Switzerland."

"You do those things? Sail and ski?"

"Yes, two of my favorite passions."

"I've never participated in either of them." She added somewhat tentatively, "although they look like they'd be a lot of fun." Sailing, skiing…both were activities that she had wanted to try. She'd even had an opportunity to go on a school ski trip when she was a senior in high school, but her mother had refused to sign the permission slip, saying it was a foolish waste of money. It was but one of a long list of disappointments and regrets that had been part of her life, most of them caused by her mother. Then there was the time her mother had refused to allow her to go to the senior prom in high school and… She shoved the memories aside. She knew they would only make her angry and would serve no purpose.

"Never? I have a small sailboat, large enough to be seaworthy but not so large that I can't handle it by myself—" He abruptly jumped to his feet, staring at her for a long moment without saying anything.

"What? What's wrong?"

"I've got it!"

"You've got what?" She looked around, but everything was just as it had been when he started talking. She didn't hear any noises coming from outside.

"Damn…it's nothing." The optimistic expression that had been on his face just a moment before had disappeared.

He dejectedly slumped back into the chair. "I thought I had a solution to where you could stay for a couple of days, but it was a bad idea—an impractical notion that wouldn't work."

"Stay where? What idea?"

"Well, I thought I could hide you on my boat for a day or two." He shook his head and took a swallow from his glass. "It wouldn't work. It was a stupid idea."

"I don't understand. Why is that impractical?"

"No one lives on my boat, so having somebody suddenly staying there would attract unwanted attention at the marina. And it certainly wouldn't be a secure location." He didn't want to upset Tara any more than she already was, but he knew that whoever was involved in this could easily have seen him with her at the restaurant and traced his car license to discover his identity, if they hadn't already. He was fully conversant with how simple it was to gather information on someone. Anyone with a computer, a modem and decent computer skills could find out that he owned a sailboat and where he kept it.

"Oh." She looked as dejected as he felt.

He moved to the bed, seating himself on the edge next to her chair. The tone of his voice provided a comforting level of intimacy. "You understand how important it is for you to stay out of sight and avoid all contact with everyone, don't you? It's the same concept as when you were under the marshals' protection before and during the trial…only for the time being it's just you and me until I straighten out a few things."

A few things, such as who killed five out of six witnesses, with two of those witnesses having been in the Witness Security Program. A few things, such as figuring out how someone had obtained the new identities of protected and relocated witnesses…whether there was someone inside the Marshals Service selling those identities. *A few things,* such as a motive for the killings. He reached out, took her hand

and gave it a reassuring squeeze. Her muscles tensed beneath his touch, telling him just how distraught she really was despite the brave facade she had been trying to display.

A few things—such as who this woman hiding inside the beautiful package labeled Tara Ford was and how she got mixed up in this mess. He continued to hold on to her hand. Warning bells sounded off inside his head telling him he had overstepped the line, but he chose to ignore them. He liked the way her hand felt in his.

"Weren't you starting to answer my question about how you became involved in this situation when I interrupted you?" He had to have information, but didn't want her to feel as if she was being subjected to an interrogation.

"It's not a very interesting story." The warmth of his touch produced a sensual flow of energy that started with her hand, ran up her arm, then quickly spread through her body. The sensation did more than excite her. It also provided an odd feeling of security that she hadn't known before. Even during the trial when she was under the direct protection on the U.S. Marshals Service she never really felt safe. For the first time since agreeing to testify against John Vincent she felt that something positive was finally being done to ease her anxieties. Did she dare to trust those feelings?

"I'd like to hear it. I need to know everything I can. Some little bit of information might not seem important to you, but it could mean a great deal to me. So, if you could start at the beginning…"

Tara shifted her weight in the chair, but allowed the comforting sensation of his hand to remain on hers. She didn't like talking about herself, certainly not to a stranger and especially not to someone like this very disconcerting man who made her heart beat a little faster and her pulse race.

"Well…I guess it started when I answered a help wanted ad in the newspaper. Green Valley Construction was looking for a secretary. I had just graduated from college with a degree in something *practical* that would guarantee me a secure future…something my *mother* had insisted on.''

She knew that bitterness had crept into her voice, but she had not been able to control it. It was an old wound and at the same time a fresh one that still hurt. From the time her father had deserted her until the time she'd made the decision to testify against John Vincent, her mother had made every attempt to control her life. All during her school years her mother had denied her permission to participate in extracurricular activities.

Her mother's excuses fell into two categories—either it was a waste of money or else her mother suddenly developed an illness and Tara had to stay home to take care of her. She knew her mother wasn't really sick, but there wasn't anything she could do about it. Things had gotten better when she had been able to get her own apartment after graduating from college and getting a full-time job, but she hadn't been able to escape her mother's continuous attempts to dominate her and the constant meddling.

''I got the job and eventually was promoted to the position of John Vincent's administrative assistant and finally the company office manager. As his assistant I had access to more company information than when I was a secretary. As the office manager I had access to all the company records including the books. That's when I came across the irregularities in his accounting.''

''What did you do then?'' Her tone of voice told him as much as her facial expression when she mentioned her mother's connection with her choice of educational pursuits and career. Part of his job was to read people quickly and make judgments based on that assessment. She obviously had a very strained relationship with the woman. How deep did the problem go and how much of her life had been affected by it? Questions he would have to put aside until some other time.

''I wasn't sure if I was interpreting the information correctly, so I finally went to the company's outside CPA with what I'd found. Phil Winthrope and I—''

''Phil Winthrope was the fifth witness killed. I didn't realize you knew him before the trial. Did you know any of the others?''

She glanced at the floor, then back at Brad. A sadness covered her face as she spoke. ''I didn't know Phil well, we only had the occasional business contact. He seemed like a nice man. Did he…uh…leave any family? A wife or children?''

''No, no immediate family.''

''I didn't know any of the other witnesses before the trial.'' She shifted her weight as if trying to find a more comfortable position before continuing. ''Phil looked over what I brought him and agreed with my conclusions. John Vincent had been systematically looting the pension fund and was also keeping a double set of books as far as taxes were concerned.''

''Did the two of you ever discuss what to do about this discovery or did you both just sort of ignore it?''

A quick flash of anger darted across her face. ''*Ignore it?* Are you accusing me of condoning John's actions?''

He remained calm despite her outburst. ''I'm not accusing you of anything. I'm just trying to get a clear picture of the sequence of events.''

She took a deep breath, held it a moment, then expelled it. ''I…I guess I'm just a little on edge.''

''That's certainly understandable.'' He extended a comforting smile and waited for her to continue.

''Neither Phil nor I had an opportunity to do anything about it. The very next day I was approached by the D.A.'s office. They said they were conducting an investigation into John's activities and questioned me about what I knew. I didn't know what to do or say. I knew the books had been manipulated, but I really didn't know for a fact that it was John who had done it. They had me served with a subpoena to testify before a grand jury along with several other potential witnesses. I gave them the information about the books. The grand jury findings were presented and John Vincent was arrested on numerous charges. I was called on to testify at the trial, and the rest, as they say, is history. At that moment my life became chaos. I thought everything would have returned to normal by now." A look of sadness darted across her features and her voice dropped to a mere whisper. "But I was wrong."

Brad studied her for a moment. She had already been through so much. In some ways she seemed so in need of protection and so vulnerable. Yet there was an inner strength that radiated from her, something he felt even though he couldn't clearly define it. Each passing minute proved to be added fuel to a flame of desire that had started as nothing more than a sensual spark. He rose to his feet under the guise of taking another peek around the corner of the drapes, all the while telling himself *this is business...this is business.* It was a refrain that continued to repeat in his mind as he stared at the parking lot.

A quick jolt of adrenaline shot through Brad's body. He stared at the car with the headlights off slowly making its way along the row of motel rooms. A flashlight beam came from the car window, shining on each of the cars parked in front of the rooms.

Chapter Four

Brad flipped off the light switch. His words came out fast and emphatic. "Get into the bathroom. Lie down in the bathtub and stay there."

"What's the matter? Is something—"

"Don't argue with me!" The demanding growl in his voice said as much as his words. "Do it!" He watched just long enough to see Tara disappear into the bathroom and close the door. He moved quickly and efficiently. He pulled the 9mm from his holster and clicked off the safety. He wedged a straight-back chair beneath the door handle. Using the large overstuffed chair as a shield, he crouched in the corner. The adrenaline continued to pump through his body.

He drew in a calming breath, then slowly pulled aside the bottom of the drape. He watched as the flashlight beam fell on his car, then continued down the row. A moment later the slow-moving vehicle made its way back up the rooms across the way, then came to a halt.

Brad scanned the parking lot, taking in everything. His senses tingled with nervous energy. Every few seconds he glanced at the bathroom door to make sure it was still closed. A shadowy figure emerged from the darkened car. His pulse rate jumped into high gear.

The figure moved toward the room across the way, then an angry female voice reverberated through the night air, accompanied by a loud banging on the motel-room door. "Open up right now, Sam...you lousy excuse for a husband. I know you're in there with that Mary Anne person. And this isn't the first time, either!"

Brad leaned back against the wall. He emitted a sigh of relief followed by an amused chuckle as he slipped the handgun back into his holster. He hurried to the bathroom and yanked open the door. Tara stood just on the other side, her startled expression showing her surprise at his sudden appearance.

Her voice quavered as she spoke. "Are you all right? Is everything—" she glanced through the opened door into the bedroom "—under control?"

"What are you doing standing here?" His words demanded without his tone being too harsh. "I told you to get down inside the bathtub and stay there."

Surprise and confusion flashed across her face. "But I'm in the bathroom like you said, and the door was closed."

"What I said was for you to lie down in the bathtub. The door and wall might not have been enough protection if bullets had come flying through the air." He eyed her carefully, making a pointed statement with his question. "Don't you agree?"

"But they didn't—"

"That's not the point. They *could* have." He grabbed her shoulders, holding them firmly in his grip. He stared at her, trying to pull together the proper words. He felt the tension in her muscles. It matched the tension that filled the air between them as they stood facing each other—a tension as much sexual energy and attraction as it was a clash of wills and the effect of the danger.

"We need to get something clear right now." Brad's words were very matter-of-fact, his attitude all business. "This is my area of expertise. I expect to have my instructions obeyed without hesitation or questions. This is very serious business. Remember the car bomb? Your life could depend on your immediate response to my orders.''

"Your *orders?*" The irritation raced through Tara's body. "Just who do you think you are to be *ordering* me around?" She scowled at him for a moment, then jerked away from the electricity of his touch and brushed past him as she left the bathroom.

He caught up with her, grabbing her arm to bring her to a halt. His response was to the point, his irritation matching hers. "I think I'm the man who's trying to save your life. Who do *you* think I am?"

She glared angrily at him, but he stood his ground and refused to back down. She wasn't sure what to make of him. He seemed to be able to turn on his aggressive manner in the blink of an eye. And giving her orders…well, it was far too reminiscent of her mother's domination and Danny's controlling behavior for her to comfortably accept it. Intellectually she knew he was right in his concerns, but her emotional reaction to his take-charge attitude left her uneasy. And her reaction to the magnetic sex appeal of this dynamic and very handsome man left her equally uneasy.

Tara held his eye contact, refusing to look away. A shiver crept up her spine. It was more than the tantalizing physical contact where he still had hold of her arm. He seemed to be looking inside her as if searching out her hidden secrets. The intensity in his blue eyes sent an uncomfortable tremor through her body. He was right about the danger, but obeying his orders without question called for a level of trust she wasn't sure she knew how to give regardless of whether she wanted to or not.

Brad Harrison had her confused. He was a virtual stranger who burst uninvited into her world, tried to take control of her life and demanded that she trust him. Yet his unwavering gaze sent a ripple of desire through her body unlike anything she had ever experienced. She realized there was a lot more at stake here than a question of control. The concerns for her safety and the need to identify a murderer had already begun to take a toll on her nerves.

But that wasn't all. She feared there would eventually be a much larger toll to pay—an emotional one—if she didn't keep her desires under tight control. Every time he touched her a sensual rush coursed through her body. Her skin tingled and a shortness of breath caught in her lungs. It was totally inappropriate for the situation and equally out of character for her. But, for reasons she could not clearly fathom, she had made the decision to tentatively trust this very sexy and desirable man. Hopefully it would not be the biggest mistake of her life...or worse yet, the last decision she would ever make.

"You're right." She drew in a steadying breath. "This is your area of expertise. I, on the other hand, don't have any experience in being stalked..." Her voice trailed off as she glanced at the floor. "If that's an appropriate term for what's happening." She regained eye contact with him. "This may be business as usual for you, but it's all very new and very frightening for me."

"I know this is difficult for you." He softened his tone as he reluctantly let go of her arm, breaking the delectable physical contact between them. "These particular circumstances aren't exactly normal operating procedure for me, either."

Brad found himself in an awkward position totally unlike any situation he'd ever been in before. The heightened tension crackled in the air...a tension made up of equal parts sexual desire, emotional turmoil and professional ethics. *This is business...this is business...* The mantra played through his mind, but it did nothing to still the effect she had on him.

The stress of the situation was getting to him. It wasn't just the proximity of this desirable woman. There were the suspicions and confusion that had been mounting ever since he made the connection between the deaths of the witnesses.

His supervisor, Thom Satterly, had dismissed his concerns as not valid for reasons he still found very perplexing and difficult to accept. The fact that two of the witnesses had been put into the Witness Security Program was enough for Thom. He declared that no one would be able to find them, therefore the conspiracy Brad thought he had uncovered didn't exist. Thom pronounced it a strange coincidence and nothing more.

He had been disturbed by Thom's flat refusal to look into the case further, a factor that continued to pick at his consciousness. Without Thom's authorization, there would be no official consideration given to the plot Brad believed existed. He found Thom's actions very perplexing and highly suspicious. He could take his suspicions over Thom's head, but not without some solid proof, which he didn't have... yet.

He didn't know who he could trust or where he could turn for help in protecting the one remaining witness. And running beneath all that was an ever-increasing attraction to this beguiling woman who didn't seem to have any idea just how attractive and tantalizing she was. He reached out and lightly touched her cheek, allowed his fingertips to linger for a brief moment, then quickly withdrew his hand. He grabbed his jacket from the foot of the bed and pulled it on.

He turned toward her, brushed his fingertips gently against her cheek, then placed his hands on her shoulders. "Tara..." He plumbed the depths of her eyes. She exuded a fascinating combination of inner strength wrapped in vulnerability that did not diminish the sensual pull she exerted on him. He drew her closer, almost an involuntary gesture. "Get some sleep tonight and try not to worry. Everything is going to be all right. I'll stop by first thing in the morning and bring you some breakfast."

And then the desire he couldn't stop, an impulse he couldn't resist. He leaned his head toward hers and brushed a soft kiss against her mouth. It was all he had intended to do, just a quick gesture. But the moment his lips touched hers he knew he wanted far more. He captured her mouth and immediately felt her body stiffen, but she did not pull away. A moment later she responded to his kiss, sending an earthy sensuality through him and igniting every nerve ending in his body. He hadn't known what would happen when he gave in to his desires, but this certainly exceeded any expectations on his part. He wrapped his arms around her, pulling her body against his as the kiss deepened.

The breath caught in her throat and her heart pounded. He had caught her completely off guard, sweeping her away on a heated wave of exhilaration. As handsome, sexy and desirable as she found him it never crossed her mind that he would try to kiss her. It seemed so out of place considering the circumstances, but she couldn't have stopped him even if she'd wanted to. And wanting to stop him was the last thing on her mind. She had never had anyone convey such a level of sensuality with just a kiss.

It was Brad who came to his senses and finally broke off the delicious kiss in an attempt to cool down the burning desire churning deep inside him. He took a step back as he tried to catch his breath. He cupped her face with his hands. A slight flush spread across her cheeks. Her hazel eyes sparkled. His gaze dropped to her slightly parted kiss-swollen lips. He wanted more, so much more, but he knew he didn't dare.

"Uh...Tara..." He dropped his hands to his sides and took a couple of steps backward. "I...uh...well, I'll see you in the morning." Without waiting for her to respond, he turned and went out the door. He walked straight to his car while raking his gaze across the parking lot. Everything appeared exactly as it had when he'd left the room to get the ice and soft drinks. He slid in behind the steering wheel, took a calming breath and started the engine.

Brad drove his car to the entrance of the motel, parked and sat there. He watched the cars passing by on the street while trying to collect his thoughts. The sensation of his lips on hers still lingered with him. And he wanted more. He knew he had to get out of her room as much for his own well-being as anything else. He had overstepped the boundaries and now he needed to get his priorities in order. Her life was in danger and it was up to him to protect her, not take advantage of the situation.

He had never conducted himself in anything less than a strictly professional manner, had never allowed himself to become personally involved with any of the witnesses. His only personal involvement had been his pride in his work. But somehow, after only a few hours of face-to-face contact, Tara Ford had gotten under his skin. She had become very personal for him...far more than simply a case number.

He shoved his thoughts back to the situation at hand. She had to be the key to what was happening. She was certainly the easiest of the witnesses to find, yet she was the only one still alive. There had to be a reason and he had to find out what it was. And as much as he didn't want to believe, there was still a possibility that her involvement wasn't completely innocent.

"WHAT THE HELL'S going on? I turn on the television to get the late-night news and plastered all over the screen is a news story about Tara Ford's car blowing up in the parking lot of a restaurant. Only she's still alive and well. And she isn't home. I told you there was a deputy marshal who was suspicious. Well, any suspicions he may have had will now be clearly confirmed. Is that what you call *taking care of things?*"

"I swear I didn't know Pat was going to do that. He didn't let me know what he had planned."

"You were supposed to have handled this a long time ago and you didn't. Okay, I let you go to the outside and get someone to do it. Granted, he did a good job with Phil Winthrope, but this time he screwed up big. It was a very sloppy job handled like a rank amateur. Do I have to do everything myself?''

''I'll set something up with him. Give me a couple of days.''

''Another couple of days? Why not a couple of weeks or a couple of months? We don't know where she is other than the fact that she's obviously in hiding. This has gone from bad to worse.''

He heard the click then the phone line went dead. He nervously drummed his fingers against the desk, then reached for his little black book, looked up Pat's number and dialed the phone.

GET SOME SLEEP TONIGHT *and try not to worry.* Brad's words from the night before echoed through Tara's mind as she stepped out of the shower. If only it was that easy. She had just spent a restless night, getting very little sleep. The reasons were twofold.

First and foremost in her mind was the lingering sensation still on her lips as a result of his kiss. It had been the most wonderful kiss she had ever experienced—a heart-pounding, take-your-breath-away excitement that left her weak in the knees and wanting more.

But on a more practical note, she had also spent part of the night worrying about what the day would bring. She glanced at the clock—it was six-thirty. She didn't know when to expect Brad other than his mention of bringing her breakfast. She dressed quickly so she would be ready for whatever he had in mind when he arrived. She looked around at the meager necessities she had purchased. One thing for sure, it wouldn't take her very long to pack.

The motel room came equipped with a small coffeepot. She turned on television and made some coffee. She tried to relax, drink her coffee and watch the early-morning news, but her mind kept wandering as one concern after another invaded her thoughts.

Suddenly Tara jerked upright in her chair. A picture of the restaurant parking lot and the burned remains of her car filled the television screen. She listened intently as the reporter talked about the explosion. A cold stab of fear pierced her body as she continued to watch the news story.

The registered owner of the vehicle, Tara Ford, and her fiancé, Don McMillan, had just finished dinner at the restaurant when the explosion occurred.

The reporter had given her name on the air. Why hadn't Brad just insisted they leave right away before the police arrived rather than stay so that she had to give her name? Surely the car was beyond being identifiable and couldn't be traced to her. Foreboding jittered through her body, followed by a sick churning in the pit of her stomach.

A noise from outside startled her. She peeked out the side of the drapes, but it was just the normal morning activities. Every time she heard voices or car doors she jumped to attention only to find it was nothing more than the occupants of the other rooms checking out. She paced up and down the small room, peeking out from behind the drapes every few minutes. And each time she did, her anxiety level increased.

She didn't know what she felt, but whatever it was, she didn't like it. One moment it seemed like trepidation, then the next it turned to panic. And underlying all were thoughts of Brad Harrison. He charged into her life, told her she was in danger right before her car blew up, then he rushed her away to a motel—all within a few short hours. Everything had happened so fast that she didn't have time to really consider all her options...or even if she had any.

A soft knock on the door sent a nervous rush through her body. She looked through the peephole. The relief flowed over her when she saw Brad standing on the other side of the door.

"Come in." She stepped aside so he could enter.

"Good morning." Brad quickly closed the door behind

him. "I brought breakfast." He indicated the paper bag and the two foam containers as he set them on the table.

He turned to face her, captivated by her natural beauty yet bothered by the apprehension that covered her features. "Did you sleep okay last night?"

"I suppose so." Her answer lacked any enthusiasm.

"You sound less than sure." The thought danced through his mind that her wakefulness was due to the kiss he had initiated. She had been upset by his actions. He tentatively reached out and touched her cheek. "Are you all right?"

"Just a little on edge, I guess." A tremor of anxiety jittered through her body. "The truth is, I didn't sleep very well at all. I've been awake since about five this morning." She looked up at him, trying desperately to maintain her composure. She gestured toward the television. "I saw a story on the news this morning about my car. They said my name." She saw a hint of displeasure dart through his eyes, but his expression gave away nothing about his inner thoughts or feelings. "Why couldn't we have left before the police arrived?" Her frightened words pleaded with him for some sort of explanation. "My car was burned beyond recognition. No one would have known we were there."

"That's not true. If we had simply disappeared, you'd now have the police looking for you. The people in the restaurant knew you by name and saw us together. And even though your car was a mess, the vehicle identification could still be established and the registered owner determined without much difficulty. Our having left the scene before talking to the police would have created more problems than just a news story. We have to maintain as low a profile as possible—" he glanced at the television "—even though it seems to be getting harder to do, and that does not include having your name on a police bulletin as being wanted for questioning in connection with a car bombing."

He drew in a deep breath and slowly expelled it. He wanted to be able to bring her some good news, but that wasn't the case. "I'm sorry, Tara, but you'll need to stay here another day. By tomorrow I should have other arrangements that will be safe."

"I see." The disappointment rang clearly in her voice. She seemed to withdraw inside herself, as if all the life had gone out of it. Her gaze lingered on the floor, then she looked up and made eye contact with him.

"What's...what's going to happen next? When will I be able to go home? To go back to my job?" A little sob caught in her throat. "To go back to a normal life?"

Her obvious distress tugged at his emotions. He'd been in similar situations before with protected witnesses who were feeling the pressure of the circumstances surrounding the trial, but she had already been through that. It wasn't fair for her to have to be going through it again.

"I don't have an answer for you. This is a unique situation, at least it is for me. The steps normally taken to protect a witness don't apply here. I'm not able to make use of the vast resources of the Marshals Service, not yet—not until I'm sure of who I can trust."

He placed his hands on her shoulders, then drew her into his arms in an attempt to provide her with some comfort. He gently hugged her, holding her trembling body against his as he spoke in a soft, soothing voice. "I know this is very difficult for you and I'm sorry you have to go through it. With someone having placed a bomb in your car it's no longer a matter of *if* you're in danger. You *are* in danger and I have to do everything I can to protect you."

The car bomb...his wife dead...his failure to protect her. The guilt he continued to carry around with him surfaced again but slowly gave way to the memory of the heated kiss he had shared with Tara. As much as he didn't want it to be so, he could not deny his very real attraction to her. He had dated several women since his wife's death, but it had been as much out of loneliness as out of any real interest in any of them beyond the superficial. But Tara was different. Somehow he had to make sure that he didn't fail again. He had to see that no harm came to her.

He lifted her chin until he could see her eyes. "You do understand why you need to stay here for another day, don't you?"

"Yes." There was nothing left for her to say. She had resigned herself to the situation. Circumstances forced her to place the ultimate trust in this stranger...to trust him with her life. Could she be allowing a physical attraction to a sexy man cloud her thinking? She wasn't sure. She hoped not.

He reluctantly released her from his embrace and tried to inject a lighter mood with an upbeat attitude. "Come on, let's eat the breakfast I brought before it gets cold." He put his arm around her shoulder and walked her to the small table. "I brought some coffee, orange juice, yogurt, French toast and bacon. I hope there's something here that you like."

"That sounds fine. I'm hungry."

Those may have been her words, but her actions said otherwise. He watched as she spent more time poking at her food than eating anything. He tried to alleviate the tension by making idle conversation, but he had difficulty drawing her out of her shell. Even though he wanted to stay with her, he knew he couldn't. He finished eating, then stood up to leave.

"I have things I need to do in the office, but I'll be back at lunchtime. Is there anything special you'd like for lunch?"

"I noticed a coffee shop across the street. Couldn't we go there for lunch? I don't know anyone in Tacoma, so there's no reason for anyone to recognize me. We'd be there less than an hour." She offered a hopeful smile that came off as more strained than anything else. "It feels like the walls are beginning to close in on me."

"I'm sorry, but we can't take that chance. I'll get you out

of here by tomorrow. Just hang in for one more day." He put his arm around her shoulder again and gave it a comforting squeeze. "Do you think you can do that?"

She attempted a chuckle, but it came out more bittersweet than upbeat. "Do I have a choice?"

He saw the resignation in her eyes and heard it in her voice. As it had the night before, it tugged at his emotions in a way that made him decidedly uncomfortable. "No, I'm afraid you don't. I'll see you in a few hours."

Tara watched as he climbed in his car and drove out of the parking lot. As soon as his car was out of sight, she slumped into the large chair in the corner. She couldn't even open the drapes to let in the daylight for fear someone would see her. He had also cautioned her about letting in housekeeping to clean the room.

She closed her eyes. The heated kiss from the night before still lingered on her lips and burned in her senses. It fueled her desires where Brad Harrison was concerned...desires she knew were totally inappropriate and equally impractical. He was not the type of man for her. She wanted someone settled, someone who would treat her as an equal partner in a relationship, someone whose life wasn't filled with danger. She shook her head in an attempt to rid her mind of the errant thoughts.

She had to pull herself together. For someone who had lived a life devoid of taking chances, the last year had certainly made up for that. Sitting around feeling sorry for herself was not going to accomplish anything. Somehow she had to make a contribution to Brad's efforts to protect her, not just sit by, doing nothing, with her fate in someone else's hands. There had to be something she could do other than hiding in a motel room. She glanced at her watch. It was eight o'clock and time for her to be at work.

Her gaze moved from the motel phone to Brad's cell phone. She had to call to say she wouldn't be at work. Just not showing up was unacceptable, irresponsible and wasn't fair to her employer. She had to notify Judy, but what should she say? She couldn't tell her the truth even though she was sure it wouldn't matter to the situation at hand. After all, there wasn't anyone she worked with who had any connection to this mess from her past. She thought of several explanations and finally settled on one. She placed the call from Brad's cell phone, mindful of his instructions about not using the motel phone, which would give the front desk a record of the number she had called.

"Judy…it's Tara. I'm afraid I won't be at work today…or for the next few days, either."

"What's the problem. Are you sick?"

"No…" Tara paused a moment. Something in Judy's voice sounded strange. "It's a family emergency. My mother is in the hospital and—"

"Which hospital is she in? I'll have some flowers sent from the company."

"Uh…no, I don't think you should. We don't know how long she'll be there. They might be moving her to another facility tomorrow. I won't know until later today." A headache pounded at her temples. She had never had a talent for lying. What if she didn't sound believable? Would Judy suspect she was lying?

"Where are you now…at home?"

"Uh…yes, but I have my car keys in hand and I'm running late. I'll be leaving here as soon as I hang up." Car keys in hand…that was a laugh. Her car was probably still smoldering in the restaurant parking lot.

"You're driving? Didn't I hear on the late news last night about your car and an explosion? That you had been having dinner with your *fiancé?* I didn't realize you were engaged to anyone."

Was it her imagination or had she detected a hint of accusation in Judy's voice? No, that wasn't it…not accusation. Perhaps Judy was hurt that she didn't know about Tara's supposed engagement. Surely that's all it was. There was something there, though, something that wasn't right. Maybe Judy was upset because she had to hear about the car explosion on the news.

"I...I didn't realize there was anything on the news about it. It was just some kind of freak accident. The...uh...gas tank somehow exploded. I have a rental car supplied by my insurance company."

"Well, I had assumed you were all right." Judy's apparent resentment over not being personally notified came out in her voice. "The news story said no one was injured. I called your home but didn't get an answer so I left a message on your machine. Didn't you get it? I was worried when I didn't hear back from you."

"I've, uh, been having trouble with the machine. I need to replace it."

"Will you be here in town?"

"No, I'll be out of state." More lies. She had not been prepared for Judy to ask so many questions or bring up the news story about her car. Nor had she been prepared for her friend's off-putting attitude.

"Do you have a phone number where I'll be able to reach you in case of a work emergency?"

"I'm not sure where I'll be staying. I'll call you when I have more concrete information."

Tara quickly concluded her conversation. She sat on the edge of the bed and thought about what had happened. Something about the conversation left her uneasy, but she wasn't sure exactly what it was.

She shook her head. No...she was just being paranoid. She had lied to her friend and was now suffering pangs of guilt. That was all there was to it. She needed to get her nerves under control. She glanced around the room, then cleaned up the breakfast remains.

Her fingers moved to her lips, the sensation of the kiss

still very real for her. What would it be like to have Brad Harrison as a part of her life? She didn't have an answer for the question. She wasn't sure she really wanted to know the answer.

Chapter Five

As soon as Brad arrived at work he grabbed a cup of coffee, took several file folders from the file room and settled in at his desk. He took advantage of Thom Satterly's momentary absence to dig out more information on the John Vincent case. The deputy marshals assigned to protect the witnesses had been headed by Ralph Newman. He had worked with Ralph on a couple of cases.

Although competent in handling assignments, at forty-eight years of age Ralph hadn't progressed as far up the ladder as he probably should have and made no secret of being disgruntled by his lack of advancement. He didn't socialize very much with his co-workers and had a known proclivity for poker and racehorses, a pastime that had put him in a precarious financial situation on more than one occasion. The latest office gossip had him owing thousands of dollars to a bookie, an allegation which, if proven, could cost him his job. Brad took the Vincent file and wandered casually over to Ralph's desk.

Ralph looked up and quickly shoved something in his desk drawer, but not before Brad recognized it as a racing form. "You need something, Brad?"

He carefully worded his comments to make it appear that he had just started to work on the file. "I've been assigned file follow-up duty until the doctor gives me a medical release to go back into the field.''

A hint of confusion crossed Ralph's face. "So what is it I can do for you?"

"One of the files I'm working on is the John Vincent case. You headed the team in charge of protecting those witnesses, didn't you?"

Ralph regarded Brad warily for a moment before answering. "Yeah, that was me. It says so in the file." He leaned back in his chair, his tone and manner becoming defensive. "Why do you ask? Is there a problem of some sort?"

"Problem?"

"Why is there a follow-up on the case? Everything was closed out, Vincent was convicted and sent to prison, all my paperwork was completed in a timely manner." Ralph gestured toward the file folder in Brad's hand, his voice taking on an edgy quality and growing louder. "Everything's in there that's supposed to be. My reports are always thorough."

"Calm down, Ralph. I'm not accusing you of anything. John Vincent died of a heart attack while in prison. I'm going to be contacting the witnesses to let them know that he's now permanently out of the picture. Just a courtesy thing, that's all. Is there anything special about any of the witnesses that I should know?"

Ralph shifted his weight in his chair and creased his forehead in concentration, his manner and voice still guarded. "I can't think of anything special. Certainly nothing that's not in the file."

"Okay. Since you were involved with the original case, I just wanted to touch base with you before you left for the day. You're on the Judge Allen protection team, aren't you?"

"Yeah, the judge has been getting death threats. I'm covering him from noon until eight o'clock."

Brad retreated to his cubicle. Ralph's behavior struck him as odd, almost adversarial, as if he had accused Ralph of something. If Ralph had any information, he had chosen to keep it to himself. He gave no indication that he was aware of any of the witnesses being dead or for that matter that John Vincent had died almost six months ago. Brad filed that bit of information away in the back of his mind.

"How are you doing with those files?" Thom Satterly's sudden appearance startled Brad out of his thoughts. He closed the Vincent file and stacked it with four other folders.

"Everything's coming along fine, but this is boring stuff. I'll be glad to get back in the field."

"Just as soon as the doctor gives you a medical release for that shoulder wound." Thom pointedly stared at the two stacks of file folders on Brad's desk. "Do you still have all of these to go through?"

Brad gestured toward the larger pile. "These are done except for some final entries."

"Then those five are all that's left?" Thom started to reach for the smaller stack of folders, but Brad quickly snatched them up.

"Yes, just these five."

Thom's eyes narrowed as he stared at the file folders clutched in Brad's hand. He lowered his voice to the point where no one else would be able to hear. "You're not following up on that cockeyed theory of yours about the witnesses, are you?"

"Hey…you're the head of the Seattle office and you said there was no case. So, that means there's nothing to look into."

Thom pointed to the Vincent file. "Then why is this in your office?"

"Just bringing it up to date like the others." Brad drained the last drop of coffee from his mug. He held it up toward Thom. "I think I need a refill. Can I bring you something?"

"No." Thom continued down the hallway toward his office.

Brad grabbed another cup of coffee, then settled in behind his desk again. He had gone through proper channels by taking his suspicions to his immediate supervisor, but had been shut out as far as pursuing it. He still found Thom's attitude very strange and highly suspicious.

Thom had already been head of the Marshals office in Seattle for five years before Brad was assigned there eight years ago. At age fifty-seven Thom had probably advanced as far as he could within the U.S. Marshals Service. Brad had heard from other deputy marshals that Thom had at one time been a real hotshot with an unlimited future. Then a couple of bad breaks came his way, a couple of botched assignments, and his career had stagnated. Like Ralph Newman, Thom Satterly was someone Brad never would have been friends with away from work.

And also like Ralph Newman, Thom had money problems. A year ago he had taken on the financial responsibility of caring for his invalid father and paying his father's considerable debts.

Brad tapped his pencil against his desktop as he thought about his next move. Once again the image of Tara Ford popped into his mind accompanied by a sudden shortness of breath and an increased heartbeat sending a heated surge through his body. Even though their kiss had become emblazoned in his memory, having it pop into his mind while he was trying to work was not a pleasant diversion—a serious distraction was a more apt description, one that did not sit well with him.

He had refused to consider the possibility of a serious relationship since his wife's death. Intellectually he knew that carrying around guilt because she died from a car bomb meant for him was neither healthy nor realistic. But emotionally…well, that was another matter. So how could he explain such an intense attraction to Tara Ford? He told himself it was only physical, nothing more. She drove his senses wild, made his blood rush and his heart pound. And kissing her had only reinforced how much he wanted more of her.

Being personally involved with witnesses under his protection was strictly forbidden, both as Marshals Service policy and by his personal code of ethics. Tara was no longer a witness and he was not *officially* protecting her, but it presented an awkward situation nonetheless. He had put her in a position where she was isolated from everything and everyone and was totally dependent on him for the time being, which made her vulnerable.

He allowed the mental picture of her kiss-swollen lips and the sparkle of excitement in her eyes to linger for a moment longer, then forced his attention back to the problem at hand.

He made up a list of possible suspects. At the top of the list was Danny Vincent, John's nephew, who had a criminal record consisting of numerous misdemeanors when he was younger. Did he also have the same connections with organized crime as his uncle? Even though he had no arrests during the past ten years, his name had come up several times in various investigations. *Always look for a motive*— it was rule number one for his good friend Steve Duncan, a homicide detective with the Portland, Oregon, police department. It was Steve who Brad had called in an unofficial capacity to request that a very thorough investigation be made of the *accident* that killed the fifth witness.

The U.S. Marshals Service was a protective agency, not an investigative one. The FBI was the investigative arm of the Justice Department, but this was something Brad could not take to the FBI without Thom Satterly's approval. So he had turned to his friend. And as Steve said…*always look for a motive.*

And Danny Vincent had motive written all over him. First and foremost would be revenge. He was an only child whose mother was dead and whose father, John Vincent's brother, had been in bad health. He may have concluded that his uncle would not have died if he had not been in prison...that the stress of the trial and then imprisonment had been too much for his heart. He could very well have held the witnesses responsible for his uncle's death.

Another possibility for a motive also presented itself. Perhaps Danny's involvement in his uncle's criminal activities was much deeper than anyone realized. He might have been worried about the information the witnesses had about him, believing that it was only a matter of time before he became the target of an investigation the way his uncle had.

After careful thought Brad had reluctantly added two more names to that list—Ralph Newman and Thom Satterly. Someone inside the U.S. Marshals Service had to be providing information on witnesses, especially with the two men who had been in the Witness Security Program. Ralph and Thom were the most obvious candidates at the moment. Each of them had money problems and were in desperate need of the kind of payoff that could be elicited for that type of information. Both men had displayed unusual behavior in response to Brad's questions and speculations.

And then came the name that concerned him the most— Tara Ford. He knew in his gut that she couldn't be involved in any wrongdoing, but as a professional he had to put his personal feelings aside and look only at the facts. As the only witness who chose to remain in the Seattle area, she was the easiest one to locate yet she was the only one still alive. What had been carefully constructed murders made to look like accidents in the cases of the other five witnesses had been a very sloppy attempt on her life with no attempt to disguise it—a lot of fireworks without any harm to her. He had notified her that he believed she was in danger, and within hours there was a bomb planted in her car. It was almost as if someone had gone to a great deal of trouble to make her *appear* to be a target.

The circumstances were very suspicious to say the least. The only thing that relieved his anxiety over her possible involvement was that he couldn't find any motive for her being involved with the murder of the witnesses. There was nothing he could see that would make the elimination of the other witnesses be to her advantage. Someone had to be the last of the witnesses and it could just have easily been one of the others rather than Tara.

He tried to use that logic to ease his apprehension, but it didn't help very much. A shortness of breath caught him by surprise. Every time he thought of her, he relived every heated moment of their kiss and the way it set his soul on fire.

He had not yet had the opportunity to look into other members of John Vincent's family and he needed to be careful about how much investigating he did in the office. So, for now, Danny Vincent was his first choice as the person ultimately responsible for five deaths whether he committed the murders himself or hired someone to do them. He was the logical candidate to receive leaked information and if that was the case, it would mean he was working with someone on the inside. But would the death of his uncle while in prison be enough for a revenge motive? It would depend on how close Danny and John really were. Danny's whereabouts needed to be verified for the times of the witnesses' deaths.

Brad could understand a possible motive for Ralph or Thom, that of a large monetary payoff. Either one of them could be providing information to Danny. Or a more disturbing thought, either one of them could be directly responsible for the deaths as a contract hit. They each had a background of training with the Special Operations Group that would provide the type of expertise needed to carry off the clandestine function. But try as he might, he could not think of a motive for Tara, a reality that sent a wave of relief through him.

Three suspects, four if he counted Tara. Who else could he add to that list? He would need to dig deeper into John Vincent's family, find out who else besides Danny would have a motive that would put them on his suspect list. He folded the list and put it in his pocket. Right now he had another lead to follow.

The murder of Phil Winthrope had been the work of a highly skilled professional, so there was a good chance that the bombing of Tara's car was also done by a professional, even though it appeared to be a hasty and sloppy effort. He procured a list of known car bombers from the Bureau of Alcohol, Tobacco and Firearms. The ATF also provided him with the information they had on recent suspected activities, criminal records, current status and whereabouts and a list of known associates. He searched out connections with anyone in the Seattle office of the U.S. Marshals Service through past cases. It was an impressive list of bomber suspects, one that could take some time to carefully decipher and narrow down the possibilities.

This non-case had become more and more complex with each new discovery. He knew he had stumbled across a very devious and well-constructed plot, yet he didn't dare take his suspicions to anyone higher up, at least not yet. And especially not with Thom Satterly being on his suspect list, as well as Ralph Newman—not without some sort of proof to back up his speculations. A wave of sadness swept through him. He found the idea of anyone from the Marshals Service being involved to be very distasteful, but he couldn't ignore the possibility, especially in light of the mounting information pointing to a leak of information from within the Marshals Service.

TARA ANXIOUSLY PACED the floor in the small motel room, glancing at the clock every few minutes. If her nerves had been drawn any tighter they would have snapped. Brad had told her he'd bring lunch. As much as she wanted something to eat, she wanted someone to talk to even more. The room had become smaller and smaller with each passing hour since breakfast.

She stared at the door as if trying to force him to appear through sheer willpower. Her gaze fixed on the door handle. The sound was almost imperceptible, but the movement was very real. Someone was at the door, someone who had not announced their presence, someone who was slowly turning the doorknob.

A hard lump lodged in her throat. Her mouth went dry. She felt frozen to the spot. She knew she had to move, had to take action, but she couldn't. All she could do was stare. Fear churned in the pit of her stomach and quickly rose up her throat. Whoever was on the other side of the door twisted and rattled the doorknob.

It was panic and a strong sense of survival that finally spurred her into action. The only way out was through the very same door where an unknown person stood. She took a step backward, then another until she bumped into the bathroom wall. It was her only chance...she could try to get out the bathroom window. She turned toward the bathroom door giving up a silent prayer that the window could be opened. Her pulse raced and her heart pounded so hard it seemed that it might actually rip out of her chest. Then she was stopped short in her tracks by a woman's angry shout.

"Jimmy! Get away from that door. You get over here right now or you'll get a spanking!"

Then there was the sound of a child running. Tara's legs turned to jelly. She leaned back against the wall, but her legs refused to support her. She slid down the wall to the floor and sat there in silence. She felt numb all over. Was this what her life had come to? Even the misadventures of a small child were enough to throw her into panic. The tears welled in her eyes, finally overflowing the brims and trickling down her cheeks.

She slowly wiped them away and tried to regain her composure. Brad would be here any time. Tara couldn't let him see her like this. She couldn't let him know how she had fallen apart over such a trifling matter. Finally managing to get to her feet, she went into the bathroom where she splashed cold water on her face. She took several deep breaths and felt a little better. A calm began to descend over her rattled nerves. Stretching out on the bed, she closed her eyes. Brad would be here soon and then everything would be all right.

The soft knock grabbed her attention. She peered out the peephole in the door just as Brad announced his arrival. She quickly opened the door for him.

"I've got lunch." He set the paper bag on the table, placed a large thick envelope on the dresser, then took off his jacket and tossed it across the arm of the corner chair. He removed the contents of the sack. "Cheeseburgers, fries, a couple of milk shakes...definitely not health food, but from the best hamburger joint in town."

"It smells good and I'm hungry." Her stomach growled as if to confirm her words. She glanced down sheepishly. "I didn't eat much for breakfast and now I'm paying the price."

They ate quickly. Tara cleared away the remnants of lunch while Brad opened the envelope and took out several files.

"I have the reports on the accidents that killed the witnesses. Victim number one is from Dade County in Florida. The coroner attributed death to poisonous mushrooms. The report states that the deceased had been entertaining a woman in his house. His neighbors said he fancied himself a gourmet cook. He had apparently prepared dinner for two as a prelude to the evening's activities. A couple of X-rated tapes were found in the bedroom on top of the television and another one in the VCR. It appeared he had very definite tastes as evidenced by the handcuffs and other paraphernalia on the nightstand."

Brad skipped ahead a couple of pages. "His companion of the evening was never identified, but described by his neighbors as a woman in her early thirties with short red hair, but no one got a good look at her face due to the large sunglasses she wore. They found bright red lipstick on one wineglass and coffee cup. The same shade appeared on his shirt along with the strong scent of cheap perfume. They found some short red synthetic hairs in the bedroom and a couple of long blond human hairs with blond the natural color rather than bleached. They concluded that the woman was wearing a short-haired red wig.

"She apparently didn't like mushrooms, which they believe is what saved her life. The dinner plate next to the wineglass and coffee cup with the lipstick had the mushrooms shoved to one side with a couple of bites of steak remaining. The official report stated that the woman is believed to be a prostitute, which explains why she never came forward to offer any information."

He put that file back in the envelope, then picked up the next folder. "This one is from the Los Angeles County sheriff's office and is a report on a fall from the cliff above the Pacific Ocean just north of Malibu. It seems that victim number two was known to go jogging early in the morning along the beach cliffs. That particular morning was foggy. It appeared that he had simply gotten too close to the edge, lost his footing and fell to his death on the rocks below. There weren't any witnesses to what happened, but nothing at the scene indicated a struggle or an encounter with someone else."

He put the file aside and reached for the next one. "Here's where it gets really interesting. This report comes from the Dallas Police Department. With victim number three we have another case of food poisoning. This time it was a plant called cassava. When cooked properly it doesn't pose any danger. But in a raw state it contains high concentrations of prussic acid sufficient enough to cause death from cyanide poisoning. Death comes very quickly. The victim was found in the bedroom and there was evidence of a half-eaten raw fruit. They also found some short red synthetic hairs on the pillow.''

Brad picked up the fourth file. ''This one is from the Cleveland Police Department. Victim number four was bitten by a coral snake. While poisonous, the bite is usually not fatal for humans unless it isn't treated with antivenom. And that was the case here. The snakebite was in the victim's neck, injecting the venom directly into the bloodstream. They found the snake in the bathroom.''

He set the file aside. ''What I found particularly interesting was that victims number one and three were the witnesses in the Witness Security Program and had been given new identities and relocated. Both of them died from eating poisonous foods. Short red synthetic hairs were found at the scene of both deaths. In both cases the cause of death was ruled as self-administered but not a suicide—in other words, apparent accidental death. That in itself is suspicious without even taking the other deaths into consideration.''

Brad added the file to the envelope with the others. ''And that brings us to Phil Winthrope's death in Portland, Oregon, another that would have gone down as an unfortunate accident. He had been pronounced dead at the scene from what was at first called a really weird accident. His front tire had apparently blown out, causing his car to veer sharply into the river, according to witnesses. He was trapped inside as a result of a jammed door and malfunctioning seat belt. Death was due to a blow on the head that seemed to have been sustained during the impact. If that hadn't killed him, he would have drowned since he was trapped inside his car underwater.

''After giving it a second look—a very thorough scrutiny—the Portland lab technicians found where and how the seat belt had been tampered with and that the tire was blown by a remote-control device so that the where and when of the accident was determined by the perpetrator. It was a very slick and highly professional job, the kind of thing where someone really had to be searching with the knowledge that it was not an accident in order to discover how it had been rigged. Without the extra investigation it would have gone down as an accident just like the other four. It's the only one where there is concrete proof of a premeditated crime— that and the bombing of your car.''

Tara didn't say anything. She seemed more stunned than anything else. Brad reached out and touched his fingers to her cheek. ''Are you all right?''

''I…I guess so.'' She looked up at him, a combination of despair and trepidation covering her features. ''I had no idea—''

He pulled her into his arms and held her, trying his best to comfort her while staving off his personal desires. She definitely stimulated his senses and aroused his physical desires, but her inner turmoil also touched him on an emotional level. He ran his fingers through her hair and cradled her head against his shoulder. She felt good in his arms, as if it was meant to be. He kissed her forehead, then fought the temptation to do more.

''Tara…''

''Yes?'' She liked the sensation of being held by him. It made her feel safe, even if only for a few minutes. What would it be like to have Brad Harrison as part of her life on a daily basis? No…she couldn't start thinking along those lines. She didn't really know anything about him except that he made her pulse race and her heart pound every time he came within three feet of her. His life was unpredictable and filled with danger. He carried a gun. He was nothing like the type of man she wanted, but still…

She also knew that his only purpose in being here was because someone was trying to kill her. It was his job. Nothing more. She couldn't even say with certainty that he wasn't already married, maybe engaged or at the very least involved in a relationship.

"Uh...I need to get back to work." Those may have been his words, but he made no effort to release her from his embrace. "While I'm gone I want you to think back over the past few months, anything you can think of, any sort of unusual situation that had the potential to be a fatal accident. We can talk about it this evening."

He stroked her hair, reveling in the silky texture. "What do you want me to bring you for dinner?" He couldn't force himself to turn loose of her even though he knew he should. Then the temptation that he had been fighting finally won out. He placed his fingertips beneath her chin, lifted her face, lowered his head and placed a gentle kiss on her lips. The tender kiss quickly deepened as he pulled her body tighter against his.

Again, her response surprised him...at first hesitant, then accepting and finally willingly involved. As before, a hard jolt of lust traveled through his body. But this time there was an undeniable rush of emotion attached to it. The words played through his mind...*this is business, this is business...* but he quickly shoved the annoying mantra aside.

Then he reluctantly broke the kiss. He rested his cheek against her head, took a deep breath and forced a calm to his growing desires. He mentally kicked himself for his totally unprofessional behavior. This woman was in danger and needed his help. And what had he done in response to that? He had allowed his physical desires to distract him from his duty.

A wave of emotion swept over him, something he didn't want to acknowledge. He abruptly turned away. "I'll see you this evening." He peeked out from behind the closed drapes. Then, when he was satisfied that everything outside was okay, he opened the door and left before the temptation to stay became overwhelming.

TARA HAD NEVER FELT so restless or uncomfortable in her life. She had been confined inside the small motel room since about eight o'clock last night, over twenty-one hours, and apparently she would have to stay there yet another night. She had managed to put off the maid and hadn't used the motel phone. There was that one call she'd made on Brad's cell phone, but that had been a necessity. She had to call Judy to let her employer know she wouldn't be at work. Surely Brad couldn't object to that. She felt a frown wrinkle her forehead as she tried to shove down a twinge of anxiety. So why was she trying so hard to convince herself that making the phone call was okay?

She peeked out from the edge of the drawn drapes for what seemed like the fiftieth time since Brad left following lunch. Even something as simple as being able to take a walk around the block would help. She slumped into the large chair, leaned back and closed her eyes. Her fingertips went to her lips. She could still feel the heated excitement of his kiss. It did far more than singe her desires on a primal level. It touched her emotions in a most profound way. It didn't make any sense. She barely knew this man, yet he ignited the very depths of her soul beyond her ability to clearly comprehend.

Her eyes snapped open. She didn't like the direction her thoughts had wandered. She needed to keep a clear head, to keep her emotions tucked safely away. He was not the right man for her regardless of how his kisses swept her common sense out the door.

She glanced at her watch, then peeked out the window again. A wave of relief settled over her when she saw Brad pull into the parking space. She noted that he parked a couple of doors down from her room even though there was a spot right in front of her door, another simple precaution that hadn't occurred to her.

Brad quickly entered the room, closing the door behind him and turning the bolt lock. "How are you doing?"

"Okay, I guess." She tried to keep her nervousness out of her voice without much success.

He set the food on the table, then tossed his jacket across the foot of the bed before turning to face her. He shot her a teasing grin that could not erase an undertone of seriousness. "Have you gone bonkers from the stress of being confined to a small room or are you managing to hang on to your sanity?"

"I'm not sure." She tried to fall in with his teasing manner, what was apparently his attempt to lighten the mood. "I think it could go either way. I was tempted to take a walk around the block just to rid myself of these four walls for a little while."

A quick flash of alarm covered his face. "You didn't, did you?"

"No." His sudden change and the implications it conveyed were hard to ignore, reinforcing her anxiety. "You said not to leave, so I didn't. It was just that I wanted to." She paused as she turned the thought over in her mind. "There was one thing, though…this morning…I did make a phone call."

His gaze flew to the telephone sitting on the nightstand. An uneasiness welled inside him. He didn't like what he heard. "You used the motel phone?"

"I remembered what you'd said about using the phone here, so I used your cell phone." She looked up at him, hoping he was not too angry with her or, worse yet, that she had done something that would backfire on them. "I needed to let my employer know I wouldn't be at work for a few days. They had to be notified. If I just didn't show up they would have come to my house looking for me. I could have lost my job. When this is all over, I'll need my…" Her words trailed off. Perhaps a more accurate phrase would have been *if* this is ever over.

"You should have mentioned this to me at lunch. Who did you call and what did you say?" Brad turned on his professional business mode, his expression giving no evidence of what was going on inside his head.

"I called Judy Lameroux. She's the office manager. You met her sort of. She's the woman I was having lunch with the day you bumped into me." It had been yesterday, but it seemed like such a long time ago and a world away. Her entire life was in turmoil and she didn't seem to have any control over it.

"The woman with the long blond hair? Yes, I remember her. What did you tell her?"

"I said I had a family emergency, that my mother was in the hospital and I needed to leave right away...that I wouldn't be at work for a few days."

"What did she say?"

"Well..." It had been an odd conversation, but she was sure it was only because Judy had been surprised by the call and upset that Tara had not called her after the car bombing, nothing more. "She did mention that she had seen the news story about my car and that she had tried to call me, that she left a message on my machine. I told her I'd been having trouble with it and hadn't gotten the message."

He pulled out his notepad, his face an impassive mask. "How does Judy spell her last name?"

"Surely you can't suspect her of anything. She's my friend. I didn't even know her when all this began." She quickly explained her coincidental meeting with Judy in her favorite bookstore and how Judy had gotten her a job at the same company where she worked just before the start of John Vincent's trial. She studied the skeptical expression that covered his features. What was he leading up to? She suddenly felt as if she were being interrogated rather than simply answering a few innocent questions.

He stood with his notepad and pen still in his hands. It was almost as though he hadn't heard a word she said. "How do you spell her last name?"

He wrote down the name as Tara spelled it, then changed

the topic so quickly that it caught her off guard, making her wonder what was really going through his mind. "Let's get to the food while it's still hot. We can talk while we're eating."

Chapter Six

Brad unpacked two complete meals from the plastic bag consisting of salad, baked chicken, vegetables and dinner rolls. Tara stared at the dinners, then looked up at him. "It looks good, but it's a lot of food."

Brad ripped open a packet of dressing and put it on his salad. "Have you thought about any unusual incidents that have happened to you since the trial ended? Any near misses or accidents that could have been fatal?"

Tara wrinkled her brow in concentration as she took a bite of her chicken. "Well, there isn't anything that leaps to mind as some sort of horrendous happening, but there were a couple of bizarre things. I was walking down the street and a large urn—a flowerpot type of thing—fell from the roof of an apartment building. It missed me by only a few feet. There were several urns along the edge of the roof. I assumed one had simply come loose and had fallen over."

"Is that a block where you often walk? A route that was normal for you?"

"Yes. It's between my house and the little neighborhood market a couple of blocks away. It gave me quite a start. I didn't think my heart would ever stop pounding. I considered myself lucky that it missed me, but didn't attach anything sinister to the occurrence." She hesitated as she recalled the moment the urn crashed behind her. A little shiver of trepidation made its way across her skin. It was an incident that now carried a far more sinister implication. "At least not at the time."

Brad watched her as she took another bite of food. What were the odds of an urn on the top of a building, something that had apparently been there for a quite a while, suddenly coming loose and falling just as she walked by? Probably about the same as five out of six witnesses from the same trial dying of accidents during a six-month period of time.

He buttered his dinner roll. "When did that happen?"

"I'm not sure. I think it was about a month ago, maybe five weeks or so."

"You said there were a couple of incidents. What about the other one?"

"I was crossing the street—"

"Were you in a crosswalk?"

"No, I was leaving my dentist's and had parked across the street, so I checked for oncoming traffic and started to cross where I was rather than going down to the corner. I had just stepped off the curb when a car came screeching out of the alley and nearly ran me down. I jumped back just in time. The car kept on going."

Brad reached for his notepad and pen. "What kind of car was it? Do you remember? Was there anything special about it? Did you notice the license tags?"

Tara placed her fork on the plate. "Things like that happen all the time..." She looked up at him as if she was seeking validation for her assumption. "Don't they? And I was in the wrong since I was jaywalking. I just chalked it up to being lucky that the driver didn't hit me and I went on about my business. I think the car was brown—" She suddenly sat upright, her intense expression boring into him.

Brad jerked to attention, his senses alert for anything amiss. "What's wrong?" He glanced toward the window then the door. "Did you hear something?" He started to reach for the lamp to turn it off.

"No...nothing like that. It just occurred to me. It wasn't a brown car." She stared at him, the light of recognition shining in her eyes. "It was dirty...mud spattered all over it, even the side windows. I couldn't see the driver because of the dirty windows. Even the license plate was covered with mud so that I couldn't read it. I think the car was green, a medium green rather than a dark color. It was a four-door model, but I don't know what kind it was. It seemed pretty new."

"That would certainly be a means of disguising the car to keep anyone from being able to identify it or the driver. He could run it through a car wash a block away then drive right back to the scene and no one would spot it as being the same car."

"Do you mean that it was a deliberate attempt on my life?" She nervously bit at her lower lip, then regained eye contact with him. "It was shortly after the car incident that I began to have the feeling that someone was watching me." A shiver of fear darted through her body. "Are the two things connected?"

"It's hard to say, but I think it's a distinct possibility." He watched as she toyed with her food. Where her manner had been cautious when he arrived, it had suddenly turned fearful. He wanted to tell her there was nothing to worry about, but he knew it wasn't true. He took another bite of chicken followed by some vegetables as he formulated his next comments.

"I want to know everything about John Vincent that you can think of, in particular any personal information that wasn't brought out during the trial. I haven't read the trial transcript. I've only been able to go through the files we have in our office and what's accessible on the computer. I haven't had time to dig into John's background in great detail, so anything you can tell me will be a help, especially since you worked for him for several years. You saw him every day and must have acquired a great deal of personal insight into the man beyond his business dealings.''

Tara took a bite of salad before answering him. Her voice held a resignation that hadn't been there before. ''I obviously didn't acquire enough personal insight since I had no idea he was a crook and, worse yet, was connected to organized crime.''

''That's not what I want to know about. I want information about his background, his friends and family, his personal likes and dislikes, his temperament—personal information.''

Tara looked up at him, a hint of confusion darting across her features. ''You mean things like his hobbies? He played golf.''

''His hobbies…his family.'' Brad watched her for a moment as she ate her dinner. ''Tell me about John's nephew, Danny Vincent. He worked for his uncle. What exactly was his job with the company?''

She hesitated, as if trying to get her thoughts together. ''Danny used to hang around the offices quite a bit. He eventually went to work for the company a little over three years ago. He carried the title of sales manager and he received a very healthy weekly paycheck. He wasn't in the office very often after he went on the payroll and I never really saw any results of his sales efforts.''

''How well did you know Danny?''

Her expression said it all, and if that hadn't been enough, there was the guilt that showed in her eyes and finally the crimson flush of embarrassment that spread across her cheeks. He had hit a nerve. She had been holding something back from him. A tremor of wariness rippled through Brad. He hadn't expected that. It left him strangely unnerved— and very disappointed. He kept telling himself that she couldn't be involved, regardless of the circumstantial evidence he'd been struggling with. Had he just been kidding himself? A tickle of anxiety told him how unsettling he found the notion.

He maintained a strictly professional outer calm as he looked at her questioningly. "Yes? There's something?"

Tara squirmed awkwardly in her chair trying to find a more comfortable position. She didn't know what to say, or more accurately, *how* to say it. She should have told him, but it had been a long time ago. It hadn't seemed relevant— until now. "Uh…well, I guess I know Danny pretty well. I was, well, I was engaged to him for a while."

She saw the shock dart through his eyes. She hastened to offer an explanation before he had an opportunity to say something. "But it's been over for a long time. I broke off the engagement about three years ago, shortly after he went on the company payroll, and haven't had any personal connection with him since that time…just the strictly business situations when he was in the office." She scrunched up her mouth, not sure how much she should say. The words came out softly, almost as a whisper. "Until a few days ago."

"A few days ago?" He tried not to show any personal reaction to this startling piece of new information, but hadn't been able to keep the edge out of his voice. "What happened a few days ago?" He now had something he didn't have before and that something was a motive for considering Tara a suspect. A sick feeling swept through him as he considered the reality. Once she knew there was a deputy marshal interested in what was happening, she could have easily worked with Danny to stage the bombing of her car in an attempt to throw him off the track. He didn't like where his thoughts were going, but he had to reluctantly admit that her involvement was now a real possibility.

"I hadn't seen Danny or heard from him since the day I quit Green Valley Construction, the same day I agreed to testify against John. Then a few days ago I got a phone call from him."

"Did he say why, after all that time, he had suddenly decided to give you a call?"

"He said it had taken him all that time to track me down and get my unlisted phone number. I asked him if he was the one who had been following me and making anonymous phone calls—"

Brad's words spilled out along with his surprise, irritation and even a hint of anger. "What anonymous phone calls?" He fixed her with a hard stare. "Why didn't you mention any of this when I asked you about strange occurrences?" He fought to keep the skepticism out of his voice, but knew he was not very successful. "You didn't consider anonymous phone calls as being anything *unusual?*"

"I'm sorry. I guess I didn't realize..." She heard the suspicion in his voice. How could she have dismissed such an important thing? What must he be thinking? A stupid question—she could see what he was thinking, the accusation in his eyes as if he was somehow blaming her for what had happened.

He took a deep breath, held it a moment, then exhaled. "Okay, the most recent call—what did Danny say he wanted?"

She heard the exasperation in his voice, a reality that left her torn between embarrassment about her oversight in not mentioning it and her annoyance at his sudden change of attitude. "He asked me to go to dinner with him. He said he just wanted to talk. I told him we had nothing to talk about and that I didn't want him calling me anymore, then I hung up. That was all there was to it."

Brad's manner was all business. "These anonymous calls, when did they start and what did the caller say? Did you recognize the voice? Was the caller a man or a woman?"

"Whoever it was never said anything. There was just silence and breathing...not heavy breathing like an obscene phone call, just the sound of someone breathing."

"Was there any background noise? Anything that might give a clue as to where the caller was?"

"Nothing that I can remember."

"Is that all of it or is there something else you've *forgotten* to mention or didn't think was important?"

She bristled at his thinly veiled accusation. "I don't know what you want me to say. I don't know what's important for you and what isn't. Do you need to know about every minute of my life? Are you trying to pry into my most private moments?" Her nerves had stretched almost to the snapping point. She knew she had gotten louder, but couldn't seem to get any control over her tone.

She jumped to her feet and leaned forward with her hands against the table. "I've already had too many people trying to control my life. I don't need it from you, too!"

He rose to his feet, his aggressive manner matching her anger. He didn't say anything, but the intensity in his blue eyes bored into her consciousness along with the heat of heightened emotions.

A second later a wave of regret swept through her. She hadn't meant to say those words and certainly not in that manner. They had just sort of slipped out before she could stop them. What started as polite dinner conversation had gone from innocent to loud and accusing without any stops in between.

What would happen if she just walked out the door? Could he legally stop her? How much danger was she really in? No...that was a dumb question. She was there when her car exploded. The danger was very real. One thing was for sure, though—no matter how much the heat of his kisses still lingered in her consciousness, she could never allow anyone else to control her life the way her mother had and the way Danny had tried to. And no matter how desirable she found him, that applied to Brad Harrison, too.

He didn't respond to her ill-timed outburst. His intense gaze continued to bore into her as if he was reading her innermost fears and desires. The quiet began to chafe her taut nerve endings. Her newly formed anxieties churned in her stomach, feeding the turmoil that already lived there. He claimed to be trying to save her life. And with every passing minute she became more and more aware of just how much danger existed around her. She had put the reckless driver and the falling urn out of her mind as being just accidents. Now she wasn't so sure. Ten minutes ago she had been hungry. Five minutes ago she became angry and defensive. Now she was just plain scared.

Then an entirely new sensation invaded her consciousness when he placed his hands on her shoulders. She felt herself being drawn to him, then his mouth was on hers. All the heat of her angry outburst transferred to the emotional turmoil churning inside her—and the passion his kiss created. Her response was almost involuntary as she reached her arms up around his neck. The excitement raced through her body, touching every corner of her consciousness.

He caressed her shoulders then wrapped her fully in his embrace. This was as wrong as anything he had ever done in his entire life, but at that moment he didn't care. The flare of her anger, the flashes of independence in her eyes, the energy of her outburst all combined to spark his desires beyond the place where he thought they were safely contained. And once let out, those desires turned into their own force of life.

The taste of her mouth, the sensation of her body pulled tightly against his, the fervor of her response—it acted like an aphrodisiac on his already stimulated senses. He ran his fingers through the silky strands of her hair. Everything about her—

The explosion of glass ripped through the drapes and flew across the table into their food. Brad winced in pain, grabbing his left arm where the bullet grazed him. There was no time to give it any further attention. He moved quickly, almost instinctively. He shoved Tara to the floor and protectively covered her body with his. He yanked the lamp cord from the electrical outlet, plunging the room into darkness.

"Are you all right?" His words were rushed as his mind raced to evaluate the situation.

"Yes...I think so." Her voice quavered and showed her distress, but it didn't reveal any panic.

"Stay here, don't get up."

Brad pulled the weapon from his holster and crawled to the side of the window farthest from the door. He flinched when he put his weight on his left arm. Experience told him it was only a minor flesh wound, nothing serious. He rose on his knees just enough to look out from beneath the drapes. He quickly scanned the parking lot, then looked again, carefully taking in everything—each car parked in front of a room, the possible presence of any people. Nothing moved. Nothing seemed out of place.

"This location is blown." He rushed his words, but his voice held control and presence. "I've got to get you out of here...now."

Tara swallowed hard. Her heart pounded in her chest and her pulse rate jumped off the scale. A minute ago it was Brad's kiss that had sent her blood racing. Now it was stark terror.

"Is...is he still out there?" She knew her voice gave her away regardless of how composed she tried to sound.

Brad crawled back to where she crouched on the floor. "I don't think so. I doubt that whoever fired the shot stuck around to verify the results. The risk of exposure would be too great."

He glanced around the room, the only illumination being the light filtering in around the closed drapes. "We've got to leave before the police show up. We walked away without any hassle from one encounter with them at the restaurant. We won't be as lucky a second time. I'm going to get my car and pull it in front of the room. As soon as I open the passenger door, keep low and make a dash for the car.''

He slowly opened the motel-room door. He maintained a low crouch as he peered out. Lights had gone on in rooms. It would be only a minute or two before people started questioning what had happened…before someone called the police.

He dashed down the walkway toward his car. A few seconds later he leaned across the seat and opened the passenger door for Tara. In less than sixty seconds from the time he slipped out of the motel room, they were on their way out of the parking lot. But now what? Somehow he had to make sure no one followed them, a task made much more difficult by having no idea who or what to be watching out for. His mind searched for a viable plan. He pulled onto the interstate and headed north.

Tara watched him as they drove toward Seattle. Tension etched his face. The hard line of determination showed in the set of his jaw. He gave up no hints of what was going through his mind. Although she managed to compose her outer appearance and sat quietly in the car, her insides alternately twisted into knots and churned violently. Her heart still pounded and her pulse had not yet settled back to normal. Even though the bombing of her car had been traumatic, the circumstances of this incident had left a more intense impact on her. The fear tried to climb up her throat, a fear she seemed to have little control over.

She tried to concentrate on where Brad was going as he exited the freeway. To her surprise he immediately got back on at the next entrance. Her confusion spun around inside her head as he repeated the procedure at each off-ramp he came to. The first time he did it she thought he had changed his mind about exiting and decided to continue north on the freeway. After the third time it dawned on her what he was doing. Their volatile exchange of words earlier in the evening did not diminish her admiration for the tactic he had chosen to determine if they were being followed. Anyone trying to tail them would need to exit each time they did and then follow them back onto the freeway again, an action that he could easily detect.

Several minutes passed before she attempted any conversation with him. She took a steadying breath, not wanting to add to his burden by showing how frightened she was. "Where are we going?"

He glanced at her then returned his attention to the road. "We're going to eventually end up at my place, but first I have to make it appear that I've stashed you elsewhere. We're going to downtown Seattle, then up into one of the many multilevel parking structures attached to one of several major hotels. At that point, you're going to have to complete the journey in the trunk. It has to appear that I dropped you off at the hotel and left alone. If asked, the parking garage attendant can say he saw me arrive with you, then leave alone a few minutes later. When we get to my place, we can enter directly from my garage into the kitchen without anyone seeing you. It's not an ideal plan, but it's the best I can come up with at the moment."

Thankfully she accepted his explanation without asking any more questions. He had too many details to work out in his mind before speculating out loud. Was the close call at the motel merely a random shot, someone taking advantage of a possible silhouette on the drapes of two people in an embrace? Or was the shot actually meant for them? And if that was so, how would anyone know they were there? Had he been followed from the office? But if that was so, then why did whoever it was wait so long to take a shot at them?

He glanced at Tara again. Or maybe the shot had been part of a plan to mislead him, just like the car bomb, by diverting his suspicions from Tara and sending him down a wrong path. Whoever had murdered five witnesses with such skill had suddenly become very sloppy with two unsuccessful attempts at Tara in as many days. First the bomb in her car that totally missed its intended target and now this. And to that he could add the other two attempts with the falling urn and the speeding car that she had told him about…four in all.

He didn't like where that thought took him, but he knew he couldn't afford to ignore it, either. He knew in his gut that she was innocent, but he couldn't just sweep aside the facts. He was a professional and he had a job to do. He could not allow himself to be influenced by the way her taste continued to fill his senses and the memory of her body pressed against his. It was as distressing to him as it was confusing.

He picked a downtown hotel at random and drove into the parking structure, taking the ticket from the attendant. He drove up three levels, finally pulling into a parking spot when he was confident no one had followed him into the garage.

Brad turned in the seat to face her. He gave her hand a reassuring squeeze. "I hope you're not afraid of the dark or suffer from claustrophobia."

She attempted a confident smile, but it felt as if someone had pasted a stupid grin on her face instead. "Couldn't I just scrunch down in the back seat? It will look like you're the only one in the car."

"Not to the attendant collecting the parking fee at the exit. He'll be on a level a step or two up from the driveway and in a position where he can look down and see everything inside my car. You'll have to be in the trunk or this won't work." He leaned forward with his face almost at hers when a flash of headlights grabbed his attention.

"Duck down." He tugged on her hand. They both remained motionless with their heads below window level. The sound of a car grew near, then passed without slowing down. He cautiously raised his head and looked around, sitting up when he was satisfied that everything was all right.

He leaned forward and brushed a soft kiss against her lips. He lingered a second longer, wanting to taste more of her. "Tara..." *This is business...this is business. Back off, you idiot, before you totally mess up.* He shoved his desires aside. "Into the trunk with you." She climbed out her side of the car, taking the plastic bag containing the belongings she had able to gather before leaving the motel room.

Someone had already killed five trial witnesses, planted a bomb in Tara's car and had just taken a shot at them. Passion-filled kisses were not the solution to catching a killer and unmasking a very clever scheme. He took a steadying breath as he unlocked the truck.

Tara peered inside. As trunks went it was pretty clean. There was a small toolbox, a couple of blankets and a duffel bag. She glanced at Brad, fought off an uncomfortable ripple of trepidation and climbed into the trunk. Brad showed her the release handle on the inside, then closed the lid.

The panic grabbed her the second the trunk lid clicked shut. Her mouth went dry and her throat began to constrict. She wasn't afraid of the dark. That wasn't the problem. But the other? That was a different matter. It's not that she was really claustrophobic...she didn't have any problems with elevators. She could stand up and move around in an elevator and there was light in an elevator. But this was different, being confined in a space as small as a car trunk. She had to maintain control, no matter what. Her heart pounded. She felt cold and clammy. *There's plenty of oxygen in here. There's nothing to be concerned about. It will all be over soon.* She tried to shove away her fears by visualizing mountain meadows, beaches, wide-open spaces, blue skies, sunshine...anything with a large expansive feel to it.

The car began to move, down the ramp then around corners then down the next ramp. She squeezed her eyes tightly shut and tried to focus on taking slow even breaths, but it didn't help her racing pulse or pounding heart as she felt the panic closing in on her.

Chapter Seven

The car came to a halt. Tara strained to hear the exchange of words between Brad and the parking attendant—the attendant's comment about him not being there very long and Brad's response that he had driven up to the level of his friend's floor and walked her to her room. Then the car moved again. The bump jostled her when they left the parking garage and turned into the street.

"Are you okay back there?" His words were a little muffled, but she could understand them.

She tried to project as much calm as she could muster. "Yes, I'm okay." A lie, for sure, but she couldn't let him know that she was barely keeping her panic at bay. He had enough to worry about without needing to deal with irrational fears on top of real ones.

"It won't be long."

She tried to take her mind off the rapidly encroaching walls of the trunk by concentrating on something else. Is this what her life had come to? Constantly looking over her shoulder to see who was watching her? Afraid to answer her phone? A bomb planted in her car? Someone taking a shot at her? And now being transported through town locked in the trunk of a car? At what precise moment had she totally lost control of her own fate? A wave of despair tried to weave its way through fear.

And what about Brad Harrison? When he found out about her former relationship with Danny, he had almost accused her of somehow being involved in a conspiracy, or at the very least knowing what was going on. He tried to dig into her personal life. And in the process he had managed to pull her life under his control just as Danny had tried to control her life. Yet when he tried to kiss her she not only let him, she willingly participated. And to make matters worse, he had ignited a fire inside her the likes of which she had never before experienced—a fire she feared could never be extinguished.

The car came to a halt, then the engine stopped. She felt the car bounce slightly as Brad opened the door and climbed out. A couple of seconds later the trunk lid popped up. The cool air rushed in at her. She quickly sat up, gasping in a lungful of air, then another and another.

A little frown wrinkled his forehead as he held out his hand and helped her out. "Are you all right?" He touched her face. "You're pale and your skin feels damp." He glanced toward the trunk, his genuine concern showing in his eyes. "You should have told me you couldn't handle being shut up inside a small space."

She forced the words in an attempt to sound casual, but it was far from what she felt. "There's enough to worry about without belaboring my short stint in the trunk." She took another deep breath. "Although I have to admit that I'm grateful to be out of it."

"You should have said something. I would have come up with another plan." He pulled her into his embrace, providing her with some much-needed comfort. It did more to calm her anxieties than all the deep breaths she could gulp in. A feeling of loss touched her senses when he released her from his arms a moment later. Without saying anything he ushered her through the garage and into the darkened condominium town house.

"Stay here." He turned on the light over the stove to

provide a bit of illumination in the kitchen. "I'm going to close the miniblinds and drapes in the other rooms before turning on any lights."

She deposited her sack of belongings on the kitchen counter. The red smear on the white plastic bag jumped out at her. She touched a trembling finger to the spot. It was wet. A lump formed in her throat. She instinctively knew it was blood. She glanced down at her shirt, almost afraid to look. A corresponding bloodstain covered her sleeve. She knew she hadn't been hit by either a bullet or the flying glass. The blood couldn't be hers. A sick feeling churned in her stomach. The shot through the motel window must have hit Brad, his blood transferring to her. He hadn't said a thing about it.

She had been so angry with him, yet he had still put his life on the line to protect her without hesitation. She wasn't sure what to think, but this time she knew exactly what she felt—it was guilt.

A light went on in another room and a moment later he returned to the kitchen. He flipped on the kitchen light. Her gaze flew to the large red spot on his left sleeve close to his shoulder. A shudder ran through her body. Her overwhelming guilt increased, building layer upon layer.

"Your arm! You've been injured."

"It's nothing. The bullet just grazed me." He winced slightly as he pulled his shirt off over his head. "It's the same shoulder as the wound that put me on the recuperative list." He dropped the shirt on the floor, turned on the water at the kitchen sink and grabbed a towel.

She took the towel from his hand and held it under the faucet. "Let me do that. I haven't been able to contribute anything very useful so far, but I can certainly take care of this." She looked up at him, another ripple of guilt and anxiety making its way through her consciousness. "In fact, you never would have been shot if it weren't for me. This is all my fault."

"It's not your fault, it's just part of the job."

She began to clean the wound, doing her best to maintain her composure and present a calm, in-control manner. He flinched slightly as she cleaned away the blood.

"I'm sorry. I didn't mean to hurt you. I'll try to be more careful."

"You're doing fine."

She was determined to show him that she wasn't helpless in a crisis. "You should have this looked at by a doctor. You'll need a tetanus shot if you haven't had one recently and you should probably have a couple of stitches."

"It's just a scratch. I'll put some antiseptic on it and a bandage. It'll be fine."

She held his arm in one hand, the sensation of his bare skin sending a little tingle through her fingers. She dabbed gently at the fresh gash. His tensed muscles made his arm feel as rock hard as it looked, and equally impressive were his broad shoulders, well-defined chest and flat stomach. Everything about him ignited sizzling desires inside her. She forced her attention and her inappropriate wandering thoughts back to the task at hand.

"There." She set the bloodstained towel in the sink. "It seems to have stopped bleeding. Where can I find antiseptic, gauze and adhesive tape?"

"I'll get it." He left the kitchen, returning a minute later with the necessary items.

She finished dressing the wound, then picked up his discarded shirt from where he had dropped it on the floor. "Do you want to have this sleeve repaired where the bullet tore it?"

"I think it's beyond hope." He took it from her hand and threw it in the trash. "I wish I had been able to grab my jacket from the motel room, though. Not only could it possibly be traced back to me, it's my favorite jacket."

She took the bag from the counter, reached inside and pulled out his jacket. "I grabbed everything I could reach while you were getting the car. I couldn't get the stuff from the bathroom, but I got everything else.''

She handed it to him. His gaze immediately captured her as tightly as if he had physically taken her into his arms... again. A shortness of breath caught in her lungs.

He brushed his fingertips against her cheek, his soft voice matching his sincere words. ''Thank you for rescuing my jacket. That was very thoughtful of you.''

She was barely able to speak. She forced out her words. ''It was nothing compared to you being shot on my behalf.'' She took a steadying breath and fixed her gaze on the floor. ''Actually you were wounded *because* of me.''

''Tara, I won't lie to you. This has turned into a very precarious situation. I don't know if the shot through the window was meant for you—or perhaps for me—or whether it was some weird random shooting and not related to the Vincent case at all. Having you stay at my place wasn't what I had in mind. It's obvious now that whoever is behind this knows I'm involved. I've got to find something a whole lot more secure than my place. But for tonight you sleep upstairs in my bedroom. Being on the second floor is more secure than being down here. I'll sleep in the den. I'll have some kind of plan by morning.''

She knew he was right about the situation having taken a turn for the worse. As unsettling as the events of the past couple of days had been, it was nothing compared to her confusion about Brad Harrison. There was no way she should have let him kiss her, no way she should have allowed that liberty. But the moment his lips touched hers she ceased to have any will of her own. She couldn't think about anything except the excitement he aroused inside her, an excitement she feared was gravitating toward an emotional attachment.

And now, seeing him standing in front of her, his blue eyes searching into her soul, and knowing the two of them would be spending the night under the same roof, did nothing to still those feelings. Only the sight of his bandaged arm and the knowledge that she was the cause of it kept her thoughts grounded in reality.

This was totally unlike her to be so immediately attracted to any man, let alone one who represented so much danger, even though this particular danger was a result of her presence. But could that danger also be equated with excitement? Was her personal life destined to continue on the path of daring that was so different from the way she had been raised? Could the real Tara Ford finally be emerging from her shell? Brad's nearness produced a quick shiver of yearning followed closely by a tremor of regret at the anger she had displayed at the motel. After all, he was only doing his job. It was a regret made all the more real by the sight of the bandage on his arm and the bloodstained towel in the sink.

"Brad…" A lump formed in her throat. "Uh…" She shifted her gaze to the floor for a moment, swallowed down her uneasiness, then regained eye contact with him. "I want to apologize for getting so angry earlier. This has been very stressful for me. Having someone wanting me dead is a difficult concept to grasp, and having the reality of that danger thrown at me in such a frightening manner…" She shifted her weight from one foot to the other in an effort to ease her mounting tension. "Well, I've been on edge. And then when you started prying into my personal life, telling me what to do, trying to *control* me…" Her words trailed off. She didn't know how to finish the sentence.

She checked the bandage on his arm, hoping it would be a distraction from the emotional confession she had almost made. "I'm so sorry you were injured. I feel responsible for this." The physical contact with his bare skin once again sent an excited ripple through her body.

"It'll heal in a couple of days." He wrapped his hand around hers and gently moved it away from the wound, then quickly turned loose of her before her touch drove him to total distraction. Her words had struck a chord with him, especially the emphasis she had put on the word *control*. It was the same impression he had gotten when she had spoken about her mother. Was it the key to understanding who she was and what she was about? He wasn't sure, but it was a start.

He wanted to get inside her head, to know what made her tick. He wanted to know everything about her. Part of it was professional curiosity. As much as the idea bothered him, there were still facts that pointed to her involvement, and now she had given him what he had been missing—a possible motive in her relationship with Danny Vincent. He couldn't simply ignore the evidence, no matter how much he wanted to.

"Grab your things. I'll show you where you're sleeping tonight." He escorted her through the kitchen, into the living room, past the door to the den and upstairs to the bedroom suite. He flipped on the light for her.

"You can sleep here." He shoved a pair of shoes into the closet and snatched up a T-shirt and an old pair of jeans from the arm of a chair. He tossed the jeans into the clothes hamper, then pulled on the T-shirt. He extended a sheepish grin. "You'll have to excuse the mess. I wasn't expecting company."

He turned on the light in the adjoining bathroom and glanced around, making a quick check to see that everything was reasonably picked up. He indicated the linen closet. "There are clean towels and washcloths in the cupboard." He looked at her questioningly. "You said you weren't able to retrieve anything from the motel bathroom?"

"I didn't have time." She held up the bag. "I was barely able to grab the things within my immediate reach."

He opened a drawer and pulled out a sack from the drugstore. "I just bought these to take out to my sailboat. Take what you need. There's a new toothbrush, still in the package, among other things."

She glanced around, then settled her gaze on Brad. A hint of embarrassment touched her at the thought of him providing her with such personal items as a toothbrush. "Thank you. That's very nice of you."

"Why don't you leave your things here? We'll go back downstairs and talk for a while. I really need some more information from you." He extended an encouraging smile, hoping he didn't sound as if he was about to interrogate her. "Are you up to it?"

Her anxiety level increased. More questions. More delving into her personal life. She understood the necessity, but it didn't make her any more comfortable with it. "I'll do my best."

Brad showed her into the living room where she settled into a corner of the couch. She glanced around, taking time to notice the decor. It felt comfortable yet at the same time showed good taste and an attention to detail.

He sat in a large chair opposite her, watching her for a moment. It was getting late. There wasn't time for any superficial conversation. "I need to know more about John's family. What can you tell me about John Vincent's ex-wife and his daughter? All I know is that he was divorced seventeen years ago and never remarried. He has a daughter from that marriage who would now be thirty-two years old. What can you tell me about them?"

"Not a whole lot. I never met his ex-wife or his daughter. His former wife died about five years ago. His daughter's name is Doreen. She was raised by her mother, sent to boarding schools then college. I don't think she and her father were really that close, although there were a few family gatherings I know they both attended. I've seen pictures of her, one in particular that John kept on his desk. It was taken at a country club, I don't know where—somewhere on the East Coast. They were having a party celebrating her college graduation. John and Doreen were standing together on the terrace. There were palm trees and ocean in the background. He did say something a few years ago about Doreen planning to get married and move to Paris.''

''You never met Doreen Vincent?''

''No. I've only seen photographs of her.''

''What does she look like?''

''She's striking-looking—very attractive with long blond hair, blue eyes and a good figure. Judging by the photograph showing how tall she was standing next to John, I'd say she stood about five feet six inches.''

''Do you know her married name?''

''John never mentioned it. I'm not even sure she really ended up getting married.''

''You don't know where she is now, do you?''

''No. She might still be in France, or maybe she didn't ever go. I just don't know. John never said.''

''Would you recognize her if you ran into her?''

''I'm not sure.'' She wrinkled her forehead and stared at him quizzically. ''I think I would. Why?''

''Just curious.'' He pondered the description. Could it be possible for her friend Judy and Doreen Vincent to be one and the same? Perhaps a little plastic surgery? After all, she said she had never met Doreen Vincent, had never actually come face-to-face with her. The story Tara related of how she met Judy and got her job seemed a little too coincidental. The sheriff's report from the first *accident* did state that a couple of long blond hairs had been found at the scene in addition to the red hairs from a wig. It was an idea he decided not to discuss with Tara—at least not yet. There was no reason to tell her of his suspicions about her friend until he had more information.

''Do you suppose we could get back to Danny Vincent without you getting angry?'' It was a loaded question and there wasn't time to make it more palatable.

She bristled at his comment while fighting off her feelings of guilt over her earlier outburst. She glanced at the bandage on his arm, a bullet that had been intended for her. It only added more guilt to the load she was already carrying. She took a calming breath. ''Yes, we can do that. What do you want to know?''

''What about Danny taking over John's illegal operations? In your opinion would he be the logical successor?''

''I haven't any idea about that. Until the trial I didn't even know John was involved in outside criminal activities, especially of that magnitude. Surely there must be someone better qualified to answer that question than me. How about the D.A.'s office? Wouldn't they know more about that? Wouldn't they have investigated Danny as well as his uncle?''

''Possibly so. What about personal matters? His temperament…is he the volatile type or methodical? Does he have a quick temper, prone to violence? Or does he hide behind a facade and carefully plan out everything he does? Is he very secretive?''

She tried to maintain an outer calm as he delved into what she perceived was her personal relationship with Danny Vincent, a situation that was over and one she didn't believe was anyone else's business. She knew her reaction was inappropriate, but that didn't stop the feelings. She didn't want to repeat her earlier outburst. She took a steadying breath and tried to speak in a calm manner. ''I guess I'm a little confused. What does this have to do with anything?''

''I'm still trying to figure out a motive for these murders. That will help lead me to the person or persons responsible. One obvious motive is revenge. I want to know if you think Danny is capable of avenging his uncle's death by murdering the people he believes were responsible for putting John in prison and thus contributing to his having a heart attack…those witnesses who provided the testimony that convicted him.''

A myriad of things swept through her mind. Danny's controlling nature, his apparent need to be in charge. She had always felt as if it was a point of contention between Danny and his uncle. A couple of times she saw him show his temper with someone else, almost like flash paper instantly bursting into anger. He had never turned that temper toward her, but had it only been a matter of time?

She tried to carefully formulate her words. "I'm not sure Danny and John were really that close, especially to the point where he would feel a need to avenge John's death."

"Then that leads us to another possible motive, which again leads me to Danny. If not revenge, then possibly Danny's involvement with John's criminal activities was known by some of the witnesses. He could have believed that it was only a matter of time before that information became public knowledge."

"I really can't comment on that, either. As I said, I'm not sure Danny was that close to his uncle and I have no idea about any criminal activities he might have been involved in."

"He was close to you, though." He knew he had to be careful in how he presented his thoughts. It was a thin line between speculation and accusation. "That could easily explain why you're still alive and the others are dead. Perhaps he still has lingering feelings for you as indicated by his phone call last week, where he wanted to get together with you for dinner."

Tara jumped up from the couch making no effort to conceal her feelings as she angrily blurted out her words. "Just what is that supposed to mean? Are you accusing me of something? Do I need to remind you that someone tried to kill me by blowing up my car?" A sob caught in her throat as the full magnitude of those words washed over her. She knew she sounded defensive, a situation aggravated by her guilt over having not been completely honest with Brad and compounded by his being shot while trying to protect her. She should have told him about her past relationship with Danny and about the anonymous phone calls, but at the time it simply hadn't occurred to her as being anything connected with what Brad had been talking about.

"I'm very aware of your car being blown up." Brad tried to keep his manner calm and in control. He could not let any emotional elements influence his thinking or actions, but had been unable to keep the accusation out of his voice. He knew he couldn't allow his desire for Tara to blind him to the facts...nor could he allow her emotional distress to tug at his senses any more than it already was. Yet there remained an undeniable question of her involvement.

"So what are you getting at?" A hint of confusion wrinkled her forehead and carried over into her voice. She shoved down the apprehension that suddenly welled inside her as she became less sure of herself with each passing second. He had sounded as if he was accusing her of something. Uncertainty surrounded her words. "Are you implying that I'm somehow involved? Are you now saying that I'm really a suspect in all of this? I don't understand. You're the one who came to me and said I was in danger and needed protection. I didn't believe you. Then my car blew up—"

A sob formed in her throat. She fell back onto the couch. Her voice again dropped to a frightened whisper that perfectly matched her despair and the fears she had been trying so hard to keep under control. "Then my car blew up and it convinced me you were right."

She closed her eyes. The memory of the explosion, the sound of that horrible moment, played through her mind. A tremor of fear darted through her body. The very man she thought was the one to help her...the man who had somehow charmed his way into her life, the man who literally took her breath away just thinking about the delicious kiss that had been interrupted by the gunshot...now seemed to be accusing her. She pulled her composure together and confronted him while trying to suppress the painful blow he had dealt her. If she had learned nothing else in her life, it was that she needed to stand up for herself because no one else was going to do it for her.

"This apparent idea that you have that I'm somehow involved is absurd. What possible motive could I have for wanting those people dead? For wanting anyone dead? Why would I have…" Her inner turmoil choked off her words, preventing her from saying any more. She had never felt as distraught as she did at that moment. She desperately needed to bring some sort of calm to her soaring apprehension.

Brad moved over to the couch and sat next to her. As hard as he had tried to keep a tight rein on his emotions, he could not ignore her obvious distress. He put his arm around her shoulder, then pulled her into his embrace. His entire reality seemed to be split dramatically along two lines… suspicions about her possible involvement in a conspiracy, something he desperately didn't want to believe, and his own growing personal involvement with her. He felt her body tremble and wished he could do or say something to make it easier for her. But instead, he said nothing. He simply continued to hold her as she touched his senses on every level, both physically and emotionally.

He took a steadying breath, then gathered the most soothing manner he could—something he hoped would soften what looked to be the beginnings of a battle of wills between them compounded by his own internal battle between the facts and his affection for Tara. "I'm not accusing you of anything. I'm merely trying to explore all the possibilities, trying to fit answers to questions, to find explanations for what's been happening over the past six months."

Even though he didn't want it to be so, in the back of his mind lurked the distasteful possibility of collusion between Danny and Tara, something that would not have occurred to him without the knowledge of their having been engaged. By being a witness against John Vincent and putting him in prison she could have helped pave the way for Danny to take over. Being on the inside at Green Valley Construction put her in a position to be able to keep Danny apprised of John's comings and goings as well as his private business matters. It was one scenario that could support the facts as Brad knew them, a scenario he did not like.

If that was what happened.

Her being the only witness still alive would also support the other possibility that Danny was the culprit and his motive was revenge, but his lingering feelings for Tara wouldn't allow him to dispose of her until a deputy marshal became involved in the matter and forced him to take action in order to cover himself. There was a great deal of what had happened that he couldn't explain, but if there was one thing about all this that he did understand, it was why Danny Vincent would still have strong feelings for Tara. There was something very special about her and it had been driving Brad to distraction from the moment he first saw her.

And then there was the third possibility, that someone other than Danny Vincent was responsible. On the surface, the most obvious motive for killing the witnesses was still revenge. Perhaps there was someone else who blamed those who'd testified against John Vincent for his death. He had to consider John's daughter, Doreen Vincent. He made a mental note to find out if there was any record of Doreen being married or any other name change, of her leaving the country as Tara mentioned and then returning. He also needed to find out if John Vincent had left a will. Who inherited his legitimate business interests? Would that person also inherit his criminal activities as well?

But regardless of who profited from John's death, how would that be a motive for killing the witnesses? In fact, it would be just the opposite. Whoever inherited would have benefited from John's death and wouldn't have a very good motive for wanting the witnesses dead. The more he tried to put logic to the problem, the more confusing it became. The murders of the witnesses had been very clever, devious and intricate. Perhaps the motive was equally intricate.

Something was missing. There had to be a key piece of information that hadn't surfaced yet, something that would tie all the loose pieces together so that the puzzle would make sense.

The entire thing had him baffled, a situation compounded by an undeniable attraction to Tara that grew more intense each time he saw her. He recognized the signs of her stress and sympathized with her plight. He had seen it with threatened witnesses and knew how it played havoc with their nerves. And for Tara, this was her second time of having to go through the pressure of being threatened and having no control over her own life. Combined with the bits of her past that he had begun to piece together from her various comments, it certainly explained her anxiety-ridden outbursts. And it made him all the more determined to protect her from harm.

The silence increased the intensity of the energy that crackled between them, fed by strong emotions on both sides—anger, anxiety, suspicion, confusion. And underlying all of that was a sexual tension hot enough to scorch everything in its path. It had been the farthest thing from his mind to have her spend the night in his bedroom. It violated all the rules of professional conduct connected with his job, but since the circumstances dictated that she be his overnight guest he didn't want to have an evening filled with undue stress and wariness. He didn't want to ask her any more questions about the Vincent family or the case...at least not that night.

"You...uh—" he gestured toward her shoulder "—have some blood smeared on your clothes. I'm sorry about that. It must have happened in the garage when you got out of the car trunk. If you'd like, we can put what you're wearing through the washer and dryer. Do you have anything to change into while your clothes are washing? If not, maybe I can find something of mine that will do in the interim."

She had forgotten about the stain on her blouse. She had

tried to forget about everything—about the trial, about the feeling of being watched, about the horror of the car bomb, about suddenly needing to flee for her life. She hadn't been any more successful at that than she was at convincing herself that being in Brad's arms didn't excite her physically and touch her emotionally.

She glanced up at him, but her attention fixated on the bandage on his arm instead. The wet red stain had seeped through the gauze, a vivid reminder of the danger that surrounded her. A little shiver darted through her body, an involuntary reaction to the knowledge that she was responsible for his injury.

"This is more important." She reached for the bandage. He started to move her hand away, but she brushed aside his effort. "You really should have a couple of stitches for the wound to heal properly. It's going to leave a scar like this."

"Another scar will hardly be noticed." He closed his hand over hers before she could undo the bandage. "You really don't need to do this. It's just a scratch."

"It's not a scratch. It's a—" The words caught in her throat. She had no experience with guns or this type of violence. The guilt welled inside her, compounded by the concern emanating from the depth of his blue eyes. She couldn't keep the quaver out of her voice. "I'm so very sorry—"

He put his fingertips to her lips to still her words. "Don't be. It wasn't your fault. It's one of the hazards of the job, nothing more."

"I'm not the type of person who takes chances. The most daring thing I've ever done was agree to testify at John Vincent's trial." Her voice dropped to a whisper. "If I hadn't testified, none of this would have happened."

"If you hadn't, a criminal might still be on the streets."

"There were plenty of other witnesses who provided much more damning testimony than I did. The prosecution didn't need me in order to get a conviction." She spoke reflectively, almost as if she were talking to herself. "The first time I ever took a risk and look what happened. I guess that should be a lesson for me."

He lifted her hand to his lips and kissed the inside of her wrist. "People who don't take risks might protect themselves from the lows, but they never get to experience the highs."

"Is that why you're a deputy marshal? You like to take risks? To experience those highs?"

A little chuckle escaped his lips. "If you're asking if I'm an adrenaline junkie, the answer is no. I chose this as a career because I wanted to make a difference, do something positive. For the most part it's been very rewarding, but every now and then I run into a situation that...well..." He couldn't find the right words without taking a chance on making her feel worse than she obviously already did. Besides, talking wasn't what he wanted to do.

He placed his fingertips under her chin and lifted until he could look into her eyes. He lowered his head and a moment later his mouth was on hers. There would be no more conversation that evening. What started as a casual kiss quickly escalated. He wanted more of her. He knew he wanted too much. He wanted what he had no business even thinking about doing. He wanted what broke every rule and code of ethics he had ever lived by.

And at that moment he didn't care.

He shoved everything from his mind except Tara Ford—how she felt in his arms, the taste of her mouth, the sensation of her body pressed against his. It was a kiss he didn't want to have end. He ran his fingers through the silky strands of her hair, caressed her shoulders, then pulled her body tighter to him. Everything about this was wrong, yet nothing had ever felt so right.

His kiss deepened, sending Tara's desire into overload. She wrapped her arms around his neck before she could stop herself. No one had ever created the depth of excitement or the height of desire in her the way he did. She had often speculated on how miserable her life would have been with Danny, but she couldn't even imagine what life with Brad Harrison might be like.

No one had ever touched her existence the way he did. She had never really trusted anyone in her entire life, especially not where personal matters were concerned. But deep in her soul she knew Brad was different. In spite of his words about her possible involvement, and in spite of her anger and resentment at those words, she knew he was only trying to find the truth and do his job. And that truth would prove she was innocent of any wrongdoing. She trusted Brad. She trusted him with more than her physical safety…she trusted him with everything.

She melted into the passion of his kiss, blocking from her mind everything other than the way he made her feel, the desires he stirred in her, the surprising emotions that pushed to the surface of her consciousness…emotions that she had never experienced before.

Brad wasn't sure exactly what to do. No one had touched him emotionally the way Tara did, not since his wife died. He had been afraid of this moment…afraid that it might happen and equally afraid that it would never happen for him again. And he didn't know what to do. He very much wanted to make love to her, but beyond that…well, he was afraid to speculate beyond that.

So he reluctantly broke off the kiss and forced his attention to what needed to be done in the morning.

Chapter Eight

"Here's a picture of her." Brad handed Ken Walsh the head-shot photograph he had taken of Tara the previous night along with the necessary vital statistics of height, weight and a fictitious date of birth. "I need an out-of-state driver's license and I need it right away." He looked at his watch. "It's seven-thirty now. Could you have it for me by ten-thirty? The driver's license is the only thing I need..." He paused a moment, concentrating, then, "Better add a couple of membership cards just to lend legitimacy and corroborate whatever name you decide to use, something like a library card and maybe an automobile club card."

Ken looked at his longtime friend and slowly shook his head. "What have you gotten yourself into, Brad? What's going on that you can't go through proper Marshals Service channels to get this done? And why the extreme rush?"

"I can't trust anyone else with this, Ken. I think there's a leak somewhere in the office and this woman's life hangs in the balance. That's all I can tell you for now other than this is, of course, strictly between you and me and it's life-and-death important. No one else can know about this."

"I don't like it, but if you say it's that important then it stays just between us. I can't have this for you until eleven o'clock. That's in three and a half hours. That's the best I can do."

"That'll be fine. Thanks, Ken. I owe you one."

Brad left the home of retired Deputy Marshal Ken Walsh, the man who had been his mentor when he first joined the Marshals Service and had remained his close friend. Ken was the only person connected with the Marshals Service that he could trust with anything having to do with Tara.

He continued on to the office. He had several things to do and not much time. As soon as he arrived he checked his e-mail. There was a message from Steve Duncan in Portland. The body of Andrew Carruthers had been found underneath a pier in the Columbia River. Andrew Carruthers had been identified as a professional killer who went by the one-name alias of Pat.

He had been the primary suspect in the contract killings of no less than thirty-five people in the last fifteen years with no two deaths being identical. He was an expert with disguises and proficient with guns, knives, explosives, poisons and had been known to use several other unique means in dispatching his victims. He had been arrested several times, but there was never enough evidence to make any of the charges stick and he was released and the charges dropped. He had been the only suspect, subsequently those murders had never been solved.

According to Steve's information, Pat had been killed by a single shot between the eyes from a small-caliber handgun at very close range. Unfortunately, with the body having been in the river, there wasn't much chance of being able to collect any forensic evidence to help with the investigation.

Brad stared at the computer screen as he turned the information over in his mind. It must have been someone Pat knew and did not fear, for the person to get that close with a gun to a professional contract killer.

It had been determined that Pat was in Portland at the time of Phil Winthrope's death and had since been in Seattle. It was unknown why he had returned to Portland, but a gas receipt found in his car placed him fifty miles north of Portland at eleven-thirty last night. The coroner put the time of death a few hours later, at approximately two o'clock in the morning.

Brad printed out the e-mail then deleted it from his computer. Steve's information had Pat in Seattle at the time of the bombing of Tara's car and would also have allowed him to have been the one who shot through the motel window and still be in Portland shortly after midnight. Had he gone to Portland to meet someone? To collect his money for killing Phil Winthrope? To explain why Tara Ford was still alive? Perhaps it was an explanation that did not sit well with his employer and had gotten him killed for his failure.

Had Pat been responsible for all the deaths? The duplication of a woman's presence in two of the deaths—both of them involving poisonous foods and a short-haired red wig—confused the issue. Did Pat work with a female partner that no one was aware of?

Brad concentrated as he tapped his pencil against his desk. He took a sip from his coffee cup while toying with a new thought. He needed more than a photo of Andrew Carruthers. He needed a physical description. Was Carruthers slight enough in stature to be able to disguise himself as a woman? The name Pat could belong to either a man or woman, which would allow him to present himself to his clients as either one, providing himself with an additional layer of anonymity. It was a thought worth following up.

Brad went to the files to see if they had a picture of Andrew Carruthers, a.k.a. Pat. He had been arrested, so there had to be at least a mug shot of him somewhere. Unfortunately it didn't exist in the U.S. Marshals' files, either on paper or in the computer. The ATF would have a file on Pat and so would the FBI, but he preferred not to draw more attention to his activities by requesting more information from another federal agency than he already had. So he did the next best thing...he called Steve Duncan and asked for a picture along with physical description including any known disguises and aliases. Steve promised to send it to Brad's home computer right away. Brad would show it to Tara. Perhaps she'd recognize him.

Brad took a deep breath, held it for a moment, then slowly let it out. Tara. He had spent a very restless night on the sofa bed in the den. He couldn't get her off his mind or out of his senses. Nor could he ease the internal conflict that had plagued him all night long. He had started something when he pulled her into his arms and kissed her, something he thought he could easily control.

He was wrong...very wrong. There had been nothing easy about putting a stop to the electricity that sizzled between them, and equally difficult had been his attempts to ignore the emotional pull on his senses—an emotional toll he knew he could not afford and wasn't sure he wanted even though he couldn't deny its existence.

He tried to shove away the distracting thoughts. He didn't have the luxury of indulging his personal desires or exploring the possibilities presented by this woman's presence in his life. A murderer was on the loose and people were still dying. Even if the now-deceased Andrew Carruthers, a.k.a. Pat, had been the perpetrator of one or more of the murders, he was now dead at the hands of someone else. Brad was sure that person was a direct link to the John Vincent case rather than someone connected to Pat's shadowy past. He couldn't trust his colleagues or even his boss with the information he had gathered...at least not yet.

Brad glanced around to make sure no one was within earshot, then made another phone call. A moment later he had the flight coordinator for the Marshals Service on the phone.

"Yes, myself and one other person. We need to leave by noon today." He listened for a moment, then responded. "No—a witness, not a prisoner in transit." There was no reason for anyone in the office to know about his plan as he was using an entirely different computer software system and he had the authority to order space on a Marshals Service flight. He gave the coordinator a job charge number used for miscellaneous transactions, confident that it was secure.

Next he phoned Tara using the agreed-upon calling code of two rings then calling back. She hadn't appeared downstairs by the time he left that morning. He didn't want to wake her, so he left a note saying he had an early meeting and would call her in a few hours. "I'll be picking you up in half an hour."

"Where are we going?"

He heard it in her voice, the anxiety tinged with despair. It tugged at his already rattled emotions. "I'll see you in half an hour." He didn't want to say any more on the phone than was absolutely necessary for fear someone would hear him. He shoved his chair back from his desk and rose to his feet. As soon as he looked up he saw Thom Satterly standing at the door of his cubicle. A quick jolt of apprehension darted through his body. How long had Thom been standing there? How much had he heard? Had he been there long enough to hear his call to flight operations?

"Did you need me for something, Thom?" He forced a calm to his voice, not wanting to alert his boss to anything being amiss. "I was just about to leave."

Thom glanced at his watch. "It's only nine o'clock. A little early for lunch, isn't it?"

"Not lunch. I've got two more of these files of yours that need follow-up and closing-out. A couple of these people aren't reachable by phone, and since I'm on restricted duty anyway, I thought I'd see them in person so I can finish up this project." He grabbed a couple of file folders and shoved them into a large envelope already stuffed full of other files and computer printouts. He added a computer diskette to the envelope.

Brad locked his desk, then glanced at Thom. "The doctor

should be giving me a release next week to return to full duty and I want everything cleared off my desk so I'll be ready for a new assignment.''

The words might have sounded convincing but Brad knew he'd have some tall explaining to do when the doctor got a look at his most recent run-in with an armed assailant. Even though it had only nicked his arm, it was still a bullet wound and one he had not seen the doctor about—or even reported to anyone.

''You'll be gone the rest of the day?''

''Yep, the rest of the day.''

He stepped into the hall and found Ralph Newman next to the cubicle door getting a drink from the water fountain. How long had Ralph been there? Things were going from bad to worse. Could either one of them have overheard him making arrangements for a flight for himself and one passenger? He wasn't sure. He had to take a chance and proceed as if everything was okay.

''Ralph, I need your signature on this report—'' Shirley Bennett emerged from the cubicle next to Brad's, stopping in midsentence when she looked up at him. She looked questioningly from Brad to Ralph. ''I'm sorry. I didn't mean to interrupt anything.''

Ralph gave a sidelong glance in Brad's direction, then addressed his comments to Shirley. ''You're not interrupting. I was just getting a drink of water.''

Brad's mind raced ahead as he left the building. That made three people who could have overheard his phone conversation. Not just anyone could call and get the information about his destination. The pilot had to file a flight plan, but someone would have to know to ask for the information and have the proper authority code to get the details. Brad didn't like the uncertainty, but there wasn't anything he could do about it right now other than try to convince himself that there weren't going to be any problems.

He hurried home. He had told Tara half an hour and it

had only been fifteen minutes. He went immediately to the den and checked his computer for the information about Andrew "Pat" Carruthers that Steve Duncan had sent him. He read the pages as they came off the printer. Steve had sent him everything he'd asked for, but it didn't answer his nagging questions.

Pat was six feet two inches tall and tipped the scales at two hundred and thirty pounds—definitely not a physical description that would suggest he could disguise himself as the woman the neighbors reported seeing at the location of the first death. It was also not a physical description associated with someone who could be easily overpowered by an assailant. So, how did Pat end up as a body in the river with a bullet hole in his forehead?

Brad looked around, the silence inside the town house finally penetrating his consciousness. Hadn't Tara heard him come in from the garage? He strained to hear any little noise, but there was nothing other than the normal sounds. An adrenaline surge hit him and a nervous jitter settled in the pit of his stomach. He pulled the 9mm handgun from his holster and clicked off the safety.

He moved quietly toward the stairs, pausing at the bottom to once again listen for any untoward sounds. He cautiously ascended one step at a time. With his back pressed against the wall next to the partially opened door, he peered around the corner into the bedroom. Tara was nowhere in sight. He stepped into the bedroom, weapon drawn and at the ready. He took a quick glance behind the door, then checked the closet. He turned toward the bathroom just as the door swung open.

Brad dropped to one knee, gun arm extended toward the door. "Hold it right there!"

The sight that greeted him immediately burned into his memory. Tara stepped into the bedroom. Her long, shapely legs extended from the bottom of the bath towel wrapped around her body. Her tousled hair gave her an appearance of earthy sensuality. His mind leaped to the passion of their shared kisses and the sexual electricity from the previous night. All he could do was stare at the incredible vision. A tightness pulled across his chest and his breathing became labored.

Her startled eyes and the quick look of panic that darted across her face finally brought him back to reality. "I... uh..." Then he realized she was staring at the gun in his hand.

He holstered the weapon, stood up and turned away from her so that he faced the bedroom door. "I'm sorry...I didn't mean to break in on you. I didn't hear you up here...you hadn't said anything when I arrived...I was concerned... uh...I was afraid something..." He glanced back toward her. The panic disappeared from her features to be replaced by the crimson tinge of embarrassment.

"I must have been in the shower when you arrived. You said half an hour so I hurried, but I guess I wasn't fast enough." Her heart still pounded from the sudden jolt of fear when she'd walked out of the bathroom and realized someone was in the bedroom pointing a gun at her. Or perhaps it still pounded as a result of the way his gaze started at the floor and traveled up her legs, her body and finally settled on her face. The look in his eyes brought back the sensation of their shared kisses from the night before...every heated moment that told her Brad Harrison was without a doubt the most desirable man she had ever met. It went far beyond his ability to send her logical and sensible life into a spiral of escalating exhilaration.

"It's only been about twenty minutes. I'm early." He finally forced himself to look away again. "I'll wait downstairs."

Brad left the bedroom, pulling the door closed behind him. He closed his eyes and leaned back against the wall. He had to get control of himself. It had gone so far beyond the physical that he wasn't sure how to describe it. When he thought she wasn't there his first reaction had been panic that something had happened to her, not as a witness, not as someone connected to a case, not as someone who was *business as usual*...but instead as a woman he cared about very much. The thought that she might have left voluntarily hadn't occurred to him. It was only fear that she had been harmed. It had all become so very personal.

He didn't know what to think about her. At first she had been angry and suspicious. Then she'd given in to her fears. And finally she seemed to have accepted that she didn't have any control over her life at the present time. But he knew he couldn't dismiss the possibility of an ongoing connection between Tara and Danny Vincent, as much as he found that idea distasteful. On an emotional level it was not even a valid consideration, but intellectually...well, he needed to keep things in their proper perspective.

"I guess I'm ready to go."

Brad whirled around at the sound of Tara's voice. She was dressed in the same clothes as yesterday, but they had obviously been run through the washer and dryer. She held the sack from the store that had become her luggage containing the few possessions available to her.

"I've got a spare weekend bag in the closet. I'll get it for you so you can throw that sack away."

She held it up and extended a shy smile. "This old thing? I think I've become attached to it."

He grabbed the suitcase from the storage closet. "This should be better. Now, what else do you need for two or three days?"

Apprehension clouded her features as her gaze locked with his. The slight quaver in her voice belied any attempt on her part to put on a brave front. "I don't know what I'll need. Where am I going?"

Once again her plight touched him on a very emotional level. He pulled her into his arms and cradled her head against his shoulder. After drawing in a steadying breath, he attempted to soothe her obviously jangled nerves.

"I'm so sorry about all this. I've never been in a situation like this before. It probably doesn't seem like it, but I do know my job and I'm very good at it. This situation is so unique. My normal sources are closed to me until I can at least figure out who's *not* involved. Right now there's only one person I know I can trust and we'll be seeing him in a couple of hours. In the meantime we'll get you what you'll need for a trip out of state. I've made arrangements for one of the U.S. Marshals planes."

She felt good in his arms. He ran his fingers through the silky strands of her hair, then lifted her chin so he could see her face. "All I can do is ask you to trust me. We'll get through this."

Her soft voice attested to her emotional state. "My father deserted us when I was a child. My mother only cared about how things affected her and what she could get. Danny wanted control of everything and everyone, he wanted a dutiful wife who would live in his shadow. I've never trusted anyone before, never completely… but I do trust you."

It was a confession that had come from a place so deep inside her that she wasn't even sure exactly where it had originated. All she knew was that it had been the truth. She did trust Brad, more than she had ever trusted anyone in her life. And right now he was the most important person in her life. Not just because he was working to protect her from harm, but because she had never cared as much about someone as she did about him. She drew in a steadying breath to calm her nerves. "What do you want me to do?"

Her confession did more than touch him. It burrowed deep inside him and became part of him on his most personal emotional level. For Brad, his relationship with Tara had moved far beyond that of a protector guarding the safety of someone in danger. But how much farther it had progressed was something he didn't want to deal with. He lowered his head and placed a tender kiss on her lips. "Time's wasting. We need to hurry."

Tara transferred her few things from the store sack to Brad's suitcase, then they left. After making a stop at a store to buy some needed items, they continued to Ken Walsh's house.

Brad addressed his comments to Ken. "This is the woman the identification is for." Ken and Tara nodded acknowledgment of each other's presence, neither registering any surprise that Brad had not introduced them by name.

Brad turned immediately to the business at hand. "Is it ready?"

"Yes. I decided to go with Canadian identification to put her one more step farther removed from the U.S. and from the availability of quickly checking out her ID. I have a driver's license, a library card and a Canadian health card— all in the name of Alice Denton from Victoria, British Columbia."

Brad inspected the documents. "These look terrific." He handed them to Tara, who slipped them into her purse.

Ken glanced at Tara, then turned to Brad. "I had to really call in some favors to get these for you so quickly. Can you at least tell me what's going on?"

"It's better if I don't. What you don't know can't come back and bite me in the ass."

Ken's expression grew somber, his tone of voice very serious. "Whatever it is you're doing, be careful. The waters are full of sharks."

Brad nodded his head. "I'll be in touch."

As soon as they had driven around the corner out of sight of Ken's house, Tara turned in the seat toward Brad. "What did he mean by the waters being full of sharks? That sounds very ominous."

"He just meant for me to be very careful and watch my back."

She stared at the road in front of them as they drove along in silence. Any thoughts of her troubles being settled sometime soon had long been abandoned. Brad was sending her on a plane to some unknown place where she would be all alone, probably confined to another motel room, without anyone to talk to...and where she wouldn't be seeing Brad for a while. And that was what bothered her the most. She took a quick sideways peek at him as he drove. In only a few days, this virtual stranger had become so important to her. The fact amazed her.

He turned off the interstate close to the airport, circling to the far side away from the main passenger terminal and the freight terminal, headed toward an isolated area.

A large dump truck filled with sand idled in the turnout at the side of the road. The reality hit him at about the same time as the truck lurched across the road in front of his car.

"Hang on!" Brad jerked the steering wheel around. He expertly worked the brake and gas pedal. His reflex actions moved faster than his thoughts. His body strained against the seat belt. The car slid sideways in a tightly controlled maneuver. The dump truck rumbled by, narrowly missing them. It ran through a chain-link fence and finally came to rest in a ditch.

Brad slammed the transmission into park as he barked out an order. "Stay here!" He jumped out of the car and charged across the road toward the now-disabled truck. He unzipped his jacket as he ran and reached for his holster. His heart pounded in his chest. The adrenaline pumped through his body. Crouching as he neared the truck, he yanked open the driver's door.

He stared into the empty truck cab. The steering wheel had been tied off so that the truck would maintain a straight course. A large rock rested on the gas pedal. The rig-up was crude, very basic...and quite effective.

The sound of screeching tires grabbed his attention. He spun just in time to see Tara jump out of the car and run toward a concrete-block wall. A hard lump formed in his throat, threatening to choke off his breathing. Near panic twisted inside him as she disappeared from his sight, then a moment later a black car sped away from behind the wall. He raced across the open field at a full run. Uncertainty rampaged through his consciousness. He rounded the corner of the wall, his nervous tension assuaged only when he saw that Tara was apparently all right.

Brad grabbed her arm and spun her around, his voice telling of his relief even though his words spit out his irritation. "What the hell do you think you're doing? I told you to stay put."

She jerked her arm from his grasp. "You're always *telling* me. Has it ever occurred to you to *ask* for a change?"

He ignored her question. "We have to get out of here. This was not an accident. Someone rigged the truck to slam into us, most likely the driver of that black car. I wish I had gotten a better look at it."

"Well—" she held up a small notebook, ripped out the top page and handed it to him "—do you think the make of car and license number would be helpful?" She leveled a steady gaze at him, almost like a challenge, while waiting for his response to this turn of events.

He took the paper from her, glanced at it, then back at her. He tried to suppress a grin and maintain a stern attitude, but it didn't quite work. "I don't suppose you were able to see the driver, maybe identify who it was?"

She stared at him for a moment before speaking, her voice a combination of teasing and sarcasm. "Well, thank you, Tara...nice work...very helpful...how astute of you to have spotted the car and realized that there might be a connection, and then on top of that to have acted quickly enough to actually get the license number."

She turned her back on him. As she walked toward his car she muttered just loud enough for him to hear. "Oh, well, I guess *what the hell do you think you're doing* probably means the same thing.''

Brad stood there dumbfounded for a moment, not sure what to say in response to her unexpected comments... unexpected but true, he reluctantly admitted. He ran a couple of steps to catch up with her. He tried to remain neutral in his outer manner, but wasn't successful in hiding his admiration for her quick thinking.

''And with all this astute observation of yours, did you happen to notice the driver?''

''Yes, but I couldn't make out anything. The windows had a dark tint and whoever it was wore a hat and had a jacket collar pulled up. I couldn't even tell you if it was a man or a woman.''

''Damn...this is even worse than I thought. Someone found out about a flight that I scheduled only a few hours ago. Somehow the flight schedule information has been accessed...'' Brad scrunched his face into a scowl and muttered under his breath. ' Or else someone overheard me making the arrangements.''

He raked his gaze across the open field, along the road, then froze on a couple of small buildings. Parked between them, nearly out of sight, was what appeared to be the same black car. He turned to Tara, forcing a calm to his voice as he spoke in slow measured words that could not hide the seriousness of the moment.

''Our assailant hasn't gone very far. It looks like the same car parked between a couple of buildings waiting for us. We need to get out of here...now.'' He grabbed her hand and raced toward his car. This was as close as he had come to whomever had been trying to kill Tara, as close as he had been to being able to actually engage in a showdown with the culprit. Only there was nothing he could do but run...and try to get Tara to safety.

Chapter Nine

Tara ran to keep up with Brad while glancing over her shoulder in an attempt to locate what had caught his attention. There was no mistaking the sense of urgency surrounding his words. She hurried toward his car without questioning his orders.

Brad headed the car back in the direction they had come from. She swiveled in the seat until she could see out the back window. The black car pulled out from between the buildings and followed them. A moment later it put on a burst of speed. The immediacy of the danger swept through her. She fought down the panic. She had to keep her head and wits together if she was going to be a help to Brad rather than a hindrance. She hoped the fear didn't show in her voice.

"The black car is behind us and it's gaining."

Brad glanced in the rearview mirror again. "Yeah, I know. Hang on." He tromped on the accelerator. His car lurched ahead, quickly picking up speed. If there was one part of the city that he knew well, it was the side roads and industrial areas surrounding the airport.

He pulled a hard left turn around the corner of a warehouse, throwing Tara against the car door. A second later he took a sharp right and screeched to a halt behind a row of Dumpsters. With it being lunchtime, the activity around the warehouses was minimal. He wasn't sure if that was an advantage or a detriment. The tension churned through his body. He waited, barely breathing, as he listened for the black car...the same sound he had heard earlier, a loud noise that sounded like a broken muffler.

"What do we—"

"Shh!" He strained to listen. "Hear that? The car's moving away—slowly, but it's going."

"We've fooled him?"

"For the moment, but whoever it is won't be fooled for long. The plane is out of the question. We've got to get out of here now." Brad put the car in gear and cautiously edged forward, carefully surveying the area for any sign of the return of the black car. Avoiding the primary road in the area, he drove through alleys and parking lots until he came to a truck delivery gate. He exited the industrial area and was back on the city streets.

Brad made a quick determination of the options available to them, then decided on a plan. He grabbed his cell phone and jabbed in a number. Impatience churned inside him as he waited for someone to answer the phone.

He almost shouted the words. "I need to talk to Lieutenant Duncan." He motioned for Tara to hand him the information she'd jotted down about the black car.

"Steve...it's Brad. I've got a Washington license plate I need to have you run. Tell the computer that the car was found abandoned in downtown Portland and you need the name and address of the registered owner. I'm in my car headed north. I'll hang on here while you make the request. And Steve, see if you can put some sort of emergency status on it."

He turned onto the interstate and headed north as he waited for Steve to come back on the line.

"Yeah, I'm still here. What did you come up with?" Brad listened for a moment. "Stolen? I'm not surprised. Where was it stolen from?" He concluded his conversation with

Steve, then returned the cell phone to his inside jacket pocket.

He shot a quick sideways glance at Tara. "I'm going to owe Steve a heap of favors by the time this thing is over."

"He told you the car had been stolen?"

"Yes. Apparently about two hours before we encountered it."

She looked at him. "You mean someone went out and stole a car for the express purpose of trying to kill us?"

"A very specific car…a muscle machine with a big engine and lots of power plus dark tinted windows to prevent anyone from seeing inside. It was made to order for their purpose, and depending on where it was stolen from, there was a good chance that the owner wouldn't have realized that the car was missing for several hours."

He took a deep breath before continuing with the rest of the information he'd gleaned from his conversation with Steve Duncan. "And that leads us to the obvious question of how someone knew two hours ago that they were going to need that car."

She didn't have an answer for his comment…other than the obvious one that somehow there was someone who had access to inside information. She didn't say anything during the rest of the drive, using the time to try to sort things out.

Brad was thankful for the quiet. He had many things to work out in his mind. One thing was for sure. Tara couldn't have had anything to do with this latest attempt. She didn't have any prior information and hadn't been out of his sight from the time he told her he had arranged a flight, a fact that sent a wave of relief through him.

Nothing had gone right from the moment he had decided to approach Tara and confide his suspicions to her. Her life was in his hands. He was thoroughly convinced of that now more than ever. He also knew that it wouldn't stop with her. He had become a target as well. He needed to present a confident front to Tara, to let her know he had things under control and she would be safe. He only wished he felt as sure about it.

They didn't stop driving until they reached Anacortes, about ninety miles north of Seattle. Brad bought gas, then bought tickets for the Washington State Ferry to Friday Harbor on San Juan Island, about halfway to Vancouver Island, British Columbia. They ate in the car while waiting for the departure time.

Tara finally ventured a question. "Where are we going?"

Brad knew the time for explanations would eventually present itself. Now he had to come up with some answers. "We're going to hide out in the San Juan Islands for a couple of days. I have some information I want to go over with you." He stole a quick glance in her direction, this time the thoughts very personal rather than business. "Hopefully we can get a couple of days where we don't need to be constantly looking over our shoulders."

"Wouldn't we be safer if we took the ferry to Canada?"

"Yes, and we may need to end up doing that. But for now I'd rather not have to identify myself as a deputy U.S. marshal crossing the border in order to explain my handgun and leave a record of my being in Canada. And I certainly don't want to get caught in a random spot-check and have them find my handgun as if I were trying to smuggle it into the country without properly identifying myself."

Tara took a moment to consider what he'd said. It made sense. She looked around at the cars waiting to load on the ferry. She scanned them a second time. "I don't see the black car." She turned to face Brad. "Do you think we lost whoever it was?"

His voice didn't sound as confident to her as she wanted it to. "I think so...for now."

The arrival and docking of the ferry drew their attention. It unloaded its cars and a few minutes later they drove on and were soon on their way. They remained in Brad's car on the vehicle deck, not venturing up to the passenger decks.

"We might as well use this time to get a little bit of work done." Brad grabbed the envelope he had taken from his office and pulled out the pages he had added when he printed out the information Steve Duncan had sent to his home computer.

"I have a couple of pictures here that I want you to look at. One of them is a police mug shot taken three years ago and the other one is a photo of a body pulled out of the Columbia River at Portland early this morning."

He handed the pictures to her. "Do you recognize this man? Maybe someone you've seen in the past couple of months? Try to picture him with long hair, his hair a different color, maybe even a mustache, possibly glasses... anything that would have altered his appearance from what he looked like when they fished him out of the river. There's a physical description there, too...height, weight, eye color and so on."

Tara accepted the pieces of paper from him. She closed her eyes for a moment as she took a calming breath. She had never seen a dead body before other than in a casket at a funeral—certainly not one that had been murdered and found in the river. A little tremor of anxiety made itself known. She slowly opened her eyes. The gasp escaped her throat before she could stop it. Someone had put a bullet hole in the middle of his forehead. One side of his face appeared battered, probably from the river banging the body against the pier pilings or maybe against some rocks.

She looked at the other picture, the police mug shot. She read the physical description, then tried to picture what the man would look like standing on a sidewalk or sitting in a car. Something about him caught her attention but she wasn't sure exactly what.

"He does look sort of familiar, but I can't place where I've seen him. I'm getting the impression of something from a while back, not anything as recent as in the past couple of months." She shook her head and held the pictures out to him. "I'm just not sure." Her voice dropped to a whisper. "I'm not sure of anything anymore."

"You keep hold of the pictures for a while. Maybe it will come to you later." Once again her plight touched a deeply emotional response in him. He put his arm around her shoulder and drew her body next to his. "Everything's going to be okay. Whoever is behind this is desperate. What had been carefully planned-out crimes that were made to appear as unfortunate accidents, such as the near misses you had with the careless driver and the falling urn, have since turned into a blatant assault on your life with no attempt to make it appear to be an accident.

"And now that I'm on the scene there have been two attempts when we've been together, both true signs of desperation—" he indicated the photos "—capped off by the killing of one Andrew Carruthers who went by the name of Pat—a man who I believe was responsible for the very least for the murder of Phil Winthrope and possibly the rest of the witnesses as well. I also think he planted the bomb in your car, something I believe he was rushed into doing. It didn't have the same sense of careful planning associated with his other jobs."

She looked at the photo of the corpse again. "And now he's dead, too."

"It's my guess that his failure to eliminate you probably cost him his life."

She furrowed her brow in a moment of concentration. "If the hired killer is dead, killed by the person who hired him, does that mean that whoever is behind this will be coming after us directly rather than hiring someone else?"

"I think so. The attempt today with the truck almost had to have been handled by them directly. There wasn't enough time between my phone call to schedule the flight and the run-in with the dump truck and black car for them to have located and hired another contract killer to do the job."

"You keep saying *them*. Do you think there's more than one person behind this?"

"It seems as if there has to be at least two people. Whoever found out about my arrangements for a plane...whether it was someone who hacked into flight operations' computer schedules or someone who overheard me on the phone...pretty much had to call someone else to handle the details, steal a car, rig the truck—"

The words froze in his throat. He forced them out as he shoved her toward the floorboards. "Get down. There's someone moving between the cars."

Tara's pulse raced as she crouched down as low as she could get. How could someone have followed them onto the ferry boat? She watched as Brad again pulled the 9mm handgun from its holster, the sight of the weapon becoming more familiar to her with each passing day. He slowly opened the car door and slid out, keeping low to the ground. As soon as he moved away from the car, she lost sight of him. Her heart pounded so hard it felt as if it might burst from her chest, or at the very least be heard by someone passing by.

She attempted to force a calm to her rampaging trepidation. She strained to hear anything out of the ordinary. The only sounds to reach her ears were the churning engines that propelled the boat through the water, accompanied by the rolling motion of the ocean swells. The one thing that did capture her conscious thoughts was the realization that she was not experiencing the same all-out fear and panic as she had on earlier occasions. Was it her belief in Brad Harrison and trust in his ability to protect her? She didn't know, but the idea brought her some comfort.

The car door flung open. "I don't know if I'm getting jumpy or what—"

The sudden intrusion startled her out of her thoughts. She jerked to attention, banging her shoulder sharply into the car door. She let out a little yelp of pain as she looked up at him.

"Are you all right, Tara?" His manner softened, his concern real as he leaned inside the car and helped her back into the seat.

She rubbed her hand against the sore spot on her shoulder, then extended a sheepish smile. "You startled me." She scanned the rows of cars on the vehicle level of the ferry, a hint of nervousness showing in her voice. "What did you find? Who was out there?"

He slid in behind the steering wheel. "As I started to say, I guess I'm a little too jumpy. We're approaching Friday Harbor. It was just a couple of crew members preparing for arrival at the dock." Then, as if to give validity to his statement, several passengers returned to their cars in preparation to disembark. A short while later they drove off the boat and proceeded directly to a motel.

He checked them into connecting rooms. Tara used her new name of Alice Denton provided by Ken Walsh. Brad registered using the name Martin Bronson. He reluctantly put both rooms on the Martin Bronson Marshals Service credit card he carried for emergencies. It was either that, or he had to use his real name and personal credit card as he didn't have enough cash on him to carry through with what he might need for the next couple of days, and he didn't want to leave a trail by using an ATM machine at Friday Harbor.

He rationalized his decision with the fact that the credit card use was part of the business records and an entirely separate system not available to the deputies or office personnel. Even if someone had managed to hack into flight operations and had appropriated information about witnesses, there wouldn't be any reason for someone to be snooping in a system that contained only accounting and other routine business records.

Brad took Tara's suitcase from the trunk, then grabbed

the duffel bag that he carried at all times. It contained clothes, personal items, the cell phone he had given to Tara to use and his notebook computer—sort of an emergency kit should he find himself in a situation where he needed to leave town immediately without being able to pack a suitcase before going. This was just such a situation.

They each settled into their assigned room, then Brad entered her room through the connecting door. He quickly surveyed the surroundings as he stepped inside. "Well, it's not glamorous but it's clean and looks comfortable. At least it's larger than the motel room in Tacoma and we do have two rooms rather than just the one."

Tara sat on the edge of the bed. She looked up at him, her eyes questioning even more than the timbre of her voice did. "What happens now? What kind of plan do you have? We can't stay here forever and you can't keep moving me from one motel to another. At some point we need to go back to Seattle and I need to get on with my life."

He sat down next to her, putting his arm around her shoulder and drawing her closer to him. He wanted to provide some comfort for her, to ease her anxieties. "This is only just for a day or two."

"That's what you said about the motel in Tacoma. Then there was a night at your condo. And now we're here. I have a job that I can't neglect if I'm going to keep it. And you—" a moment of sorrow swept through her body "—because of me your career is in jeopardy."

"Don't worry about my career. When we find whoever is behind this, no one is going to give me any grief about my actions." He tucked a stray strand of hair behind her ear, allowing his fingers to trail lightly down the side of her neck before cupping her chin.

He placed a tender kiss on her lips, brief yet meaningful. "I know your job is important to you. I'm sorry about constantly moving you around, but we need someplace where we can hide out while we put together a plan of action.

Arranging for a Marshals Service flight didn't work. Here we've got anonymity and hopefully a couple of days of breathing space before things catch up with us again."

"But is this really safe?"

It was the same question he had wrestled with, one for which he did not have a good answer. All he could do was try to reassure her. "This is an out-of-the-way independently owned motel, not part of a national chain. They aren't connected to a computer network for reservations. There isn't anything where someone can hack into the system to find out who is registered. The Washington State Ferry system doesn't log car license numbers of the thousands of vehicles they transport each day. We didn't do anything prior to our arrival that said this was where we were going. It was truly a last-minute decision made after we were already in the car."

"Okay…so, where do we begin?" She didn't want him to know just how frightened she was. She extended what she hoped came across as a confident smile. He already had too much to worry about without her dumping additional pressure and stress on him.

He stood up. "I'll be right back."

She watched as he went back through the connecting door to his room. *His* room… *her* room. Wouldn't it be more expedient if they shared a room, easier for him to provide the required safeguards and protection? But it was an idea that left her rattled and confused. She toyed with the notion that it was a much more personal reason that had her thinking about their sharing a room…an intensely personal interest in Brad Harrison, the man whose kisses drove her wild, rather than Brad Harrison the strong protector.

She closed her eyes and allowed the feelings to flow over her. Whenever he touched her she felt the soft sensation filtering through her as a sensual warmth surrounded her. Yet at the same time, her emotional turmoil fought for its place in the equation.

She was in danger. There had already been attempts on her life. Brad had put himself in harm's way to protect her, and because of that sacrifice he had sustained a flesh wound. She could not be mad about him questioning her on certain matters or even about him considering that she might be somehow involved in a scheme with Danny. He was doing his job.

So, how could she have entertained such a frivolous thought as their sharing a room, something so far removed from the reality facing them that it never should have entered her mind? She slowly drew a steadying breath, held it a moment, then exhaled. It was more than the physical desire that coursed through her body whenever he was near. There was an added level of comfort and emotional security. In other words...trust. It was an entirely new sensation, one as exhilarating as the thought of them making love.

Brad's return interrupted her errant thoughts and musings. He placed a couple of file folders on the bed then sat down next to her. "This is everything I've gathered about this mess up to and including what my friend, Lieutenant Duncan, sent me this morning. I want to go over all of it with you. Some of this we've already been through, but I want to go over it again. I want you to tell me any thoughts that occur to you, no matter how obscure or insignificant you think they are. This location might be safe, but it's possible that we've only bought a little bit of time. We can't continue to move from place to place, one unsafe location to another. We've got to get this resolved. We've got to figure out who's behind this."

A tingle of excitement flitted across the surface of her skin. He kept saying *we* need to do things. He was including her as an equal. It was a profound moment in her life, one that had her growing emotional involvement with him escalating to new heights. She stiffened her resolve to come up with some useful information, anything that would help him.

He shuffled through one of the files. "We need to either find the person in the Seattle office of the Marshals Service who is providing information or exonerate everyone. Once we've accomplished that we can utilize the full resources of the Marshals Service and you can have proper protection until the situation is resolved."

He turned to face her, the seriousness of the moment written on his face. "And the death toll is mounting. Even though the last victim was a professional killer, his death was still murder at the hands of someone dangerous and growing more desperate with each passing day. We need to get to the bottom of these crimes before another dead body is added to the list."

He grabbed a notepad and began jotting notations as he talked. "All of this apparently started as a result of John Vincent dying of a heart attack two weeks after going to prison following his conviction. There are two theories I can't seem to separate. There's equal evidence for each side. The first one says everything would have been okay if John had done his prison time and gotten out. He would have been eligible for parole in seven years. His death might have touched off the need in someone for revenge. Or, the flip side of the theory coin says that murdering all the witnesses was nothing more than a smoke screen to cover a specific murder committed for reasons not connected to John Vincent's death or to a revenge angle."

He continued to make notes as he ran down the possibilities. "Perhaps it was only the two protected witnesses who were the target. They were put into the program and given new identities because of what they knew about organized crime in addition to their specific testimony about John Vincent. It was like a half-opened can of worms. The necessary worms had been extracted, but the lid couldn't be put back on to keep the rest of them safely inside the can. It would only be a matter of time before everything came spilling out."

She tentatively ventured an observation. "If that's the case it could be someone who had nothing to do with John Vincent, someone who felt threatened by what else those two witnesses might know and used John's death as a convenient cover for the real motive. That means there isn't anything I could know or any information I could provide you that would help solve the case." Her voice dropped to a whisper. "It also means that I'm not a threat to whoever is behind this chain of events, that killing me doesn't gain anything for them."

She immediately recognized the implications of that line of speculation. The murder of the other witnesses was nothing more than an attempt to cloud the issue and obscure the real motive. The odds against solving the crimes would be greatly increased. It also meant that there might never be an end to her danger, that she would spend the rest of her life looking over her shoulder and being afraid every time she heard a noise in the shadows. It was not the way she wanted to live her life.

She picked up the photographs of Pat and stared at them. "There's something familiar about this man. I wish I could figure out where I'd seen him."

"If anything strikes you, no matter how insignificant you think it is, let me know right away."

Brad leaned back on the bed, propped up on one elbow. He studied her as she concentrated on the photos. He had watched her change over the past few days. At first she was skeptical of what he had told her, almost defiant. Next there was anger, but he had chalked that up to her attempts to cover up her fears. The anger didn't last long, quickly turning into a brave front that he found admirable. He had been right about her from the beginning—strong, independent and self-reliant.

Then there was the softness underneath, a vulnerability that was far from being a weakness. Her words still lived in his mind, her confession that she had never trusted anyone before but she trusted him. It had touched him on an emotional level in a way he had never before experienced, emotions that ran deeper than he wanted them to. He had closed off that part of his life when his wife had been killed. Brad didn't know if he could cope with that type of emotional upheaval again by allowing his vulnerability to be exposed. Their relationship had to be kept on a business level. He had to protect her from harm. No matter what, Brad had to do everything he could to justify her trust.

But how, when he didn't know where that harm was coming from or why? And more to the point, would he be able to keep his distance? That first kiss had opened a floodgate that he hadn't been able to close. She possessed a sensuality that knocked him for a loop and that had continued to keep him slightly off balance from the moment his lips first brushed against hers. He wondered what the night would bring and how much intimacy he dared pursue. The last thing he wanted was for her to feel *obligated*....

"I'm sorry." She placed the photographs of Pat on the nightstand. "I can't pull it up from the back of my mind. I've seen this man before, but I don't know where. I know it wasn't recently, not during the time frame of the John Vincent trial or since then."

Her words had cut into his thoughts. It was just as well, as he didn't like where those thoughts were going. "That's okay. Maybe if you don't concentrate on it so hard it will come to you."

"I hope so. It's frustrating knowing I have a piece of information that might help but not being able to remember it."

Brad checked his watch. It was five o'clock. "I need to make a call before it gets any later."

She listened intently as he called Thom Satterly and said he would be taking a few days' sick leave, that he'd been moving some furniture at his condo and had wrenched his shoulder, which aggravated the wound that had put him on restricted duty.

"That should do something to stir up things. At the very least it will buy me a couple of days away from the office and at the most it could smoke out whoever the culprit is within the organization."

Brad sorted through the files and notes scattered across the end of the bed. "I'm not sure which angle to pursue. If revenge is the motive, that makes it a much more personal matter for someone than it would be for one of John's business associates. People involved in John's illegal operations wouldn't mourn his death to the point of wanting to get even. With him out of the way they would be able to take over permanently without interference from him when he got out of prison. That would feed into the theory that only the protected witnesses were the target because of what else they knew and the rest is smoke screen. It would also mean that the culprit could be any of dozens of people connected with organized crime, whose only goal is to silence those on the inside of the organization who had provided information and testified.

"But, on the other hand, if revenge is the motive, it narrows down the list of suspects to a very small select group. And either way, it still leads to the very real possibility of someone inside the Marshals Service being involved at least to the degree of providing information about the protected witnesses. So..." He leveled a steady gaze at Tara. "Any thoughts or suggestions you'd like to contribute?"

"Well..." She hesitated as she tried to organize her thoughts. "It seems to me that for someone to be able to locate and hire a contract killer of the caliber of Pat, that person would need to have some sort of organized-crime connections of their own. You can't look up *hired killer* in the Yellow Pages."

"A very good point. So, using that premise, we'd go with the idea of the majority of the murders being a smoke screen to hide one or two killings and we'd eliminate the revenge motive.''

She glanced at the floor for a moment, then regained eye contact with Brad. ''Does this mean I'm finally off your suspect list? That you believe I didn't have anything to do with these events?''

''It was a possibility I had to acknowledge, otherwise I wasn't doing my job properly.'' He leaned forward and brushed his lips against hers. His voice dropped to a seductive whisper. ''You were never a serious suspect.''

''I have another question.'' An emotional lump formed in her throat, almost as if it was an attempt to keep her from speaking. But it was a question she needed to ask, something she needed to know. She looked up, her gaze locking with his for an intense moment.

Brad frowned in confusion. ''Tara?'' He reached out and brushed his fingertips against her cheek, then slid his hand along the side of her neck and finally cupped her chin. ''What's wrong? Is there some problem I don't know about?''

He sounded so genuine, his conscientious concern for her safety so real. No one had ever cared about her this much even if it was only his job and not a personal involvement. But when he kissed her...every time his lips touched hers...it all seemed so very personal and incredibly exciting.

She forced out the words. ''I'm still worried about whether this—'' she gestured around the room, encompassing everything ''—would put you in trouble with your boss. Will what you're doing, going against what you said were specific orders not to pursue this case, cost you your job...your career?''

He wasn't sure how to respond to her concerns. Her own life was in constant danger yet she was concerned about his career, about whether he was burying himself in a hole. He had wondered the same thing, but had tried not to let it show in front of her. The emotions tugged at his senses. She was, indeed, a very special woman.

"There's no reason for you to worry about my job. There are far more important things to be concerned about and better places to use that energy than worrying." He couldn't resist the temptation of her nearness any longer. He pulled her into his arms and claimed her mouth. Perhaps it was a temporary sense of safety that propelled his actions, a feeling that they were secure for a while hidden away on an island—just the two of them with no one else able to find them. Whatever the reason, he had started something he didn't want to stop.

A tremor of excitement rippled through his body when she ran her fingers through his hair, then wrapped her arms around his neck. He sank back into the softness of the bed, taking her with him. He held her close, pulling her body on top of his. Her taste was every bit as addictive as any drug. He caressed her shoulders, then ran his hands beneath her blouse. He skimmed his fingers across the smooth skin of her back before rolling over so that his body covered hers. His thoughts became fewer and farther apart, except for the one that told him how much he wanted to make love to her. He knew where he wanted the evening to go, but the final decision would be up to Tara.

He pulled back just far enough to break the connection of the kiss. The flushed excitement of her face, the fire of passion that danced in her eyes—if there was any chance to put a stop to this it would have to be now. He tried to bring some control to his ragged breathing, at least enough to talk.

"Tara…" He smoothed her hair away from her face, kissed her cheek, then nuzzled the side of her neck. "Do you think we can set aside the chaos and uncertainty of what's going on around us and for a few hours create a little world of our own? I want to make love to you. I've wanted to almost from the first moment I saw you, but it can't be one-sided. I don't want you to feel obligated. I don't want you to think that you need—''

She placed her fingertips against his lips to still his words. A moment of uncertainty clouded her thoughts. ''I think you should know that I haven't had very much experience.'' It was the type of confession she thought she'd never make to anyone, let alone the most exciting and sexy man she'd ever met. Did she feel obligated? No way. Did his touch thrill her? His kisses excite her beyond words? More than anyone she had ever known. Did the prospect of having him make love to her surpass everything else at that moment? Without a shadow of a doubt.

She smiled at him. ''I also think you're talking too much.''

''You're right—'' his words were soft as a caress ''—I'm definitely wasting too much time talking.''

A moment of uncertainty clouded his thoughts. He had thrown his professional ethics aside the moment his lips first touched hers. But there was something much more bothersome for him, something potentially dangerous. Could he make love to Tara Ford without opening his heart to her? Did he dare take a chance? He shoved aside his doubts as his mouth found hers, his tongue aggressively seeking out and meshing with the texture of her tongue.

Chapter Ten

All thoughts left Tara's consciousness except one. Only her desire for Brad Harrison remained. She gave herself over totally to the delicious sensations coursing through her body and the excitement he stirred deep inside her. Her pulse raced as she ran her hands beneath his shirt and up his tautly muscled back.

All the rules faded in an excited heartbeat. He recaptured her mouth with a new fervor, one that left nothing to the imagination about his intentions. Their clothes were soon scattered across the floor at the foot of the bed.

The excitement grew inside her. The passion of his kisses exceeded anything she had ever before experienced. She wanted him to touch her, to caress every part of her body, to stimulate her senses even more than they already were. She ran her hands across the hard planes of his chest, her fingers exploring lower and lower until she touched the hardness of his arousal.

He felt the growl of pleasure leave his throat as much as he heard it. Her touch inflamed his desires even more than they already were, if that was possible. He cupped her breast in his hand and teased her nipple with his tongue before drawing the taut bud into his mouth. She tasted good. She felt good. He knew they would be good together. He ran his hand across the curve of her hip, then tickled his fingers up the soft skin of her inner thigh.

The moist heat of her excitement radiated to him when he reached her feminine folds. Her breathless gasp further stimulated his senses. His chest heaved as his breathing became more labored. He released her nipple from his mouth, quickly substituting the other one. He had never wanted anyone as much as he wanted her.

Wave after wave of intense sensations crashed through her body. She moved her hips to meet the manipulations of his fingers, each movement adding to the building layers rushing toward ecstasy. She brazenly stroked his rigid sex, something she had never done before. With him, everything seemed so natural and right. Her excitement combined with his.

Brad shifted his weight, then nestled his body between her legs. He paused for a moment when her words about her lack of experience came back to him. A hint of doubt jabbed at his consciousness. He wanted so much to please her. Her legs wrapped around his hips. His doubts vanished as he penetrated the depths of her femininity.

Her moist heat tightly encased his hard sex. The intensity nearly took away what little breath remained in his lungs. It was so much more than the physical pleasure. It went all the way to his heart and soul. He started a slow, even pace that quickly escalated as his excitement grew. Her hips rose to meet each of his downward thrusts.

He captured her mouth, his kiss every bit as passionate as his lovemaking. His hardened length filled her with deep sensations unlike anything she had ever experienced. The euphoria grew and expanded until it touched every part of her…body and soul. Then the rapture claimed her. The convulsions started deep inside her and spread quickly throughout her body.

He gave one last deep thrust. The hard spasms shot through him. He held her tighter, not wanting to ever let go.

The profound implications of their lovemaking were not lost on him. She was everything he knew she would be and more. She was what he wanted…what had been missing from his life, what he needed to make his life whole again. Even after his breathing returned to normal he continued to hold her, occasionally placing a loving kiss on her damp cheek or forehead.

Tara rested her head against his chest. She listened to the strong rhythm of his heartbeat. She felt so alive and free of the restrictions that had always controlled her life. She had never been so brazen, so aggressive—and it felt wonderful. With Brad she seemed to be a completely different woman. Somehow he brought out that side of her she had always kept hidden away. And she reveled in the sense of freedom it provided. She also basked in the emotional euphoria of their closeness, which told her she just might be falling in love with him. She didn't know what the future held, but at that moment she did not want to think about it. She snuggled into the warmth of his embrace and allowed her thoughts to drift on a cloud.

When she moved he shifted his weight in order to make her more comfortable. Nothing in his life had impacted him to the degree that making love to Tara Ford had. He knew he was in way over his head. He brushed a gentle kiss on her forehead. He held her tighter, the warmth of her body radiating to him, filling his mind with the possibilities of what could be—*if* they got out of the danger stalking their every move.

He took a deep breath, held it, then slowly exhaled. He had violated every professional ethic he'd ever held about being personally involved with someone connected to a case. What had he gotten himself into? And more to the point, exactly what was his relationship with her now? How had making love changed it? What would she be expecting from him and, more importantly, was it something he would be able to provide?

He looked at her, at the gentle rise and fall of her perfectly formed breasts. Her slow, even breathing told him she was asleep. He glanced over at the clock-radio on the nightstand. It was nine o'clock and they hadn't eaten dinner yet. He was hungry, but he didn't want to wake her, nor did he want to leave her alone while he went out and brought some food back to the room. So he stayed, Tara cradled in his arms and his thoughts wandering toward what would happen in the morning. It was both an exciting prospect and a worrisome situation that left him very confused—*she* left him very confused.

THE FOG OF SLEEP lifted from Tara's mind. She didn't open her eyes or make any attempt to move. Brad's arms were still around her, still cradling her against his body. She had never felt as protected or cared for as she did at that moment. She liked the way he was concerned about her, the way he made sure she was okay. In short, she liked the feeling of Brad looking out for her well-being.

She thought about that for a moment. It wasn't the same thing as Danny Vincent's need to control her like a possession. With Brad, she knew he had her best interests at heart rather than his own selfish concerns. She knew she had choices. Even if protecting her was only a job to him, he made her feel warm and cared for. He treated her with respect. He didn't act as if he was threatened by her need for independence.

It was far different than when all the witnesses were under the U.S. Marshals protection before and during the trial. A man named Ralph Newman had been in charge. He was cold and distant at a time when she'd needed some sort of reassurance that everything would be all right. The entire traumatic event had been something she'd endured alone without anyone to turn to for solace.

She finally opened her eyes just enough to see the gray early-morning light filtering in around the closed drapes. A little tingle of excitement ran across the surface of her skin when Brad's hand slid across her hip. She instinctively moved, snuggling closer to his touch.

The smooth texture of her skin sent a tremor of excitement through his body. All the passion they had shared came rushing back at him, flooding him with the feelings he had been trying to fight. When emotions were involved, people didn't always think clearly or logically. He didn't have the luxury of allowing that to happen, not if he was going to keep her safe.

As much as he was enjoying the quiet moments of early morning, the sensual energy building inside him said he'd better turn his thoughts to the business at hand before he ended up making love to her again—an idea that touched him on every level. She nestled her back against his chest and rested her hand on his thigh. That was all it took. He wrapped his arms around her, cupping her breasts in his hands. He placed a soft kiss on her bare shoulder.

He had to admit, if only to himself, that he liked taking care of her. Not as part of his job and not because she was in danger, but because it felt good to have someone to look after, someone to share with. However, from his experience with her so far she didn't seem like the type of person who wanted someone to take care of her under normal circumstances.

She had already taken him to task for making decisions and telling her what to do without consulting her about it. A warm spot grew inside him as he recalled the sparks of anger in her eyes and the defiance in her voice. She was independent and strong, two qualities he greatly admired. She also possessed a passionate nature and a sensuality that touched him as deeply as anything ever had.

And as much as he wanted to stay right where he was, in bed with the most desirable woman he'd ever known, it was something he couldn't afford to indulge. Well, maybe he could…just for a moment. He kissed behind her ear, then ran the tip of his tongue along her shoulder blade. He reluctantly turned loose of her and sat up. There was something else on his mind, something he needed to talk to her about.

"Tara…"

"Mmm…yes."

"As much as I'd like to stay here all day, I'm afraid we have work to do. We need to get busy. And I don't know about you, but I'm hungry. We didn't have any dinner last night."

She sat up. "I'm hungry, too."

He leaned forward and placed a tender kiss on her lips. "Tara…about last night…I take my responsibilities and my job very seriously. This is not the type of behavior that's standard procedure for me. Witnesses need protection, not to have a precarious situation exploited for personal reasons. I hope you didn't feel pressured—"

Once again she placed her fingertips against his lips to still his words. "No, I didn't feel pressured, obligated or coerced in any way."

"Are you sure?" A wave of guilt crashed through him. He had been wrong in what he'd done, but nothing had ever felt so right.

She leaned forward and returned his kiss. "I'm sure."

He held her a moment longer before releasing her, reveling in the warmth of her bare skin against his. Then he reluctantly turned and slid out of bed. He went back to his own room to shower and dress while Tara did the same.

Brad agreed to her request to go out for breakfast rather than eat in the room. Each felt a degree of safety in their hideaway on an island, something that had been missing from the time he had approached her in the parking lot after work. Being able to breathe without constantly checking over their shoulders was a nice break, an opportunity for nerves to settle and anxieties to lessen.

They gratefully took advantage of the reduced stress although they were each acutely aware that they were far from being safe. After breakfast they went for a walk along the waterfront, watched the boats and did some window-shopping. Then it was time to go back to the motel and return to reality. They knew they couldn't let the relative feeling of security cloud their senses to the danger that still existed.

As soon as they arrived back at the room Brad started making calls on his cell phone and connected his laptop computer to his other cell phone that he had given Tara. He wanted to check on the location and movements of everyone he felt could be involved with the case for the dates of the various accidents. Another connecting thread he had noticed was that each of the accidents had occurred on a weekend, thereby allowing anyone with a regular job to hop on a plane Friday evening, do the job and be back at work on Monday morning. Even though he was convinced that Pat was responsible for Phil Winthrope's murder in Portland, that still left the other four witness deaths. As far as he was concerned, the accident explanation was out of the question.

Top on his list was Danny Vincent and then Thom Satterly and Ralph Newman. A check of credit card transactions would show plane tickets, rental cars and hotel rooms. He wanted to know about any out-of-town trips to the cities in question whether they corresponded with the date of the deaths or not. A check of gasoline credit card transactions could also be used to place the suspect in another city or state. The other thing he needed to track down was the whereabouts of Doreen Vincent, John's daughter. So far a superficial search had not turned up any trace of her in the past year.

Utilizing a special computer program for tracking fugitives, he provided Tara with instructions for accessing various information sources from his computer, including pass-word-protected connections. They worked quickly and efficiently through the morning as a team, crossing item after item from Brad's list.

SHIRLEY BENNETT CARRIED the computer printout into Thom Satterly's office. She placed the paper on his desk.

"I was running a test program at the request of the accounting center and I came across something unusual. Since it involves this office I thought you'd want to know about it."

Thom looked up at her. "Is there a problem?"

"I don't know." She pointed to the specific entry. "Right here. This credit card in the name of Martin Bronson is assigned to Brad Harrison. I'm showing that it was used at a motel in Friday Harbor on San Juan Island yesterday afternoon. Since the schedule shows Brad assigned to office duty, I thought there might be something here that you should know about. Has the card been reissued to someone else who is out on assignment?"

Thom picked up the paper and studied it for a moment. "Brad is taking some recuperative time off. He probably decided to get out of town for a couple of days."

"But that wouldn't explain his using the Marshals Service credit card rather than one of his own. Do you want me to bring this to the attention of the accounting office?"

"No." Thom placed the sheet of paper in the tray on his desk. He looked up at Shirley. "I'll keep this until I've had a chance to check it out with Brad."

"Very well." Shirley turned to leave, running into Ralph Newman at the door of Thom's office.

"Excuse me, Ralph." She brushed by him and continued down the hall.

The two men stared at each other for a moment. It was finally Thom who spoke first. "Is there something I can do for you?"

Ralph hesitated for a moment. "If you don't need me

here for anything, I want to take an early lunch. I have some errands to run.''

"Sure, go ahead.'' Thom watched Ralph walk down the hall.

As soon as Ralph disappeared from sight, Thom retrieved the computer printout from the tray, folded it, put it in his pocket, made a quick phone call, then left the office.

KEN WALSH OPENED the front door. "Thom? This is a surprise.''

"May I come in? I need to talk to you.''

Ken stepped aside to admit Thom Satterly into the living room. As soon as the two men were seated, Thom went immediately to the purpose of his visit.

"I need to talk to you about Brad Harrison. I have a problem that I hope you can help me with. I know the two of you are very close. He's been exhibiting some odd behavior the last few days and I was hoping you might be able to shed some light on it.''

Ken leaned back in his chair, hesitating for a moment before responding to Thom's question. "Is this an *official* inquiry?''

"No, I'm asking on a personal basis. Is there anything you can tell me about what's bothering Brad? What he's involved in?''

"I'm not sure what you mean by *odd behavior*. Can you give me an example of what he's doing?''

Thom slowly shook his head. "I think that answers my question. Whatever it is, you're not going to tell me. There's only one thing Brad has presented to me lately and that's the dead witnesses from the John Vincent case. Did he mention anything to you about following up on that?''

"No, I can honestly say that he never mentioned the John Vincent case to me.''

"I turned down his request to look into it. Apparently he's decided to do something on his own in spite of my decision that no case exists and my specific orders to drop it.''

"I'm afraid I can't help you, Thom. As I said, he never mentioned anything to me about John Vincent or any dead witnesses.''

BRAD CROSSED the last item off his list, tossed the pencil on the table and leaned back in his chair. His exasperation covered his features and filled his voice. "Well, that accounts for everyone's location at the time of the murders. It leaves us with Danny Vincent unaccounted for at the time of two of the murders, the two where there was no evidence of any woman being present. There's no way to prove that he was out of town on those dates—no records of Danny being on a flight, at least not under his own name or paid for with his credit card. The same with hotels and rental cars, also no gas receipts from any of the locations. So, unless he drove his own car and paid cash for everything, I've got a cold trail for the time being. Nothing conclusive from phone records, either.

"Doreen Vincent is unaccounted for totally. It's as if she ceased to exist. There isn't a current driver's license issued to her in any state under that name. No passport, either. Also nothing on a death certificate for that name that fits her age.''

"I wish I could remember the name of the man John said she was going to marry. Maybe the passport would be in that name.''

"There's no marriage certificate for her, either, although that's not as accurate a search as tracking down driver's licenses and passports.''

"Does that mean Danny is still on your list of suspects? There's proof that he wasn't in the cities where two of the deaths occurred and there isn't any conclusive proof that he was in the other two cities at that time.'' Tara hadn't wanted to ask the question. It left her uneasy, but she wasn't sure why. Was she trying to kid herself into believing that Danny wouldn't harm her? Was she closing her eyes to reality? Refusing to accept the truth?

He looked at her quizzically. "Is there some reason why he shouldn't be on my suspect list?"

"I don't think he could be responsible for any of this. If you want to go with the revenge angle, Danny isn't the type who would go out on a limb for anyone. He certainly wouldn't to the point of committing murder for an uncle who was dead, especially when that death probably benefited Danny. Besides, he and John weren't really that close personally. They were related, not friends. Danny was a very controlling person. Being in charge was something he wouldn't want to give up just because John had gotten out of prison. I'm sure John dying in prison suited Danny just fine."

She jerked to attention, sitting up straight in her chair as the idea hit her. "Green Valley Construction, John's legitimate business, would probably have been left to his most direct heir, his daughter, rather than Danny. If Danny took over anything, it would be the illegal operations such as the loan-sharking and bookmaking, which would be a valid reason for him being pleased that his uncle was out of the way. And if Doreen did inherit, then maybe you can track her down through John's attorney. He would have needed to get in touch with her for the reading of the will and the transfer of the property."

Brad regarded her for a moment as he turned her words over in his mind. "That's very logical reasoning and a good point, especially about John's attorney knowing how to contact Doreen. Do you know his attorney's name?" The logic also applied to her comments about Danny, but it didn't remove him from the suspect list. Was he pushing at Danny because of a bit of jealousy over the past relationship between Tara and Danny? He wasn't sure of the answer.

The thought of a weasel like Danny Vincent making love

to Tara was a truly disturbing thought. He tried to shove it away, which only went to tell him just how much he had become emotionally involved with her, something that could be very dangerous for both of them. It also diluted his claim that protecting her was his job and made the entire situation very personal.

"I can't think of the attorney's name right now, but if I had a Seattle phone book I could find it. I'd know it as soon as I saw it."

Brad stood up and stretched his arms over his head, then tried to work the kinks out of his back. He'd been sitting too long, hunched over a table that was not intended to be a working space. "Then we'll get you a Seattle phone book. There has to be one somewhere on this island."

She shoved back in her chair and rose to her feet. "Are we getting any closer to solving this?"

He took her hand in his. He heard the anxiety in her voice even though she was trying to put on a brave front. "Yes, we're getting closer. We're obviously making someone very nervous. Whoever it is has lost the edge of secrecy and the ploy of using accidents to commit murder and is now operating out in the open. That will make the culprit careless and the mistakes will be in our favor. Just like the murder of Pat. That was a foolish and desperate move."

She scrunched up her face and creased her forehead. "I wish I could remember where I'd seen him. I know it's important, and I know if I could remember it would answer some questions."

He placed a kiss on her forehead, then pulled her into his embrace. She slipped her arms around his waist and rested her head against his shoulder. He allowed the moment of intimacy to continue. She felt good in his arms. She belonged there. "Don't try to force the memory. It'll come to you."

He finally released her. "Come on, let's see if we can

find that phone book. There must be a library here. Surely they'd have a Seattle phone book.''

He grabbed the local phone book from the nightstand drawer and found a listing for the library. It was only three blocks away. They set out on foot, holding hands and walking along the sidewalk at a leisurely pace that belied the urgency of their quest and the seriousness of the danger. He kept a watchful eye on the street, the passing cars and other pedestrians, but it was more out of habit than immediate concern. The majority of his attention centered on Tara's hand clasped securely in his.

They located a Seattle phone book at the library. Tara turned to the listing of attorneys and carefully scrutinized each name.

''Here it is!'' Her excitement carried over into her voice. ''Gardner and Culbertson—Leo Gardner was John Vincent's personal attorney.'' She took a notepad and pen from her purse and jotted down the information, then handed the sheet of paper to Brad.

He stared at it for a moment. ''Let's go back to the room. I'll call him in my official capacity. Hopefully he'll be willing to answer my questions, especially in light of the fact that his client is now dead, which should absolve him of attorney-client privilege.''

They walked back toward the motel, but had only gotten a block down the street, when a sudden movement in the driveway between two buildings across the street caught Brad's attention. A shadowy figure darted from behind a large Dumpster to a position behind some stacked crates on the other side of the opening between the buildings.

Brad shoved Tara inside an antiques store, barking out orders as he unzipped his jacket for quick access to his gun. ''You stay here.''

Her senses shot on alert. ''What's happening?'' She stared out the window, her gaze darting up and down the street in an attempt to discover what had prompted his actions.

"I'm not sure...maybe it's nothing." He quickly surveyed the inside of the store. He looked in the storeroom, immediately spotting an exit door. "I'm going to check something out. I'll be right back."

He slipped out the back way and ran down the alley, each stride hitting the pavement with a thud. He continued to the side street, then up the sidewalk to the main road where they had been walking. He took a calming breath before peering around the corner of the building. He carefully scrutinized each person and every doorway. The adrenaline surge shot through his body. He had been so comfortable with Tara that he had let down his guard. He could not afford to let it happen again.

Brad darted across the road, then down the side street to the alley that ran behind the buildings across the street, parallel to the main road. He paused, took a steadying breath, then cautiously made his way down the alley, keeping close to the back wall of the buildings. He came up behind the Dumpster, all the while maintaining a clear view of the stacked crates.

The empty driveway that greeted his efforts increased his anxieties rather than calming his nerves. Someone had been skulking in the driveway and now whoever it was had disappeared from sight. It was only a shadow, a brief glimpse of movement. He couldn't tell if it had been a man or a woman.

He leaned back against the wall. The adrenaline surge subsided, allowing his heartbeat to return to normal. Had he actually seen someone or merely imagined it? Had he made something sinister out of something commonplace? He shook his head, hoping to clear the uncertainty. He couldn't afford doubts. He needed to be sure about things. Lives depended on it. Tara's...and now his.

Brad took one last look around the area, then crossed the street to the antiques shop where he had left Tara.

She stepped out onto the sidewalk as he approached the door. A little wave of relief passed through her when she saw he was okay, but it didn't relieve her anxieties. "What was it? Did you see someone?"

He glanced across to the driveway, his gaze shifting up and down the other side of the street. "I'm not sure. It was probably nothing." He turned to face her. "Let's get back to the motel. I have a couple of phone calls to make."

Instead of proceeding down the sidewalk, he led her inside the store and out the back door into the alley. "It's two blocks to the motel. Are you up for a little jogging?" They started down the alley at an energetic pace until they reached the motel. They slowed to a walk, crossing the parking lot toward the building at the far end where their rooms were located.

Brad heard the sound of the broken muffler before he saw the car, the same black car with the dark-tinted windows they had done battle with the day before. With a screech of tires and the roar of a powerful engine, the mysterious car leaped forward, rapidly closing the distance to the spot where they stood.

A fraction of a second was all it took. The car window went down. A figure behind the steering wheel dressed entirely in black and wearing a ski mask extended an arm and aimed a gun in their direction.

"Duck!" Brad pushed Tara to the pavement behind a parked car then dived for cover as he reached inside his jacket for his gun. A shot rang out, ricocheting off the concrete with a loud ping. A second shot and then a third followed before the black car sped out of the parking lot and down the street toward the harbor and ferryboat dock.

Brad jumped to his feet, yelling at Tara over his shoulder as he charged across the parking lot. "You stay here."

He ran out into the street, gun drawn and the safety off.

He came to an abrupt halt. A raging frustration coursed through his body as he stood in the middle of the street and watched helplessly as the car disappeared around the corner. A quick glance around told him there weren't any witnesses to what had happened. Being the off season, the island population had drastically decreased. He holstered his gun and returned to the parking lot...only he didn't see Tara.

He ran toward the car where he had shoved her out of the way. He froze in his tracks. The acrid taste of fear filled his mouth. She lay on the ground where he had left her, a red smear of blood on her forehead.

Chapter Eleven

"Tara..." Brad kneeled beside her, a sick feeling rising in his throat. His hands trembled as he touched his fingers to her neck. A wave of relief settled over him when he found a strong pulse. He carefully cradled her limp body in his arms. A hollow sensation started in the pit of his stomach, then guilt shoved it to every part of his consciousness. He quickly and efficiently checked her before trying to move her. The blood on her forehead gave the only evidence of any type of injury.

He smoothed back her hair and found the source of the blood. It appeared that a ricocheting bullet had grazed her forehead close to the hairline. It was a minor superficial injury that was no more than a scratch, so why was she unconscious? He made a quick survey of the parking lot. The confrontation, screeching tires and shots hadn't aroused any curiosity.

Brad scooped her up in his arms and carried her the few remaining yards to the room. He placed her on the bed, then dampened a washcloth and gently dabbed at the blood on her forehead until he had it cleaned away and could get a clear look at her injury. No new blood appeared. It was a good sign. He took the first-aid kit from his duffel bag and applied antiseptic. She was still unconscious.

He touched her cheek and hair. Someone had managed

to track them down in a location that had been a last-minute decision on their part for a place to go. How had that happened? A flash of anger ignited, followed by a feeling of helplessness and frustration. Part of his job entailed protecting people, yet he had not been able to keep his wife safe and now he had not been able to keep Tara safe. And he had compounded matters by taking advantage of her vulnerability. He had made love to many women in his time, but none had impacted his life the way she had. She trusted him and he had betrayed that trust.

He didn't know who was trying to kill her, he didn't know why someone wanted the witnesses dead, he didn't know who within his own office he could trust. And even more perplexing was that he didn't know why someone would still be blatantly trying to kill her since the appearance of accidental death was no longer valid. Why would the person continue to take the risk?

All he knew at that moment was how frightened he'd been when he saw her crumpled on the ground with blood on her forehead. He touched her cheek again. For someone who was accustomed to being in charge and making split-second decisions, he found himself at a complete loss. He didn't know what to do.

A soft moan escaped her lips. She stirred, then slowly opened her eyes. She tried to sit up only to fall back into the softness of the pillow with her hand pressed to the top of her head. She looked up at him, her gaze locking with his in an emotional moment. A surge of excitement pushed at him. She had regained consciousness and didn't seem to be disoriented.

"Welcome back to reality. Do you remember what happened?"

"Well…" She shook her head to clear the confusion, then tried to collect her thoughts. "You shoved me behind the car…shots rang out…something hit my forehead…then I heard the car drive away. I started to stand up and banged my head hard on something. I think it was the side mirror on the car. I went down. Next thing I knew, I opened my eyes and I was here.''

A tender smile spread across his face. "You had me worried. It was a bullet that hit your forehead." He saw the immediate shock dart across her face. "It's not serious." He tried to make light of the event, to calm her fears. "The bullet barely grazed you...nothing any worse than scraping your knee on the sidewalk. I've had paper cuts worse that that. The wound shouldn't even leave a scar."

She sat up and swung her legs over the side of the bed. He helped her to her feet. "I've never been shot before." She touched her fingers to the small wound, wincing at the quick jab of discomfort it produced. Her words came out tentatively, the emotion attached to them clearly evident. "I guess I was lucky."

He wrapped his arms around her and brushed a tender kiss across her lips. "Why don't you stay here and rest for a while?"

"Oh? And what are you going to do while I'm *resting?*"

"I'm going down to the ferry dock before our suspect and his stolen black car can get off the island. The next departure back to Anacortes is in half an hour."

She stepped away from the inviting warmth of his embrace. A new determination swelled inside her. "I don't need to rest. I'm tired of resting." She looked him in the eyes, making sure he was paying attention to what she said. "You were shot because of me. Your career is in jeopardy because of me. And now you want me to rest some more."

"You've been through—"

"What I've *been through* is clumsily banging my head on the side mirror of a car. I'm fine. Now, let's get over to the ferry dock." Without waiting for him to respond she headed for the door. She glanced back over her shoulder. "Are you coming?"

He took hold of her arm and stopped her from going

outside. "Listen to me. You're in danger and today's incident only goes to prove that I've been too careless, that I've allowed you to be too exposed. I thought we'd be safe here for a couple of days, but I was obviously wrong. Someone has been able to track us here. I don't know exactly how it happened...yet."

He pulled her into his arms. "I've been giving this a lot of thought the last few minutes and the only connecting thread that anyone could have followed was the credit card. Several people would know that credit card and name had been assigned to me, but only a select few would have approved access to information saying that the card had been used and where...at least that quickly. And none of those people are on my list of possible suspects. That leaves us with two possibilities. Either someone within the Marshals Service who's unknown to me is involved with this and has been feeding information to Danny Vincent, or someone on my suspect list has managed to gain unauthorized access to privileged information. I'm not happy with either option."

He released her from his embrace, but continued to hold on to her hand. "So, what I want you to do is stay here out of sight."

"But whoever it is knows where we're staying. He attacked us in the parking lot of this motel. Couldn't he still be watching? If he sees you leave by yourself, wouldn't he assume I was here alone? Wouldn't that be more dangerous for me than being with you?"

He stared at her, then slowly shook his head. "I can't find any fault with your logic. I don't like it, but I can't refute it."

"Good. Now, let's get going before he gets away again."

They drove to the ferry dock. There were a minimal number of cars in the staging area waiting to board the ferry. They immediately spotted the mysterious black car with the tinted windows waiting in line with the others.

Brad parked on the street. He sat for a couple of minutes,

his gaze furtively darting from place to place...scrutinizing everything he saw, searching for answers. He finally opened the car door, but turned toward her before getting out.

"You stay here. If you see me walk on the ferry as a foot passenger, pull the car in line and board with the rest of the vehicles. Stay in the car and I'll come down to the vehicle level and find you."

"What are you going to do?"

"I'm not sure. Right now I'm just going to look around."

Brad wandered over to the vehicle staging area. A tingle of nervous energy ran through his body as he tried to appear casual, just one more person returning to his car in preparation for the arrival of the ferry. He approached the black car from behind. He tried to see in the rear window but the tint was too dark.

He purposely dropped his keys. When he bent down to get them he leaned against the back fender so that the car bounced, then waited for any movement from inside the vehicle. But nothing happened—no indication of anyone being inside the car. He grabbed his keys from the pavement, taking a second to run his hand by the tailpipe to feel for heat. It was cold. He strolled toward the front of the car until he could see in the front windshield. It only confirmed that the car was empty. He felt the hood. A slight warmth told him the car had been there for a while, probably only minutes following the attack in the motel parking lot.

He scanned the surrounding area, but didn't see any familiar faces. The sinking feeling in the pit of his stomach told him the car had been abandoned with the driver possibly being one of the anonymous faces waiting to board the ferry as a foot passenger. Or the other possibility said the driver had already taken a commuter flight from Friday Harbor's small airport to Seattle. Either way, the culprit had eluded him once again. It appeared to be a dead end for the time being.

Brad returned to his car and slumped in behind the steering wheel. Just about everything had gone wrong. No matter what he did, it seemed that the suspect was one step ahead of him. He sat there staring at the black car.

After several minutes of silence Tara finally spoke. "Is he gone?"

"I think so. We'll wait until the cars load, but I don't think there will be anyone showing up to claim the car."

She studied him—the frustration that covered his features, the determined set of his jaw, the tautly drawn muscles. She wanted so much to be able to contribute something helpful, to be more than just excess baggage. She leaned back in the seat and closed her eyes. If only she could remember, if only…

The image popped into her mind as clear as if it had been just yesterday. She jerked to attention, turned to Brad and grabbed his arm. The words spilled out in an excited burst. "It was a couple of years ago…he was in our offices!"

He creased his forehead in confusion. "Who?"

"Pat…he was at Green Valley Construction. He met with John Vincent. I was never given his name, but he's the one."

Brad sat up straight. Her animated features spoke as much of her excitement as her voice did. "Are you sure?"

"Yes. The memory just popped into my mind. I can see him walking in the front door. He stared right at me with cold dark eyes. He just kept staring until John called him into his office."

Brad's excitement level increased, although tempered by caution. He pulled out a pad and began making notes. "Was anyone else at that meeting?"

"There was another man who came in right after Pat. I was never introduced to him, either. I don't know who he was, and to the best of my knowledge I haven't seen him since then."

As more of the memory returned to her, a sick feeling began to churn in the pit of her stomach, then rose in her throat. She actually felt the color drain from her face accompanied by a cold shudder. She tried to blink away the tears welling in her eyes. She looked at Brad. She made an attempt to speak, but no words came out.

"Tara?" Deep concern blanketed his face as he moved closer to her. "What's wrong? Are you in pain?" He smoothed her hair away from the place where the bullet had grazed her. "Is it the scrape on your forehead?" A hint of panic crept into his voice. "Do you need medical attention?"

"Uh…" She forced the words. "No…it's not that."

"What is it? You look like you're about to pass out. What can I do to help?"

She swallowed several times in an attempt to stop her throat from closing off. "That meeting in John Vincent's office—" she locked eye contact with Brad "—Danny was at that meeting. He knew Pat. Whatever they discussed behind that closed door, Danny was part of it." She desperately needed some type of emotional support. She wanted Brad to hold her, to tell her that it really wasn't true. Danny Vincent wasn't trying to kill her. It was all some huge mistake…some horrible nightmare. He had continually said Danny was at the top of his list of suspects, but she had refused to accept it…until now.

Her feelings of betrayal, the emotional turmoil…every painful moment of her trauma reached out to Brad to the point where it nearly overwhelmed him. He put his arms around her, drawing her close to him. He cradled her head against his shoulder.

"I'm so sorry, Tara. Is there something I can do to ease—"

She looked up at him, her eyes pleading for understanding. "Why would Danny want me dead?"

"We don't *know* that it was Danny. We still have things to check out. We still need to call John's attorney and see if we can get a location on Doreen Vincent. We still haven't determined a clear-cut motive for the murders yet. And if it is Danny, then he's not in this alone. Someone has to be providing him with information and whoever that person is could have much more involvement than merely being a source of Marshals Service information and someone who is tracking our movements. This is far from over.''

He continued to hold her, sensitive to her needs while at the same time keeping an eye on the black car. The arriving ferry docked, cars disembarked, foot passengers boarded and still no one returned to claim the black car. He kissed her on the forehead. Her life was still in danger and he couldn't afford to let down his guard, no matter how much he wanted to give her his full attention.

''Well, that's it.'' He watched the last of the cars being loaded onto the ferry. ''Whoever was driving has definitely abandoned the car. There's nothing more we can do here. We need to get busy.''

She sat up and stared out the window at the lone car remaining in the vehicle staging area. She visualized the driver, dressed all in black, wearing a ski mask and pointing a gun straight at her. Had it been Danny? If she had agreed to meet him for dinner when he called would she now be dead? A man she had once been engaged to, a man she thought she had once loved, a man who had professed his love for her…could he be the same man who had just tried to shoot her down in a parking lot? A hard shudder of fear shook her to the very depths of her soul.

They returned to the motel, packed and checked out. They boarded the next ferry to Vancouver Island in British Columbia, headed in the opposite direction of Anacortes and the Washington State mainland.

Knowing that they would be going through a customs check twice, once entering Canada and the second time reentering the United States, Brad reluctantly removed his gun and holster and hid them in the trunk under the spare tire. Unless the border officials had some specific reason to make a thorough search of the car, they would clear through customs without any problems and without the need for him to identity himself as a deputy U.S. marshal.

From the city of Victoria on Vancouver Island, they took a different ferry to Port Angeles, Washington, on the Olympic Peninsula, then drove to Seattle, arriving late in the evening.

Brad pulled up to an ATM machine and withdrew as much cash as he could. Anyone checking transactions would find that he had withdrawn the cash within ten miles of his home, which would give no hint of his comings or goings. He turned to Tara. "How about you? Do you have an ATM card? We need as much cash as we can get our hands on. We can't take a chance on using any credit cards for anything, including the Marshals Service credit card assigned to me. That card had to be the means of someone being able to locate us."

"Didn't you say that the financial operations were a separate system from what your office computers could access? We only checked in to that motel late yesterday afternoon. How could someone have known about the use of that card so quickly?"

The frown that spread across his face said as much as his words. "The motel must have run the card to get an authorization rather than waiting to put the charge on it when we checked out. I don't know how, but someone managed to get their hands on that information. So, from here on out we're strictly cash. The ATM system only allows so much cash to be withdrawn each twenty-four hours. I can make another withdrawal tomorrow but I'd feel better if we had some more cash now."

"Of course." She retrieved her ATM card from her purse and made a cash withdrawal from her account. She held out the money toward him.

"You keep it. That's only for backup emergency."

She stifled a yawn. It had been a long day and the stress had added to her exhaustion. "Where are we going now?"

He brushed a soft kiss against her lips. "I know you're tired, but I'm afraid we still have a couple of hours of driving ahead of us yet tonight. We're going someplace where we don't need reservations, where we don't need to check in, where we won't have to pay and where we won't leave a trail."

She looked over at Brad, at the determination covering his features. "That sounds like a camping trip...a tent in the wilderness."

"No camping, but we are heading for the great outdoors. My sister and her husband own a cabin at Mount Rainier. I have a key for it and they're in New York right now so they won't be using it. I should have thought of it earlier. My name isn't on any records connected with the property...not on the deed, the utilities, the tax rolls."

It was late, but he wanted to be on familiar ground before stopping for the night. He gave her hand a loving squeeze in an attempt to instill a feeling of confidence. "Only a couple more hours, maybe a little longer depending on traffic, then we can call it a day." He bought gas, then headed toward Mount Rainier. In a little over two hours they arrived at the cabin.

It wasn't as isolated as Tara had thought it would be. It was located at the edge of the village about three blocks from the general store—the area's main supplier of groceries, pharmacy items, clothing, camping equipment and it also housed the post office.

Brad put the car in the garage so it couldn't be seen from the road. He grabbed his duffel bag from the trunk, having clipped his holster back on his belt as soon as they cleared U.S. Customs in Port Angeles. Tara took her suitcase. They entered from the garage into the kitchen.

Tara looked around as Brad turned on some lights. It wasn't at all what she had expected. "This is very nice.

When you said cabin, I had something much more rustic in mind. This is really a vacation home rather than a cabin.''

''It definitely has all the amenities, including a TV satellite dish and a hot tub on the back deck.'' He led the way upstairs to the bedrooms. There was a moment of hesitation, then he put his arm around her shoulder and they walked into the bedroom together. It was late and they both needed some sleep. Brad did a quick check of the house to make sure all the doors and windows were locked, then set the perimeter alarm system.

He went back upstairs. Within five minutes Tara was snuggled in his arms as they lay in bed together. As much as he wanted to make love to her again, his mind kept going to thoughts about the case. He couldn't turn off the questions circulating through his head.

''Do you think you'd recognize Doreen Vincent if you were face-to-face with her and she was using a different name? Is the photo of her with her father the only picture you've ever seen of her?''

''I've seen several other photos. The one of the two of them was in a frame and John kept it on his desk, so I've seen it lots of times. As to whether I'd recognize her if I simply saw her…I'm not sure. I think I probably would, at least I think so if she hadn't done anything to change her appearance.''

''You said you'd never met her? You've never heard her voice? Not even to maybe take a phone message? You don't know if she speaks with a regional accent, has a high-pitched voice, a nasal quality or anything of that sort?''

''I haven't a clue what she sounds like. I've only seen pictures.''

''So, if she'd had some plastic surgery done, changed her nose and maybe her chin or something like that, you wouldn't recognize her? She could be someone you come in contact with every day and you wouldn't know it?''

Tara turned on her side, raised up on her elbow and

looked at him. "What are you getting at? Do you think someone I know is really Doreen Vincent? Do you have anyone specific in mind?"

"I was wondering about your friend, Judy Lameroux."

"Judy? That's ridiculous. She couldn't be involved in..." Tara's voice trailed off as she turned the notion over in her mind. She'd also believed that Danny couldn't be involved. Judy's physical description fit as far as height, eye color, hair color and age. Her face didn't match, but plastic surgery could have accounted for that. Was Brad desperately reaching for answers or was it something for her to be concerned about?

She hadn't thought about it until he brought up the idea, but it had been kind of odd the way they met—that Judy would be in a bookstore nowhere near her home or place of business, that they would both reach for the same book at the same time. Was she reading more into the situation than was there or was she ignoring something very obvious?

Tara shook her head, no longer sure what to think or believe. "I don't want to suspect my friend. I don't want to be so suspicious that everyone I encounter becomes someone to fear. I've lived that and I don't like it."

Brad placed a tender kiss on her cheek, then pulled her tighter into his embrace. "I don't want you to live that way, either. But I don't want to dismiss something that could be dangerous. We have to consider and be open to every possibility."

She couldn't keep the quaver out of her voice or stop the cold shiver that swept through her body. "You mean like me refusing to believe that Danny Vincent could be involved until it was so obvious that even a three-year-old could have figured it out?"

Brad knew it had been a rhetorical question, but that didn't prevent the emotional impact of her turmoil from leaving a deep scar on his consciousness. He had failed before and as a result had been living an emotionally closed-off life. Somehow he had to make sure he didn't fail again. More important to him than catching the person responsible was making sure that nothing happened to Tara.

Somehow when he wasn't looking she had managed to become the single most important person in his life and it was up to him to make sure she was protected. It had gone far beyond merely doing his job. He didn't even want to think about how personal it had become. Was it possible that he might be falling in love with her? He wasn't sure he really wanted to know the answer to that question. He wasn't sure he could handle the full implications of just how much she meant to him.

His thoughts gravitated back to the serious business at hand. Even if Judy Lameroux and Doreen Vincent were one and the same person, that still didn't tell him who within the Marshals Service had been responsible for providing classified information and then ultimately monitoring his whereabouts.

And as long as he was adding people to his suspect list, in addition to Thom Satterly and Ralph Newman, there was Shirley Bennett. Was her computer expertise good enough to have created a false identity for herself that was so fool-proof she had actually been able to procure a job with the U.S. Marshals Service without being detected? It certainly wasn't an impossible task, and if she had been able to accomplish that, she wouldn't have any trouble hacking into classified records.

He conjured up an image of Shirley. Her age was correct, but her appearance was way off. The most obvious difference was her height. Everything else could be altered, but Tara had pegged Doreen Vincent's height at five foot six and he knew for a fact that Shirley was only about five-three.

Once again too many questions and no answers. He wasn't all that easy in his mind about having chosen his sister's cabin, either. True, it had no connection directly to him, but it wouldn't take too much effort to connect him to his sister through his personnel file and her name to the cabin. It was something he had initially dismissed as not very likely, but now he wasn't so sure. It was another item on his mind that he needed to talk about with Tara.

He had become a target by virtue of being with her. He was the one they were able to track, but their ultimate goal was her. Once again the thought crossed his mind—why would they still want Tara dead when everything else was out in the open? What purpose would Tara's death serve at this point? Why take the risk for no return? As much as he didn't want to dwell on it anymore that night, he knew they needed to discuss one very important matter.

He ran his fingers through her hair, then cradled her head against his shoulder. "There's something we need to talk about." Her body stiffened in his arms in response to his words. He held her tighter, wanting so much to protect her from everything but not sure if he could.

"I think we need to separate. I'll stay here. You need to get out of the state. So far everything they've done to find you has been the result of tracking me. I want you out of the way so I can set myself up as their immediate target. They'll watch me assuming I'll lead them to you. I have two people I trust who can help you. One you met, Ken Walsh, and the other is Steve Duncan, my friend who's a homicide detective with the Portland Police Department.

"While Ken is known to some of our suspects, Steve is a new and unknown face. I'm going to have him pick you up and take you to Portland. He can coordinate with Ken in finding a safe place for you until this is over. I'll call both of them first thing in the morning and set this plan in motion."

There was a moment's hesitation, then her response came out clear and emphatic. "No."

"What?" He raised up on one elbow. Had he heard her correctly? "What do you mean by no?"

"I mean no, I'm not going to do it. You're in danger because of me. I'm not going to go and hide somewhere while you set yourself up as a target. I'm in this all the way. It won't do any good for me to be somewhere safe. If anything happened to you it would be because I was hiding away and they decided to eliminate you as the obstacle preventing them from getting to me. Ultimately I wouldn't be any safer than I am now, with the difference being that you'd be dead."

She looked up at him, reached out with trembling fingers and touched his face. Her voice was soft but it held a firm determination. "I couldn't live with myself if something happened to you because of me while I was safely in hiding. I'm their primary target and I should be the bait to draw them out into the open."

"I can't allow you to risk your life that way. I'm trained to do this type of work. It's the Marshals Service that should be protecting you and right now I'm as close to that as circumstances allow."

"As you said, it's my life and I won't have anyone else making that type of decision for me. I'm not going and there's nothing else to discuss in the matter other than how *we* are going to proceed."

A little tremor of uncertainty swept through him. She sounded so determined, so positive in the stance she had taken. He didn't like the idea of being separated from her, but the thought of her being harmed because of him was something he knew he would never be able to live with a second time. Somehow he had to dissuade her. Even though he admired her courage and respected her determination to stay, he had to talk her into letting him do what needed to be done.

"Tara, listen to me…"

"No. I'm not leaving and there's nothing more to say."

Brad knew there was no use continuing the conversation that night. He would call Steve first thing in the morning and send Tara to safety, somewhere away from the danger. But for tonight they would be safe.

He pulled her body over on top of his. He ran his hand down her bare back as he captured her mouth with all the passion and desire he had been trying to keep at bay. This could be their last night together and he wanted it to be enough to live in his memory and sustain him for the difficult days ahead.

"I'VE BEEN WATCHING the cabin for the past three hours like you wanted." He shifted his cell phone to the other ear as he reached across the car seat to grab a can of beer. "You were right. They showed up about half an hour ago. The exterior lights are on, but the house is now dark. They're still in there, probably for the night."

"You've had more than enough opportunities to do away with her, starting back when it would have been considered just another unfortunate accident before anyone had stumbled across what had really happened. It's too late to turn back now. She's become a thorn in my side, an itch I can't scratch. I want her eliminated along with her protector."

His anger flared. "You want me to kill a deputy marshal? Are you crazy? We'll never get away with that."

"I've had it with your incompetence. It's your screwups that have us in this mess. Just do it!"

"Hold on a damn minute! You don't give me orders, not now and not ever. We need to get a few things straight. You seem to have the very wrong idea that you're in charge here, and we both know that's not the way it is." He popped open the can, took a sip and listened.

"We can have this out right now—"

He'd heard enough. He clicked off the cell phone, terminating the conversation in midsentence. He tossed the phone on the car seat next to him. This showdown had been brewing for several months and couldn't be put off any longer. The stakes were too high. There was too much money at risk for him to ignore the problem any longer.

He turned his attention back to the darkened cabin. Kill a deputy marshal? That was more trouble than he was willing to take on. And as for getting rid of Tara, he'd tried three times without any success. He had even given the assignment to Pat, which had also failed. In retrospect he realized that he had rushed Pat too much by insisting that it be done that same day.

At this point there didn't seem to be any real reason for getting rid of Tara. Things had gone beyond the point of creating accidents and now there was a deputy marshal involved. Business matters were running along smoothly. The two witnesses that posed a threat were dead. There wasn't any real evidence to link him to any of it. The deaths of the witnesses had already been declared accidental and there wasn't any proof to the contrary. Maybe Brad Harrison had his suspicions, but his concerns were not supported by anyone else.

If everything just stopped right now, it would all blow over and no one would ever know what really happened. If they did some digging, the police might have been able to make a connection to Pat, but that wasn't a problem any longer now that Pat was dead.

He took another long swig from the can of beer. He needed to reassert his authority, establish once and for all that he was in charge. And somewhere in the back of his mind he knew that meant getting rid of Tara. It was a matter of self-preservation. She was a threat to him. There was no room for sentiment.

Chapter Twelve

The loud noise pierced the nighttime quiet. Brad jerked upright, shaking his head to clear the sleep from his mind. The adrenaline surged fast through his body, which put his senses on immediate alert. His heart pounded, sending his blood racing through his body. He hadn't anticipated anything, at least not this soon after their arrival.

Tara raised up on one elbow, her voice filled with the hazy sleep that circulated through her thoughts. "Brad? Is something wrong? What's that noise?"

He forced a calm to his voice, not wanting to panic her. "It's the perimeter alarm. Probably just a raccoon looking for food. It happens all the time. You stay here. I'll go turn the alarm off." He pulled on his jeans as he glanced at the clock. It read 5:20 a.m. He took his handgun from the holster on the nightstand, then moved quietly down the hall toward the stairs. After checking the control panel for the point of attempted entry, he reset the alarm.

Someone had tried to force the back door. He didn't for one minute believe the raccoon story he'd given Tara, but he didn't want to alarm her unnecessarily. The only question that needed an answer was whether the culprit was a common burglar who thought the cabin was unoccupied or someone who had managed to track them down in spite of the precautions he had taken. And if someone had tracked them down…how had they done it so quickly?

He proceeded down the stairs and through the dark cabin toward the back door, clicking off the safety on the 9mm as he went. Pausing just inside the door, he listened for any sounds that could give him some information. He reached for the bolt lock, then pulled back his hand. He had rearmed the system and opening the door would set off the alarm again. He moved to the window and peeked cautiously around the edge of the miniblinds. The exterior lights illuminated the immediate area. Whoever was there had been scared off by the alarm—at least for the moment.

Before returning upstairs he turned on a light in the kitchen and another in the living room so that it would appear to anyone who might still be watching the cabin that the occupants were now awake and downstairs. He hurried back to the bedroom. Tara had put on her robe and was sitting on the edge of the bed.

She looked at him expectantly, a hint of urgency in her voice. "What did you find? What set off the alarm?"

"I didn't find anything. Whatever it was had apparently been scared away by the noise." He returned the weapon to its holster.

Tara stood up, tightened the belt sash at the waist of her robe and took a deep breath. She tried to read his expression, to figure out what was going through his mind, but all she saw was the practiced facade that didn't give away even one thought.

"Please don't lie to me, not now…not after everything that's happened. Someone tried to break into the cabin, someone who wanted to kill us." Just saying the words out loud caused a chilling shudder to work its way through her body. Brad had thought they would be safe at the cabin, at least for a while. But the reality rang loud in her ears. She would never be safe. And because of her, Brad would never be safe, either.

He pulled her into his arms. His strength and determination radiated to her uncertainty. She felt protected in his arms, as if everything would be all right.

"I'm not lying to you. I looked and I didn't see anything or anyone. I don't know what set off the alarm. It might not have had anything to do with us. My sister and her husband don't live in the cabin and they don't rent it out, either. It could have been someone assuming no one was here, just a common thief wanting to grab a television. It could even have been someone looking for a place to sleep for the night."

She tried to take comfort from his words, but could not get past what she knew was true. "You don't really believe that any more than I do. Someone knows we're here."

He held her in his embrace, her body pressed against his and her head cradled in his shoulder. He didn't respond to her statement. There was nothing to say, nothing that could change the truth of her words or the reality of the situation—it was possible that someone had already tracked them.

"It will be daylight before long. *If* someone has managed to find us here, I don't think they'll try anything during the day. Hopefully by tonight we'll have some concrete leads to follow."

"What happens now?"

"Let's check the kitchen and see what's available for breakfast. I'm sure there won't be any perishables in the refrigerator, but my sister usually keeps the pantry stocked as well as the freezer."

Tara located the coffee canister and soon had a pot of coffee ready. They found some breakfast items in the freezer, popped them into the microwave, then sat down to eat. They talked casually over breakfast, although an undeniable undercurrent of nervous tension played through the air.

After eating, they took their coffee and went into the living room and watched the morning news on television.

Brad turned off the television as he checked his watch. It was 8:15 a.m., late enough for someone to be in the office. He grabbed the phone and dialed a number. A second later Tara reached in front of him and disconnected the call.

Her words were emphatic. "I'm not going. I thought we settled that last night."

He cocked his head and looked at her, while suppressing a grin. "I was calling John Vincent's attorney to see if I could get a location on Doreen Vincent and whatever other information he might have."

She glanced at the floor. The heat of embarrassment spread across her face, but she quickly regained her composure. "As long as you weren't making arrangements to send me away."

He flashed her a wry grin. "I'd be afraid to even try."

She made an effort to adopt a stern expression. "As long as you know where I stand on that issue. Now, I'm going to make some more coffee while you're talking to Leo Gardner."

Brad watched as she walked into the kitchen. The heat of desire settled low inside his body. Everything about her excited him more than he wanted to admit. He closed his eyes and tried to rid himself of the inappropriate feelings. It was with great difficulty that he resumed his task of contacting John Vincent's attorney.

To Brad's surprise, Leo Gardner was already in his office. He had assumed he would be talking to a secretary. At first Leo was reluctant to provide any information, but a very persuasive Brad Harrison convinced him that he wasn't breaching any client-attorney confidentiality because the information was available through public records even though going that route was inconvenient.

He made quick notes as Leo Gardner answered his questions and provided him with what he wanted. As soon as he hung up, he turned to Tara to report on what he had found. "The majority of John Vincent's estate went to his daughter, Doreen Vincent. In addition to Green Valley Construction, which was the major item in his will, Doreen inherited five hundred thousand dollars in stocks and bonds, a house in Seattle and specifically listed items of art and jewelry, in addition to the undisclosed contents of a safe-deposit box, which I assume was probably a lot of undeclared cash and hidden assets connected with his criminal activities. Whether she knew of his activities prior to his arrest and the trial is another unanswered question.

"To his nephew, Daniel Vincent, he left a car and a van plus fifty thousand dollars in stocks. Even though it's not been tested in court, we know that Danny was fully aware of John's criminal activities and was a participant in many of the jobs." Brad saw the quick look of pain that darted through Tara's eyes, a pain that he felt as surely as if it had been his own. She had been hurt by Danny on an emotional level and then had the reality dumped on her that the man she was once engaged to had been involved in the attempts on her life. He wanted so much to ease that pain and permanently erase the hurt from her memory.

Brad continued sharing the information gathered from Leo Gardner. "Then came the big question...where to find Doreen Vincent. All Leo knew was that she had been living in the house in Palm Beach that she inherited when her mother died five years ago and that she worked as a personal trainer and was considered a physical fitness guru. To the best of his knowledge the house she inherited from her father has been vacant from the time he went to prison. While the estate was in probate she stayed at a downtown hotel. She chose not to retain Leo as her attorney for her personal and business matters beyond the settling of her father's estate. Since he no longer has any business association with her, he has no idea where she is or even if she stayed in Seattle rather than returning to Florida."

"Where does that leave us?"

He drew in a deep breath, held it for several seconds

then expelled it with a sigh of frustration. "The same place we were before I talked to Leo. Other than confirming that Doreen, rather than Danny, inherited Green Valley Construction, we don't know any more than we did."

"We know Doreen was living in Palm Beach, Florida, at the time of John's death, at least that's where the attorney contacted her." She paused a moment, her face scrunched up as if something was bothering her.

"Tara? Is something wrong?"

"It just occurred to me...don't you think it's odd that she didn't bother to attend any of the trial proceedings? I never saw anyone in court during that entire time who resembled the picture of Doreen that always sat on John's desk, or any of the other photos—"

Her eyes narrowed and a frown wrinkled across her forehead as she bit her lower lip. "There's something... somewhere...a photo. I can't quite place it...something I've seen."

He stared at her. It was as if she was dragging little bits of her past to the forefront, one piece at a time as something triggered the memory. "Is it a picture of Doreen?"

"I think so. It's something about her." She shook her head. "I can't seem to get it into focus."

"Don't force it. It'll come to you. Go on with what you were saying...about Doreen not attending any of the trial proceedings."

"I was saying that I never saw anyone at the trial who resembled the photos that I'd seen of her. I know John had maintained contact with her, so they weren't estranged. I recall a couple of occasions when John mentioned family get-togethers that included Doreen and Danny. I even saw a couple of photos from one of those gatherings. They weren't a close-knit family, but they did maintain contact on a fairly regular basis."

Brad cocked his head, stared at her for a moment as he turned a thought over in his mind. He proceeded cautiously, not wanting to upset her with his line of questioning. "Do you recall seeing anyone who looked like Judy Lameroux at any time during the trial? Maybe with shorter hair? Dressed differently than you know her now?"

She pursed her lips as a slight frown wrinkled her forehead. She spoke hesitantly. "No...not that I recall. But having never seen her before we met in the bookstore, she wouldn't have been anyone who caught my attention. Having seen pictures of Doreen, that would have been someone I would have noticed."

"Well, at least we now know for sure that Doreen came from Palm Beach. We just don't know where she is currently."

"Doesn't that give you a place to start a search of some sort? Maybe phone company records showing a new phone number or a forwarding address? Property records showing whether or not she still owns that house? If she doesn't live there, then the property tax statements would have to be mailed to her somewhere. Wouldn't that be a matter of public record for anyone wanting to go to the trouble to dig it out? And, unless the house is rented to someone else, there might be utility bills that are being sent to her at another address."

He leaned forward and brushed a quick kiss across her lips, the brief touch sending a tingle of excitement through him. "You're very good at this. Perhaps you're in the wrong line of work. Have you ever considered being a detective?"

Her spontaneous laugh filled the room. "Me? Someone who has lived her entire life by the credo *don't take any chances* being a detective? That's quite a fanciful imagination you have."

"Maybe that's the way it was for you at one time, but that hardly describes your life now." He pulled her into his arms, his manner very serious in spite of her obvious amusement. "You are a very exciting and intelligent woman with a great deal to contribute to a relationship. Don't ever sell yourself short.''

The words had been heartfelt, but Brad stopped short of saying what was truly in his heart. It had been such a long time since he had opened his heart to anyone, he wasn't sure how to proceed. Nothing had been clear-cut or straightforward from the moment he first laid eyes on her. Nothing had gone smoothly. It seemed that he had totally lost control of everything around him. It was a situation that was certainly foreign to him and his way of life.

He continued to hold her for a minute, then reluctantly released her from his embrace. ''We have work to do. I can check a lot of that Palm Beach information on the computer.''

''Is it really that easy to get all kinds of personal information about someone just by sitting in your living room and punching stuff up on a computer? I know we gathered quite a bit of information while we were at Friday Harbor, but those were protected areas with passwords and things like that. What about the normal person with their home computer? Can they access all this information, too?''

''Yes. In my line of work a computer is a useful tool, but in the hands of unscrupulous people it can create untold problems such as identity theft. It's a major problem around the world.''

''You mean that whoever is behind these events could have found me as soon as I moved? That my unlisted telephone number is readily accessible to anyone with a computer and the knowledge about how to find it?'' She hesitated as another sharp barb of reality struck at her vulnerability. ''That Danny probably knew where I was as soon as I moved?''

''Yes, that's exactly what it means. I'm sure that's how the three witnesses who were not under our protection were located. But the other two who had new identities and had been relocated, that's another matter. That information had to come from an internal leak, and even within the Marshals Service that information is highly classified and hard to get at.''

Brad quickly accessed utility records for the address of Doreen's Palm Beach house. A scowl crossed his forehead as he stared at the screen. ''It appears that the house is rented. The utility bills are sent to the house, but in someone else's name. It's been that way for—'' he clicked a couple of keys then read the new data ''—almost five months.''

She leaned over his shoulder to see the information displayed on the computer screen. ''What about the property taxes?''

''I'm checking that now.''

A couple of minutes later the results appeared on the screen. Tara stared at the address, then shook her head. ''It's an address in Palm Beach and the suite number suggests that it belongs to an office building. Do you have any way of checking an address to see what it belongs to?''

''Let's see what we can find.'' Brad spent several minutes trying to track down a source that would tell him who the address belonged to, but without any luck. He scowled at the screen. ''I didn't think it would be this difficult.''

''Is there someone in Palm Beach you could call who could find out and get back to you?''

''Hmm, there just might be someone I can call.'' He reached for the phone and dialed. After two rings the call was answered.

''Steve, I need another favor.''

''You're really going to owe me big time when you get finished with this. I assume you're still involved in the same *nonexistent* case you've been working on.''

''Yes, it's the same *nonexistent* case. I have a street address in Palm Beach, Florida. I need to know who or what it belongs to. Can you make an inquiry of the Palm Beach Police Department?''

Steve's voice dropped to a conspiratorial whisper. ''I

don't know how much longer I can do these things for you without giving my captain an explanation of what's going on. He's already suspicious of my insistence that the lab boys go over the Winthrope death with a fine-tooth comb. He didn't press me, but I know he didn't buy my explanation about why I didn't believe it was an accident when that's what the initial report said. And then there was the car license you had me run. He was curious about why a homicide detective was requesting an out-of-state vehicle check not connected with any of our current cases."

"I'll see if I can find another way. I don't want you to get in trouble with your captain."

"Give me the address. I'll work something out and get back to you as soon as I can."

"Thanks, Steve. I definitely owe you one."

"You owe me a lot more than one."

"You got it. Call me on my cell phone."

Brad turned his attention to Tara. "Could Doreen be staying at Danny's house?"

"I suppose she could, but didn't John's attorney say she stayed at a hotel during the period they were settling the estate? Surely if there was a time that she would stay with Danny it would have been then. Unless..."

Brad perked up. "Yes? Unless what?"

"Well...unless they were at odds over the inheritance. Maybe Danny thought he should be getting more or possibly Doreen thought he should be getting less. Either way, it could have put them on opposite sides of an issue."

She paused a moment, then ventured a question that had been forming in the back of her mind. "Does this mean that you think Doreen Vincent is definitely involved in all this? Do you think she and Danny could actually be working together rather than being at odds with each other?"

"It's certainly beginning to look like a serious possibility. People don't decide to change their identity and disappear for no reason." He stared at the computer, slowly shaking his head while trying to organize the myriad thoughts running through his mind. "What I don't understand is how Doreen could have totally disappeared in the six months since John Vincent's death. It's as if she never existed. The timing on this said she must have been planning this prior to her father's death, possibly even prior to his trial."

He stared at Tara, his eyes questioning as much as his words. It was as if he was trying to divine some answers from her face. "And if that's the case, did she make the decision at the time he was arrested predicated on her belief that he would be convicted? And if so, then what did she intend to accomplish by the change of identity? There has to be a motive, something that hasn't come to light yet. And even more confusing is the running of Green Valley Construction."

"What's odd about Green Valley Construction?" A warm feeling settled inside her as he pulled her into his lap, accompanied by a surge of excitement the same way it did every time he touched her. It had only been a few days yet he was the most important person in her life. She tried to separate the concept of the danger surrounding them making him seem larger than life from the reality of what she knew to be true. And each time it came back the same...she wanted to build a life with Brad Harrison. Somehow it had to work out.

Brad took a sip of his coffee. "If she has totally dropped the Doreen Vincent identity in favor of whatever new one she created, then how can she continue to run the business when the person who owns it no longer exists? I haven't investigated anything having to do with the company. What I need to do is check into Green Valley and see if there's any record of a change of ownership in the past six months since Doreen inherited."

Watching his mind work had been a real education for Tara—the way he sorted through little bits of information, extrapolated what seemed significant, then built on that. And

very important to her personally was that he was sharing
with her, allowing her to know his thoughts, making her a
part of the process rather than keeping her at arm's length.
She was actively involved in searching for a solution, not
just the cause of the problem.

Then another thought tried to invade her consciousness,
one that kept shoving at her no matter how hard she tried
to push it away...she had been falling in love with Brad
Harrison from the moment he brushed a kiss across her
mouth that very first night she stayed in the motel in Tacoma. She tried to deny it when they made love the first
time, but to no avail. What she didn't know was what the
future held. A little shiver ran through her body. Or if there
even was a future for her—with or without Brad.

She tried to force her thoughts back to the problem at
hand. "How can you check on Green Valley's ownership?
It's not a publicly held company, it's privately owned."

"True, but the company is incorporated, so there has to
be a filing of corporation papers with the state which lists
the officers and which should show any change of ownership. That information should be a matter of public record."

While Brad did a computer search of corporate filings,
Tara wandered over to the living-room window and looked
outside. It was a beautiful morning, one of those marvelous
days when the residents of Seattle and Tacoma could clearly
see Mount Rainier with its perpetual snowcap glistening in
the sun.

So many thoughts circulated through her mind, each one
eliciting a different yet equally strong emotion—the immediate danger surrounding them, what her life would be
like if they couldn't identity and arrest those responsible for
the witnesses' deaths, the seemingly impossible task Brad
had taken on by himself, what this was doing to his career
and future. It wasn't fair. He'd been shot trying to protect
her. He had possibly thrown away his career trying to pro-

tect her. And all she could do in exchange was stand there and stare out a window.

She grabbed her cup of coffee and stepped out onto the large porch. The crisp mountain air filled her lungs with the clean scent of pine. She shielded her eyes against the bright morning light as she surveyed the surroundings. The business section of the village was only about three blocks down the street. A few cars traveled the road, but traffic was light. She watched as a couple of joggers ran along the trail that paralleled the road.

"I don't think you should be out here."

She jumped when the hand came down on her shoulder and spun around toward the sound of Brad's voice. The concern on his face touched her heart. Everything about him touched her heart more than she ever thought possible.

"Why not?"

"Someone we don't recognize could be watching the cabin." With a gentle nudge, he attempted to guide her toward the door.

She resisted his efforts to move back inside the cabin. "I know, but I can't stay cooped up forever. And you can't continue to move me from one hiding place to another every time you think someone might be watching us. If someone is watching the cabin, then they already know we're here. If no one knows we're here, then there isn't anyone watching. It's that simple."

He gave her shoulder a reassuring squeeze. "I admire your logic, but I'd feel better if you were inside."

She looked up at him, extending a hopeful smile. "Could we go for a walk in the woods? If we left by the back door no one would know." She forced a little chuckle. "I'm starting to go a little stir-crazy being cooped up inside all the time."

He captured her gaze, his eyes saying as much to her as his words. "You know the answer to that." He kissed her on the cheek. "I'm sorry. I know this is difficult for you.

She couldn't keep the despair out of her voice. "I suppose you're right." She gazed out over the mountains, drawing in another deep breath as she allowed the calming beauty of nature to settle over her. "I'll be there in a minute."

He hesitated before turning toward the door. The emotion in his voice conveyed the depth of his feelings. He turned back long enough to take hold of her hand for a moment. "Don't be too long. It's dangerous for you to be out here."

She gave his hand a squeeze, then watched as he went inside. It was apparently dangerous for her to be anywhere, so what could standing on the porch hurt? She turned her attention to the little bit of activity that existed along the road. Summer was over and most of the tourists, vacationers and summer residents had gone home. The smell of autumn filled the air.

Her thoughts turned again to Brad, to what this was doing to his life and career, to what she could do to help rather than feeling like such a burden. She watched the cars traveling the road. Then one caught her undivided attention.

A jolt of fear stabbed at her. Her blood turned cold as she watched the car moving slowly down the road. She tried to give the appearance of someone minding her own business and not paying any attention to what was happening. The car slowed then pulled off the side of the road across the street and a few feet past the cabin. A hard lump formed in her throat. She forced herself to move slowly, not wanting her actions to be conspicuous.

She stepped over to the door, but didn't go inside. She stood with her back to the door. With one hand she sipped her coffee. With the other she reached behind, wrapped her knuckles against the door, then grabbed the doorknob and held on to it. She pretended to be enjoying the morning. It only took a few seconds before she felt the doorknob move in her hand as Brad tried to open the door from the inside. She brought the coffee mug to her mouth to cover the fact that she was talking.

"Don't come out here. See if you can peek through the window. Across the street...the car parked there...it's the same kind Danny Vincent drives and I'm sure that's Danny behind the wheel."

His voice came back at her through the door. It carried a calm, commanding presence that immediately filled her with a sense that everything was under control. "Are you all right?"

"Yes. I'm just looking around, trying not to stare at him while pretending to be enjoying my morning coffee. What do you want me to do?"

"Can you stay there for a minute or so, long enough for me to grab the binoculars and take a good look at him? As long as you're out there he'll probably continue to watch, especially if he doesn't realize that you've spotted him. I can't imagine him trying anything in broad daylight."

"I'll stay here by the door and sip my coffee." Even though Brad instilled a feeling of confidence in her, she couldn't control the butterflies wreaking havoc with her nervous system. She moved casually, trying to make each gesture seem at ease, as if nothing was wrong. But she couldn't help herself, couldn't stop the involuntary action of casting furtive glances toward the driver.

"Tara..." Brad's words came through the door. "Get inside here as quickly as you can without appearing suspicious."

"Right away." A quick flash of anxiety hit her. The urgency in his voice was anything but calm. She pretended that her coffee cup was empty. She opened the door, breathing a sigh of relief when she was safely inside.

"What is it? What's wrong?" Her stress level rose with each breath she took. She could see it in his eyes, in the way he clenched his jaw into a hard line.

"I've never seen Danny in person, but the man sitting in the car is a dead ringer for the photos I've seen. There's a handgun on the dashboard. He's reached for it twice and each time hesitated, then pulled back and left it there. The third time he picked it up. He looked as if he was trying to screw up his courage to do something he didn't want to do. He was definitely apprehensive. He put the gun back and then just sat there, staring straight ahead out the front windshield.''

Whatever hope she held out that Danny wasn't really trying to harm her, that it was all some sort of misunderstanding, disappeared in an instant. The hurt and humiliation washed over her, the final undeniable realization that her fears had all come true—the firm knowledge that he had betrayed her and everything she thought they once had in such a cold and impersonal manner. A sob caught in her throat. She made an attempt to blink away the tears that formed in her eyes.

"I'm sorry, Tara. I wish I could have made it easier for you." He stopped short of telling her he wished it could have been different. If things had been different he never would have met her and never would have known that it was possible to open his heart again.

The ringing phone intruded into the moment.

"What do you have for me, Steve?" Brad listened intently as his friend provided the information he had requested. "Thanks. I'll be in touch later."

He turned to Tara. "Steve says the Palm Beach address belongs to a private mailbox service. Doreen Vincent could have made an arrangement with them to have her mail forwarded anywhere in the world and there wouldn't be any official trail to follow the way there would be with the post office."

The sound of car tires spinning on gravel caught Brad's attention. He looked out the window just in time to see the car across the street pull onto the pavement and disappear down the road.

"It looks like Danny decided to leave rather than staying

put. He probably realized we spotted him and now needs to stay out of sight for the rest of the day.''

Tara glanced out the window. ''Maybe he's gone to confer with Doreen.''

''From what you said about Danny being the controlling type, I don't see him needing or wanting to consider someone else's opinion and wishes and certainly not wanting anyone else's input.''

''That's true. Danny has always—'' The image popped into her mind, as vivid as when she first saw it. She whirled toward Brad, her excitement barely contained. ''That's it! The photo…it was a picture I'd seen at Danny's house. It was taken at one of the family functions that took place at John's house. Everyone was out by the pool. Danny, Doreen…and Pat! Doreen Vincent knew Pat, too.''

Chapter Thirteen

Brad felt her excitement at the new bit of information. "What were they doing in the photograph?"

Tara wrinkled her forehead in confusion. "Doing? They were..." She closed her eyes and tried to visualize the scene. "They were showing off, almost like a contest of some sort. Doreen had picked up Danny and had him slung over her shoulder like in a fireman's carry."

"Hmm...a very unusual woman. I wonder if she'd known Pat for a while or if she just met him that day."

Tara's momentary excitement faded as she considered the full impact. She looked at Brad and saw the reservation in his eyes, the hesitation that said it wasn't that simple. Her confusion and uncertainty crept into her voice. "It is Doreen that we need to find, isn't it? Isn't she the one working with Danny...the key to this?"

"That's certainly one very good possibility, but not the only one." He grabbed his notebook and a pencil and sat down at the table, indicating that she should sit down, too.

"Let's take this from the beginning. We know there was a woman involved with the witnesses on the day of their deaths in the first and third accident. Both of those witnesses were supposedly safe in the Witness Security Program with their new identities. One of those men might have let his true identity slip out in a moment of passion, but it's unlikely that both men were so careless. We also know that Danny was in Seattle on those specific dates. Both deaths were attributed to the same thing—naturally poisonous foods.

"The second and fourth deaths don't give us enough information to make an educated guess about who might have been involved, other than knowing that Danny was in a position to have been in those cities at those times, but we don't know that he was. The fifth death does give us a specific person who committed what is now officially a murder rather than accidental death as the previous four had been designated."

Tara had been following along with his recap. "Yes, and that person was Pat, who is now dead, himself a murder victim. But even if he was still alive, he's only a hired killer and not the person who wanted the witnesses dead. His only motive was money…getting paid to do a job."

"That's right. And we now have definite connection between Danny, Pat and John Vincent in that they were business associates as evidenced by you seeing them in a meeting together at John's office. We have a minor link between Doreen Vincent and Pat by virtue of them being in the same photograph along with Danny at a party. Perhaps she knew him well, perhaps that was the only time she had met him and had no other association with him.

"We know that Danny is involved and can assume that Danny is the one who hired Pat to do away with Phil Winthrope and possibly victims number two and four, also. We can assume it was Pat who planted the bomb in your car and took a shot at us through the motel window in Tacoma. We know it was not Pat who rigged the truck at the airport or who took a shot at you at Friday Harbor, because he was already dead. The time involved between my arranging the flight and our being attacked wasn't long enough for a new hit man to have been located and hired. I think we can assume that was Danny Vincent driving the black car."

Tara looked questioningly at Brad. "That leaves us with the unanswered question of who provided the flight information to him. Wouldn't it have been the same person who gave out the information about where to find the witnesses?"

"Probably, but not necessarily. The three unprotected witnesses could have been tracked down by anyone, the same way I've been tracking people using the computer. The two protected witnesses are an entirely different matter. Their new identities had to have been leaked from inside, but it's not just anyone who would have access to that type of highly classified information. It certainly isn't the type of information routinely available in any of the Marshals Service offices."

Tara leaned back in her chair. "Who does that leave? Who else belongs on our list?"

He hesitated for a moment, still unsure and unhappy about his suspicions. "Well, I've had Ralph Newman and Thom Satterly on my list of suspects for quite a while now. Thom heads the Seattle office and Ralph is a co-worker. Both are in a position to know where to start looking for classified information, have come to a standstill in the advancement of their careers and most significant is they both need money. Rumor has it that Ralph is in heavy debt to some Nevada casinos, which could give him an extra link to John Vincent through John's bookmaking operation. He could have been providing information to them as payoff for gambling debts. Thom was hit heavy by the cost of taking care of his invalid father and paying off his father's debts. He was strapped for cash, and about a year ago began selling off pieces of property that he owned."

Her voice was barely above a whisper, the emotional stress coming through. "So we really aren't any closer to resolving this than when you first contacted me and said I was in danger."

He reached over and touched her cheek. The despair in

her eyes and sadness on her face touched him on the deepest level. "That's not true. We know for a fact that there has been a conspiracy to kill the witnesses, that it's not just a wild theory. We know that Danny is heavily involved. We've also established motives for Ralph and Thom as accessories, and can assume that if either of them is involved the information they are providing is most likely going to Danny Vincent. The main task we have at the moment is figuring out where Doreen Vincent is, what her new identity is and whether she is actually involved in this or is playing out a totally separate agenda for herself that doesn't have anything to do with you or the witnesses."

Tara stood up and grabbed her empty mug. "I'm going to get a refill. Do you want any more coffee?"

He handed her his empty cup. "Yes, thanks." He watched as she walked into the kitchen. He knew about the frustration of waiting for something to happen, the boredom of sitting on stakeouts, the tedious job of sifting through seemingly endless bits of information to find the pieces that fit together into a cohesive picture. But for Tara, he knew it was frustrating and nerve-racking with the specter of death always hovering over her shoulder. Not a pretty situation for a woman who should be enjoying life rather than hiding in fear.

Brad had been toying with another idea, a bit of information that had stuck in the back of his mind as one of those little details that didn't seem to fit in with the picture that had been presented to him. While Tara refilled the coffee cups, he checked his address book for a phone number. He had been playing around with some ideas about disguises and changes in appearance that Doreen could be using and he wanted to check them out. He dialed Dr. Keeson, his optometrist. They had a good relationship and the doctor knew he was a deputy marshal.

"Dr. Keeson, it's Brad Harrison. Could I impose on you

for some help? I have a few questions about one of your patients and I need some basic information.''

"I'll give you whatever help I can, Brad. Is this something official? What is it you want to know?''

"Semi-official and confidential. I want to know about a pair of glasses purchased from you. I also want you to fill me in on some information about contact lenses.''

He gave the optometrist a list of questions and made notes of the information the doctor gave him. "I see, a brown tint. Plain glass? Isn't that a little odd? Okay. And the address you have in your records is a post office box?''

"WHAT DO YOU MEAN she spotted you? You've got to be the biggest idiot I've ever had the misfortune to be involved with! You've screwed up just about everything you've touched. It's beyond me how you've managed to survive this long. It's a simple task. All you had to do was get rid of Tara Ford. How many times have you tried and failed? Four? Five? If you'd gotten rid of her in the beginning there wouldn't be a deputy marshal involved now.''

Danny Vincent bristled at the harsh words, his anger exploding as he talked. "I don't take that kind of crap from anyone, least of all from the likes of you.'' He leaned forward across the table in an aggressive manner, his voice dropping to a menacing rasp. "We wouldn't be in this fix if you hadn't insisted on killing all the witnesses. If you'd left well enough alone like I said to, all we'd have is two accidental unrelated deaths with no connection to anything or anyone.''

Danny straightened up, his attitude as condescending as his words. "You think you're so damn clever, but it's your overinflated ego that put us in this predicament. You may have inherited the construction company, but Uncle John put *me* in charge of the important stuff when he was convicted and that still applies. *I'm* the one who runs the loan-sharking, the bookmaking operation and the other extracurricular activities. *I'm* the one who gives the orders here, not you."

"Daddy never would have left the construction company to you because he knew you were too incompetent to run it successfully. He only allowed you to take charge of the other operations as his outside contact. He fully intended to run things from prison until he got out and could take personal charge again. No way did he *give* you those operations to run on your own."

"He certainly wouldn't have left his illegal business affairs to someone who hasn't been involved in any of it, someone who doesn't know how we operate, doesn't know any of our people and doesn't know our privileged contacts or which politicians and police we own. You don't for a minute think my associates would be interested in doing business with a woman, do you? And I can assure you, none of them would ever take orders from a virtual stranger, regardless of whose daughter you are. It will never happen."

"How dare you talk to me in that manner!"

"I've tried to accommodate your obsession with getting rid of all the witnesses following Uncle John's death, but I'm through. You want Tara dead? Then you take care of it. I've got more important things to do with my time. I'm washing my hands of your mess." With that, Danny turned his back on Doreen Vincent and walked angrily toward the door.

"WELL, that's it on the corporate search." Brad started to shut down his computer, then changed his mind. "I've plowed through all the state records I can access and all I've found out is that Doreen Vincent has a very smart attorney. She's managed to hide ownership of Green Valley Construction behind a maze of corporate changes and holding companies. I couldn't find anything that confirms what name she's personally using or a valid address for her. I had three different company names that led me back to the mail service address we had already uncovered in Palm Beach."

"So you're at a dead end on tracking her down?"

"I have something else I want to try. So far, I've been searching for her new identity by using her real name and going forward in an attempt to find when she adopted a new identity and what it is. I have a new idea that might get us somewhere. Maybe if I started with a different name and tried to backtrack it to Florida as Doreen's last known address." He entered the name Judy Lameroux and started a search for a Florida driver's license.

Tara leaned over his shoulder to read the screen. "You're doing a search of Judy?" A hint of anxiety made its way into her voice. "Do you really think she could be Doreen with some plastic surgery? Wouldn't she be afraid that I'd recognize her if she were so bold as to be in daily contact with me?"

"Not necessarily. She's never met you and probably doesn't have any way of knowing if you've seen pictures of her, and if so then how many and whether you actually paid any attention to them."

"But if she is behind this, then why would she work with me for nearly six months, be a guest in my home and socialize with me without any attempts to harm me? That doesn't make sense."

"It doesn't make sense when applied to the facts we have, but we don't know everything." He continued with the computer search, checking property tax rolls and utilities. "Well, I'm not showing anything in Palm Beach for Judy Lameroux and I don't find a Florida driver's license for her, either."

"Is that it then?"

"Not yet. I have one more name I want to check."

She watched as the name came up on the screen. "Isn't that the name of—"

"Yes, there's something that's been bothering me and I

want to check it out.'' He did a background check looking for addresses and any type of records he could find to confirm the identity.

After a few minutes Brad leaned back in his chair and scowled at the screen. ''That's odd.'' He pointed to the screen, then turned toward Tara. ''Look at this...two entirely unrelated bits of information yet they're supposed to be the same.''

''Where does that leave us?''

''Much closer to the truth, but only through circumstantial evidence. We still need some solid facts and to nail down a motive.''

Tara awkwardly shifted her weight, her thoughts pushing at her. ''What do we do now as far as the investigation is concerned?''

He eyed her curiously. ''You look like you have something on your mind. Do you have a suggestion?''

''Well...'' Tara rose from the chair and walked over to the living-room window. She stared out at the landscape, a little twinge of nervous energy working its way through her body. She wasn't quite sure how to say it, how to tell him about the decision she'd made. One thing was for sure. He wasn't going to like what she was about to say. ''There has been something kind of running through my mind for the past couple of hours.''

He walked over to the window and perched on the edge of the credenza. ''Is something wrong? You look like you've got something serious on your mind.''

She turned to face him, sucked in a steadying breath, then plunged into what she wanted to say. ''I've been wondering if we should maybe rethink what we've been doing, how we've been handling the situation.''

He cocked his head and leveled a questioning look at her. ''In what way?''

Doubt suddenly welled inside her. He was the expert. What in the world made her think she could offer a suggestion that was in direct opposition to the way he had been handling things? She took another steadying breath and nervously cleared her throat.

"Uh...it seems to me that we've spent the entire time running and hiding and no matter where we've gone or what we've done they were able to find us right away. So...well, I thought that maybe we should just stay put instead of leaving and trying to find someplace else to hide out—confront them on our terms rather than constantly looking over our shoulders. I'm the one they want dead."

Saying the words sent a cold chill through her body, but she knew it was true and there was no purpose in trying to deny it or sugarcoat the reality. "You wanted to send me somewhere else to hide. Well...maybe it would be better if we made them believe I was here alone, that you had gone for some reason, then they would feel confident that they could get to me...and then, well maybe—"

"No way!" His words were emphatic, his expression stern and unyielding. "If I wanted to use you to draw them out I would have done it that first night by simply letting you go back to your house."

He drew her into his embrace. His voice softened. "I won't allow you to purposely expose yourself to danger, to be in the open and vulnerable. My job is to protect you, not use you as bait."

Her resolve started melting the moment he pulled her body against his. She steeled herself against the warmth, against the emotional pull of his touch. She stepped back, breaking the physical contact between them before she succumbed totally to the magnetism of his presence. She looked into his eyes, into the concern she found there. "It's not your decision to make—it's mine."

He presented a businesslike attitude, crossing his arms in front of his chest while continuing to lean back against the credenza. "That's very altruistic, but not very practical. The

U.S. Marshals Service does not allow witnesses under our protection to dictate the terms of—''

''Do I need to remind you that I'm not under the protection of the Marshals Service?'' She met his attempt at a stern manner with one of her own. ''As you said, there's nothing official about this. It's just you and me and because of that your entire career is hanging by a thread. And as a result of your attempts to protect me you're now in as much danger as I am. They can't get rid of me without eliminating you, too. Our fate seems to be tied together...'' She felt the heat of embarrassment flush across her cheeks as she glanced down at the floor. ''At least for the time being.'' And maybe forever? It was a question she wished she had an answer for, a commitment she wanted very much.

''Tara...'' He reached out, grabbed her hand and pulled her back into his arms. ''There may be a hint of truth in what you say, but that doesn't change anything. I'm the professional. This is what I do for a living.''

''And I'm the reason for all this trouble, which gives me some say-so in the matter. I'm not going to—''

''No...you're not the reason for the trouble. Whoever is behind this is the reason for the trouble. You are the person who has been placed in danger through no fault of your own.''

''I'm not leaving. This is as good a place to take a stand as any. By being here at the cabin we have what could be considered the home court advantage. The security system is excellent, as evidenced by the alarm going off early this morning. You have three cell phones, a Marshals Service one and two personal ones, so it will do no good for someone to try to cut the phone lines to the cabin. I noticed that there's a battery backup system for the alarm should there be a power failure. All in all, I think we're probably as safe here, if not safer, than anyplace else we could go.''

Brad stood up. He silently regarded her, then turned to stare out the window. She was right. He didn't like it, but she was right. They were probably as safe at the cabin as anywhere else. There had to be an end to this. They could not continue to run. He had never run from anything before and he didn't like the way it made him feel inside. It had been a choice between standing his ground so he could confront the trouble or retreating in an attempt to protect Tara. He had chosen the latter.

He carefully measured his words. ''And if we stayed here, just how exposed do you propose to be? You don't have anything in mind, such as parading around in the village or taking that hike in the woods you were talking about, do you? Because if that's your idea of acting as bait then I definitely veto the idea.''

''But I have to be someplace where I can be seen. It's the only way to draw them out into the open.''

Brad considered her comments, turning the possibilities over in his mind. ''Maybe if I could get some help, someone to back me up.''

''Who could you get to help us? Who do you trust?''

''I trust Steve Duncan and Ken Walsh. Steve is much younger than Ken—quick, strong, well trained and with the added advantage of having no connection to the U.S. Marshals Service, which makes his face unknown to anyone connected with the office. And then there's Ken. He has more savvy and experience than anyone I know, but I don't want to jeopardize his relationship with the Service by dragging him into this any more than I already have. Steve, on the other hand, said his captain has already gotten on his case about the favors he's been doing for me. I certainly don't want to compromise his job by putting him in the position of being caught between a friend and his captain in this matter.''

''Where does that leave us?''

A soft chuckle escaped his throat. ''As someone who professes her entire life has been based on not taking chances, doing what others have expected of her and always playing it safe, you've certainly gone out of your way to disprove all those claims.''

She offered a shy smile. "You bring out the adventuresome spirit in me."

He reached out and took her hand, his features showing the seriousness of the situation. He considered the possibilities. "Well...you seem to have your mind set on this. So, I guess we need to figure out how we're going to do it. Have you already formulated a plan of some sort?"

A bit of the apprehension lifted from Tara's nerves, leaving a new feeling of confidence. He was going along with her suggestion, allowing her to truly be part of what was happening rather than a spectator, someone to be shoved out of the way of harm and kept from danger as if she were incapable of making a contribution. He was right about her lifestyle having been *don't take chances.* But now that seemed like such a long time ago, a place where she didn't want to return. His words came back to her. *People who avoid risks don't suffer the lows, but they never get to experience the highs, either.*

"Well, I thought we might start by making it appear that you'd left me on my own. Maybe if you stopped at the gas station to fill your car and mention something about needing to be in Seattle for a couple of days. That would leave me here alone and without a car. Then I could walk the three blocks to the store and do some grocery shopping, stop at the post office to mail a letter and walk back. That should give me high visibility to anyone watching."

"It also leaves you very exposed, especially on that three-block walk between the cabin and the village. The return trip would be the most dangerous because you'd be carrying groceries, so your hands would be full and your mobility would be somewhat restricted."

"I could pick a high-traffic time when there would be lots of potential witnesses. If they were watching me, then they probably wouldn't be paying attention to anyone else

You could parallel my route on the opposite side of the road, maybe keeping back in the trees so you wouldn't stand out.''

''Okay…you walk into the village, do some shopping and walk back to the cabin with them tracking your moves. Then what? You can't keep going outside without arousing suspicion.''

Tara glanced at the floor as she thought about what he had said. She looked up and recaptured his gaze. A bit of a self-conscious smile tugged at the corners of her mouth. ''I guess I didn't think it out all the way through.''

He put his arm around her shoulder and gave a reassuring hug and a kiss on the cheek. ''For your first attempt at subterfuge you did a very good job. All we need to do is give it a little fine-tuning. But—'' he gave her a stern look ''—that doesn't mean I'm happy about your decision to place yourself in this much danger.''

The pleasure of his approval swept through her consciousness, warming every part of her that it touched. He had taken her plan as being valid, had accepted her ideas, treated her as an equal in a partnership. At that precise moment she knew just how much she loved him.

''I'll be careful. That's something I'm good at. I've spent my whole life being careful about everything. So, what do we need to do to make the plan work?''

''The first thing I need to do is make a couple of phone calls and then we'll go from there.''

Brad dialed the number. His call was answered right away. ''Steve, before you say anything…yes, I know I'm pressing my luck and I already owe you big time. I'm going to need some backup starting this evening, maybe continuing for a couple of days. We're at my sister's cabin at Mount Rainier. Can you take some time off? When this is over, I'll see that you get the use of the cabin for a week…a little vacation for you and your family.''

''What's going down?''

"We're going to draw them out and I could use a face no one knows that belongs to someone I trust. Right now the number of people I can trust has been reduced to just two and you're one of them."

"I'm sorry, Brad. I wish I could help out. We had a multiple homicide go down last night. We know who did it and have a hot tip about where he's going to be. I've pulled stakeout duty starting in about three hours. I'm rotating shifts with two other detectives and we're staying on it until this guy shows. I'll give you a call on your cell phone if something happens and I can get free, but it doesn't look very likely."

Brad quickly terminated his conversation with Steve, then dialed another number.

"Ken...I need some help. We're going to try to force this out into the open and I could use some backup. I can't trust anyone else, not until I know for sure who's behind this and who inside our offices has been working with them. I'm at my sister's cabin and would sure appreciate it if you could head up here right now."

"If you recall, you never gave me any information about what you're doing. I don't know what *this* is that you're forcing. I had a visit from Thom Satterly. He was checking up on you. He mentioned the John Vincent case and something about dead witnesses and alluded to you overstepping your authority and possibly ignoring direct orders. Just exactly what's going on? What kind of trouble are you in?"

"It's a long story, Ken."

"Well, try to condense it into a couple of sentences. Just give me the highlights."

Brad gave Ken a quick rundown, promising to fill in the details when he arrived at the cabin. He terminated the conversation a couple of minutes later, then turned to Tara.

She looked at him expectantly. "Well?"

"He'll be here about four o'clock tomorrow morning."

She frowned in confusion. "Why is he waiting until tomorrow morning? Can't he drive up here this afternoon?"

"It's a matter of precautions. Ken said Thom Satterly went to his house to specifically ask him about me. There's an outside chance that someone is aware of my visit to Ken and has been watching him. Whoever it is will be much easier to spot if Ken leaves home about one-thirty in the morning when there won't be many cars on the road. If he leaves this afternoon when there's a lot of traffic, anyone deciding to follow him could blend in with all the other cars and be difficult to detect."

"What do we do until then?"

"We'll plan out the exact moves we're making tomorrow and in the meantime stay inside and out of sight. I'll pretend to leave about nine o'clock in the morning, which will make it appear that you're here alone. That will give us about five hours of overlap time from Ken's arrival to my departure. After that you can take a leisurely stroll into the village to do your grocery shopping. Ken will stay in the cabin out of sight in case anyone tries to break in and wait for you to return. I'll be able to shadow you along the trail and into town."

He took a calming breath, reached out and brushed his fingertips across her cheek. Just touching her took his breath away and caused his pulse to race. If anything happened to her...he shoved the distasteful thought aside. He didn't even want to consider the possibility, but the apprehension kept coming back to him. "For the record, let me once again say that I'm not comfortable with you making yourself an easy target. If they decided to take a shot at you from a distance, there wouldn't be anything I could do to prevent it."

He pulled her into his arms. His voice dropped to a whisper. "I don't want anything to happen to you." He brushed a soft kiss against her lips, then captured her mouth with the emotion that coursed through his body, telling him just how devastated he would be if anything happened to her.

Chapter Fourteen

Brad checked the caller ID on his ringing cell phone, immediately recognizing Ken Walsh's phone number.

"Ken...what's up?"

"Do you have access to a television set?"

A quick jolt of apprehension hit him. "Yes. What's going on?"

"Turn on the local evening news."

Brad clicked on the television and turned to a Seattle station. The unfolding news story hit him square in the face. "I'll call you right back." He quickly disconnected the call.

"Tara..." The urgency carried over into his voice as he motioned for her to join him in front of the television. He put his arm around her shoulder and watched the news footage showing a body being taken from Puget Sound a couple of hours earlier. Then the evening news broadcast cut back to the reporter who continued with the story.

"Police report that the victim had been shot once in the back of the head. He has been identified as Daniel Vincent of Seattle. Sources in the police department tell us they don't have any suspects at this time. They have ruled out robbery as a motive for the murder. The victim was the sales manager for Green Valley Construction."

Tara's eyes grew wide as shock spread across her face.

"Danny? Someone killed Danny? But he was just here, just this morning he sat in his car across the street."

Brad led her over to the couch, where she sat down. "Are you all right? Can I get you anything."

"No…I mean, yes, I'm all right, and no, I don't need anything." She sat in stunned silence, staring straight ahead without moving.

As much as he wanted to comfort her, the situation called for immediate action. He grabbed his Marshals Service cell phone and called the Seattle Police Department, asking to speak to the detective in charge of the Vincent murder.

"My name's Brad Harrison. I'm a deputy U.S. marshal. I have been conducting an investigation involving Danny Vincent. It came as quite a surprise to me to see him all over the evening news. Is there any information you can give me other than the sketchy details provided on the news broadcast?"

He listened to the reply, not happy with what he was hearing. "Okay, let me give you my cell phone number." Again, he listened to the response. "I'm not in the office. When you call, ask them to transfer you to my cell phone."

An edge of frustration shoved at him. He understood the necessity of not giving out information over the phone just because someone they didn't know claimed to be in a position that made it okay. What he didn't like was the delay of waiting for the detective to get around to calling the Marshals Service office to verify his identity…and whether that phone call would be brought to Thom's attention.

He turned toward Tara. She sat on the couch in the same position as he'd left her. He sat down next to her, putting his arm around her to provide some comfort. "How are you doing?"

She leaned her head against his shoulder. "I'm doing okay. It was just such a shock about Danny."

"It sure was. I was totally unprepared for that step. The only question is whether it relates to what we're working on or did someone else from his past have it in for him, with the timing of the reprisal being unfortunate.''

She looked up at him. ''Isn't that the same thing you said about Pat's murder? You wondered if it was connected with this or an unrelated incident from his past?''

He jerked to attention, then stared at her as if he was trying to comprehend what she had said.

She sat up straight, glanced toward the door, then back at him. ''What's the matter? Did you hear something?''

''You said it…is this the same as Pat. Of course!'' He grabbed his personal cell phone and punched in a phone number.

''Steve…they fished Danny Vincent out of Puget Sound this afternoon. He was shot. Could you contact the Seattle police and see if you can get a ballistics match with the slug you took out of Andrew Carruthers? I have a witness who confirms that they knew each other and puts them together in a closed-door meeting with some other people. It's just too coincidental having the two of them both shot and dumped in the water within days of each other…the same as having five out of six witnesses in the same case all die of accidental deaths in less than six months. Since you're currently investigating the Andrew Carruthers's murder, your captain couldn't possibly object to you following up on a lead, especially if it helps get you closer to solving your case.''

He quickly terminated his conversation with Steve, then placed a call to Ken Walsh. ''Someone out there must be truly desperate to have depleted their ranks this way, or else whoever it is has such a huge ego that they think they don't need anyone else. First Pat and now Danny. Andrew 'Pat' Carruthers was a top-notch hit man with an impressive record of successful scores. Danny was John Vincent's nephew and probably the one who took over the illegal operations…'' He paused a moment as a new line of thought occurred to him. "Or perhaps he tried to take over and failed, with this being his reward."

"One thing's for sure, Brad. Whoever is behind this has ice water for blood. Very cold and calculating, highly ambitious, with no loyalty to anyone. A power struggle could certainly explain the reason Danny was eliminated...kind of a winner-take-all situation. But to do away with someone as useful to the criminal element as Andrew Carruthers was a truly ruthless act probably born of desperation."

"How's your schedule? Do you still anticipate arriving at the cabin about four o'clock in the morning?"

"Yes. I'll see you then."

"Give me a call when you hit the village. Cut your headlights when you get to the driveway. I'll have the garage open for you so you can get your car out of sight."

"IT'S GOOD to see you again, Ken." Brad shook hands with his friend. The retired marshal stood just under six feet tall. With his distinguished looks and dark hair graying at the temples he had the appearance of a banker or judge, but the steely glint in his eyes clearly said he was not to be taken lightly in spite of his sixty years of age. "Did you have any problems on the way up?"

"Nothing. No suspicious vehicles in my neighborhood and no one followed me. I doubled back a couple of times to make sure."

Tara walked into the kitchen, drawing both men's attention. "Good morning." She poured herself a cup of coffee, then held up the coffeepot toward Ken with a questioning look.

Ken extended a warm smile. "Yes...I'd love some coffee."

"I suppose I should officially introduce the two of you. Ken Walsh, this is Tara Ford." Tara and Ken shook hands. "Tara is the one and only remaining witness from the John Vincent trial. She's what this is all about."

Ken seated himself at the kitchen table. "All you gave me on the phone was a quick overview. Now that I'm here, do you suppose you could fill me in on the details? You needed some false identification for this young lady and Thom Satterly is curious about your activities and it has to do with the John Vincent case. And now Danny Vincent has been murdered. So, how does all of this come together?"

Brad filled Ken in on the details of how he had stumbled across the case and what had happened since he'd started poking around. "And that brings us up to now. Tara has insisted on putting herself out in the open as bait." He shot a pointed look in her direction. "A situation I'm not happy with, but have reluctantly agreed to try."

Ken regarded Tara. "That's very brave of you, young lady."

Tara slowly shook her head. "I'm hardly brave. It's just that things can't go on like this. I can't live constantly looking over my shoulder, running from one hiding place to another..." She glanced at Brad, but had to quickly look away as emotion welled inside her. She addressed her comments to Ken. "Brad was wounded because of me and his career is in jeopardy. I can't let the situation continue. There has to be an end to all of this and it isn't going to happen if we continue to run and hide. I'm the one they want, so it's up to me to take a stand."

Ken threw an admiring glance in Tara's direction, then looked at Brad. "You were wounded?"

"It's nothing, just a little scratch. Of greater concern to me is a leak of privileged information from our offices. Danny Vincent was at the top of my list as the person receiving the information. Right now my money is on Doreen Vincent, but she's completely disappeared—which is the main reason she's now at the top of my list. She constructed a new identity for herself, even going so far as to hide own ership of Green Valley Construction behind a maze of dummy corporations and holding companies.''

''I assume you've tried all the regular avenues of investigation in trying to locate her?''

''As much as I can without going through official channels. I've come up with something that I think nails her down, one little slipup in her false trail, but it's only speculation. Right now I'm waiting to hear back from the Seattle police about their investigation into Danny's murder. They wouldn't talk to me when I called. They needed to call the Marshals Service and make sure I was who I said I was. If I haven't heard from them by eight o'clock this morning, then I'll call again. I have some questions I need answered and preferably before Tara makes herself a target. Steve's going to request a ballistics comparison of the bullet that killed Pat with the one that killed Danny.''

Ken reached over and poured himself some more coffee. ''What's your plan for today?''

''I'm going to make a show of leaving so it will appear that Tara's here alone. I'll double back on the fire road behind the cabin, leave my car parked there and wait. Then she'll walk into the village to do some grocery shopping and other routine errands. You'll stay here to cover the cabin in case anyone tries to get in and wait for her while she's gone and you'll be here when she returns, hidden upstairs, out of sight. I'll keep Tara under surveillance from the time she leaves the cabin until she returns.''

Ken frowned as he glanced from Brad to Tara then back to Brad. ''That's pretty risky. What if they take aim at her from a distance from a concealed location?''

Brad glanced at Tara before responding to Ken's question. ''That's exactly the point I made, but Tara insisted that this is what she wants to do.'' He gave her hand a quick squeeze. ''And I'm not sure I'd be able to stop her short of locking her in a closet.''

Ken directed his question to Tara. ''Is that right, young

lady? Do you fully understand the risks involved? If someone puts you in the crosshairs of a rifle scope, there isn't anything anyone can do to prevent you from being shot and most likely killed.''

Her voice was soft, but it did not contain any hesitation or uncertainty. "Yes, I fully understand the risks involved. This is the only way. It's something I have to do if we're going to put an end to this nightmare.''

A sinking feeling lodged itself in Brad's stomach. He fully understood the risks, too. He wasn't sure precisely when he began falling in love with Tara, but the night they made love for the first time had brought the realization into crystal clarity. And now the woman he loved could be killed and he would be unable to prevent it. Just as it had been several years ago with his wife. His anxiety level shot up. He had spent two hours last night trying to talk Tara out of doing this. He had even gone so far as to tell her that he forbid it. He very quickly found out what a huge mistake that had been. He had done everything he could, but she stubbornly held on to her decision.

In retrospect he had to admit to himself that he would have done the same thing if he had been in her position. But would he be able to go on if anything happened to her? It was something he had to put out of his mind before it drove him beyond the realm of what needed to be done.

The ringing of his Marshals Service cell phone interrupted the moment. He grabbed it. "Harrison.'' He listened as the Seattle detective identified himself.

"I have a very tight time frame here and appreciate you getting back to me so soon. I have questions about your investigation of the Danny Vincent murder. In order to save time, I'll give you all my questions, then we can go over what you have. Who did you notify of the death and where did you reach that person? Are there any leads on suspects or motive that you've held back from the public? The news broadcast said shot in the back of the head. Was there jus one shot? Any other signs of trauma? Do you have an autopsy report yet? If not, do you have an educated guess about the time of death?'' Brad listened as the detective gave him what information they had accumulated so far.

''I see. I can give you a little bit of help on your time frame as far as Danny's whereabouts earlier yesterday.'' Brad provided the detective with the time Danny had been sighted at Mount Rainier, then concluded his conversation.

Tara couldn't hold back her curiosity any longer. ''What did he say? Did he have any useful information?''

''Not too much. With Danny's criminal background they had the possibility of more suspects than they needed. They haven't had time to sort it out yet and narrow it down to a viable list. Apparently death was caused by one single shot to the back of the head. An initial inspection showed no other trauma such as would have been inflicted in a fight, or even any signs that he had been physically restrained. It looked as if someone walked up behind him, aimed and pulled the trigger without his being aware.

''They should have an autopsy report in an hour or so. The notification of next of kin was his father, but this is where it gets interesting. The father is in very bad health in a nursing home and wasn't able to come down to make an identification of the body. The person who showed up said she was his cousin, Doreen Vincent. She gave a phone number and address, which have since been determined to be a lie. It seems that our mysterious Doreen has a sense of humor. The phone number turned out to be an unlisted number belonging to the chief of police and the address was a cemetery.

''The description of her was short red hair and oversized sunglasses. She was dressed in jeans, a sweatshirt and boots. The morgue attendant didn't really pay much attention beyond that. He did say that he thought she was wearing a wig. It seems his wife has one just like it. That loosely fits the description of the unknown woman seen entering the house of the first witness who met an untimely demise and corresponds with the short red wig hairs found at the scene of the third death."

Tara perked up at the information. "That means Doreen is still in Seattle, or at least she was yesterday. So, we know for sure that it's a woman we're looking for, someone in her early thirties." Then a new wave of reality hit her. She went to the window, pulled aside the drape and looked out at the road. "I wonder if she's out there right now, watching the cabin and waiting to see what we're going to do."

"What we're going to do—" Brad gave a gentle tug on her hand to get her to move away from the window "—is carry out our plan just as we discussed it."

She looked at him, questioning without showing any fear. "Should I be on the lookout for someone in a short red wig wearing large sunglasses? Do you think she'll stick to that disguise?"

"There's no way of telling. You'll need to be aware of anyone who appears to be the right size and age. She could even try to disguise herself as a man, so also keep alert for someone with a beard and mustache as a disguise. Of course, she'd be short for a man..." Some little fact was trying to shove its way out of his memory and into his consciousness.

"Brad?" She touched his arm. "Is something wrong?"

"No...I was just trying to remember something." He shook his head. "It'll come to me."

Brad turned on the television. Ken joined them in the living room and the three of them watched the early-morning news. Tension coursed through Brad's body. Ken personified calm, but then Brad had never known him to be any other way. Tara's tensed muscles belied any attempt on her part to appear relaxed. He nervously checked his watch. He had set nine o'clock for the time he would make his very visible departure from the cabin.

He tried to sit still. He forced his attention to the television set in an attempt to get his mind off his worries. There was a commercial on. The product eluded him, but the content jumped out and grabbed him. A woman and man on the dance floor at a formal occasion, he kissed her and the resulting excitement was so great that it literally knocked her out of her high heels.

Brad jumped to his feet. "That's it! That's what has been bothering me."

He turned excitedly to Tara, who rose to her feet. He grabbed her shoulders. "I'm six foot one and there's nothing I can do to make myself any shorter. I can shave my head, bleach my hair, put on a false beard and mustache or even give myself a prominent scar across my face through the use of theatrical makeup, but I can't make myself five-ten. I can, however, add some height with the type of shoes I wear...how thick are the soles and how high the heels. Cowboy boots would make me a perceived couple of inches taller. It's the height that's been bothering me, but now it makes sense. When I followed up on something I thought would take me one direction, I ended up stopped by the height. I followed up with the optometrist, but was stymied by the height."

Total confusion covered her face. "What are you talking about?"

"I'm talking about Doreen Vincent! The solution has been right under our noses the entire time. You said the photograph of her and John on his desk was taken at a country club party celebrating her graduation. I'll bet she was wearing high heels...making her appear two or three inches taller than she really is. Am I right?"

Tara scrunched up her face as she visualized the photograph. Her eyes widened in surprise. "You're right...she was wearing heels."

AT NINE O'CLOCK Brad took his car out of the garage and pulled it around in front of the house. He climbed the three steps to the front porch. Tara came out of the cabin and stood on the porch with him, both of them highly visible to anyone watching.

Even though it was unlikely that anyone was close enough to hear, he spoke louder than normal so that the words would have added impact to whomever might be listening. "I don't like leaving you here all alone, but I have a lead that I need to follow in person…an informant who has information for me about Danny Vincent's murder." Tara walked him to his car as they continued to talk.

"Make sure you set the perimeter alarm as soon as you go back inside, and keep it on. I should be back by midafternoon. Don't answer the door if anyone knocks. I'll knock on the front door, then I'll call to you to let you know it's me. Don't turn off the alarm until then. As soon as it's off let me know, but don't open the door. I'll unlock it and let myself in. Now, are you sure you're going to be all right here by yourself?"

"I'll be okay. With Danny gone, no one knows we're here."

"Don't take any chances. Right now while I'm standing here, go inside and lock the door, then set the alarm."

As soon as Tara was inside, Ken joined her, making sure he stayed out of sight from the window. They watched as Brad got into his car and drove away.

She looked at Ken. "Do you think that was convincing?"

He offered a confident smile, his voice carrying an upbeat quality obviously meant to relieve her tension. "I was convinced."

DOREEN VINCENT WATCHED from her hiding place among the rocks on the other side of the road until Brad's car had disappeared around the curve. She took off the headphone she had put on as soon as Brad and Tara stepped onto the porch and turned her attention back to the cabin. So, Brad had an informant who claimed to have information about

Danny's murder and he'd be gone most of the day. Her last-minute decision to purchase the high-powered directional microphone had been a good one. If only it was the type of equipment that could have heard what was being said inside the cabin as well. She already knew about the perimeter alarm system. Danny had told her what happened when he had tried to get in the cabin. But beyond that, it seemed that Brad had provided additional security procedures for Tara to follow.

She stood up. She had been hiding in the rocks since daylight and needed to stretch her muscles. Having Brad leave Tara alone at the cabin had come as a surprise. She needed to have the two of them together. They both had to be eliminated. Too bad about Brad. She liked him, but there was no way she could leave him out of this, not with everything he knew. He had signed his own death warrant when he started snooping around and digging into things that weren't any of his business.

A plan...she needed a plan. She couldn't do anything until Brad returned. Then her attention was drawn back to the cabin. The front door opened and Tara stepped onto the front porch. Doreen watched as Tara looked around, then left the cabin and walked along the path paralleling the road headed toward the village. What a stroke of luck, just what she needed. Tara would be her ticket into the cabin and then they'd wait for Brad to return.

Doreen had dressed in her jogging clothes. Her first thought was to wear the red wig and large sunglasses, but she quickly dismissed that idea. She had overused that disguise...two murders and a trip to the morgue to identify Danny's body. Brad would have caught on by now, maybe even warned Tara to be on the alert for someone who looked like that.

She put on a head sweatband and stuck her small .25 caliber handgun into her fanny pack. She gathered up the listening equipment, quickly deposited it in her car, locked

the door, then made her way along the opposite side of the
road from Tara. She kept her quarry in sight at all times.

KEN WALSH PLACED the binoculars on the table. He had
followed Tara until she was out of sight. He hadn't seen
Doreen at first, but caught sight of her when she stood up.
He watched as she put on the headband and shoved the
handgun in her pack.

He dialed Brad's cell phone. "Tara just left here. I picked
up on Doreen across the road. She has short brown hair and
is wearing a red sweatband around her head, a gray shirt
and bicycle pants. And she's armed. She seems to be trailing
Tara from across the road."

"Can you pinpoint where Doreen was hiding?"

"Yes, I know exactly where it was. I plan to check out
the site as soon as I hang up."

"I'm taking the fire road on the same side of the street
as Tara. On the other side, a few feet back in the woods,
there's an old logging road. It's hardly much more than a
rutted trail, but it's possible to get a four-wheel-drive vehicle
back there."

"I'll look around and see if I can find Doreen's car. I'm
taking this cell phone with me."

"Tara was going to try to stay in the village for at least
three hours, making the grocery shopping her last stop."

"I'll let you know when I'm back inside the cabin." Ken
clicked off the phone. As an added precaution, he left by
the back door and circled around until he was about one
hundred yards up the road from the cabin before crossing
to the other side.

He made his way down the old logging road until he saw
the Jeep parked among the trees. He proceeded slowly, carefully checking for anyone who might be working with Doreen. When he was confident that the area was clear, he did
a quick check of the vehicle. He discovered the listening
equipment and a few items that could be considered dis-

guises, such as a short red wig. He jotted down the license number, then returned to the cabin.

Ken placed another call to Brad's cell phone. "She has a Jeep parked back there. I found some professional listening equipment, so I think we can assume she heard every word you and Tara said to each other while you were in front of the cabin. I didn't see any rental-car stickers. I'm going to run the license plate on the car."

"Good. Tara just reached the village. She's inside the coffee shop right now. She's seated where she's visible through the window, but not a convenient target. After the coffee shop she's going to a gift shop and then finally to the general store. She'll browse there for a while and end up doing some grocery shopping. That will give her a sack to carry back to the cabin. With her arms full it will appear that she has her attention focused on what she's doing rather than on what's going on around her. I haven't seen—"

"Brad? Are you there?"

"Yeah...I was about to say that I hadn't seen anyone answering your description of the way she's dressed, but I just spotted her." A bit of a chuckle escaped his throat followed by words that were spoken more to himself than to Ken. "Well, I'll be damned...slim waist and hips...a hard body with well-toned muscles. So, it was padding. This certainly explains a lot of things."

"Brad? Are you talking to me?"

"Mousy brown hair, large horn-rimmed glasses and apparently about twenty pounds overweight. It was all a disguise. The blond hair dyed brown and cut short was easy. The optometrist confirmed the eyeglasses without any vision correction along with brown-tinted contact lenses to change her eye color, which was very clever of her. But the padding of her clothes to make herself seem heavier was truly inspired."

"What are you talking about, Brad?"

"Shirley Bennett...that's what I'm talking about."

Chapter Fifteen

Tara sipped her coffee. It was all she could do to sit still and project an outer calm. The anxiety churned in her stomach along with something she didn't want to admit—a large dose of fear. She had seen the admiration in Brad's eyes when she took her firm stand on making herself a visible target and it had warmed her heart. But now, sitting all alone and knowing someone who wanted her dead was out there watching her…well, all the bravado had melted away, leaving only a thin veneer of composure.

She wanted to look around, to take in the faces of the people in the coffee shop and those passing by the window. She wanted to be able to spot Doreen, to know where she was and what she was doing. But she fought the urge. If she was being watched, she didn't want it to look as if she was aware of it. It had to appear as if she thought she was safe and didn't have any concerns. She took another sip of her coffee and pretended to be reading the morning newspaper.

A myriad of thoughts raced through her mind. If Doreen Vincent was sitting two booths away, would she recognize her? How had Doreen changed her appearance? Would it be something simple like changing the color of her hair or using a wig, maybe wearing glasses, or perhaps more drastic steps such as the plastic surgery Brad had suggested?

She paid for her coffee, then continued on the route that Brad had laid out for her. She forced herself to casually stroll along the sidewalk, pausing to look in windows. She felt someone's eyes on her back, an uncomfortable presence that left her heart pounding and full-blown anxiety coursing through her body. It took a concentrated effort to keep from turning around. Was it her imagination? She tried to convince herself it was Brad keeping tabs on her, but in her gut she knew that wasn't it. The hair stood up on the back of her neck and a shiver of trepidation ran up her spine. A foreboding of things to come? She tried to shake off the sensation as she continued on her route, doing everything Brad had instructed her to do.

Tara glanced at her watch while looking through the magazine rack in the general store. It was time to buy the groceries and return to the cabin. The feeling had stayed with her, the uncomfortable sensation that someone was staring at her, watching her every move. She took a grocery cart and slowly pushed it down the aisle, selecting a few items as she went.

Her gaze darted from place to place until she located what she had been looking for…one of the large round mirrors mounted near the ceiling that allowed the employees to view areas of the store behind shelves and around corners. If she could get into the right position, she could use the mirror to see who and what was going on behind her.

Not sure if it would really accomplish anything, she moved in that direction while constantly checking the mirror. She spotted three women who appeared to be the right age, but couldn't get a good look at any of their faces. One was wearing a T-shirt and jeans, another was wearing a jumper and the third one was dressed in jogging clothes with a red headband. None of them had blond hair. She didn't spot anyone with the short red hair of the wig, either. She looked in the mirror again. If Brad was watching her, he had managed to stay out of her line of sight.

She continued up one aisle and down the next, adding only a few items to her cart as she went. She was sure that nothing would happen while she was in the store. The plan was to have Doreen follow her back to the cabin. She knew Ken was there and Brad was following her, but it didn't stop the trepidation that had been building inside her from the moment she started toward the village.

She made her purchases and carried the sack out the door. She walked to the corner, then set the sack of groceries on the bench. Taking advantage of the moment, she glanced back along the sidewalk and caught sight of the woman with the red headband. It was only a glimpse, but it was enough.

A hard jolt of reality shoved through her body. Her pulse raced and her heart pounded. The long blond hair was now brown and had been cut short, but there was no doubt in her mind that the face belonged to Doreen Vincent.

Tara pretended to rearrange some of the items in the sack, then picked it up and continued walking. She didn't need to look again. She felt Doreen's stare as surely as if she could see it. She also felt the strong emotion attached to it, a sinister presence that sent a chill through her. Each step she took produced a sinking feeling of dread. Never in her entire life had she needed her trust to be valid more than right now. Her life was literally in Brad's hands and she didn't even know where he was. All she could do was believe his words, believe that he would have her in sight at all times.

She fought the urge to drop the sack and run back to the cabin as hard and fast as her legs would carry her. She took deep, slow breaths and forced herself to maintain a leisurely pace along the path. She finally reached the driveway leading up to the cabin. She juggled the grocery sack while fumbling in her pocket for the door key.

"Just keep walking, Tara. We'll go in the front door together."

Her body stiffened. The words startled her, even though she knew Doreen was behind her. She started to turn around.

"Don't stop and don't turn around." Doreen's voice held a menacing quality to it, something far more sinister than mere desperation, which she emphasized by shoving a gun in Tara's back. "Don't do anything stupid or I'll use this."

Tara swallowed down the lump in her throat. Brad had given her very specific instructions that if confronted directly she was to do exactly what Doreen said without any argument or hesitation. Her hand trembled slightly as she inserted the key into the lock. She quickly glanced around as soon as she was inside. There wasn't any sign that Ken was in the cabin even though she knew he was there. She didn't know where Brad was.

She couldn't keep the quaver out of her voice. "Is it all right if I take the groceries into the kitchen?"

"Just put the sack on that chair."

Tara did as she was told. After depositing the bag, she turned around to face her nemesis. Her gaze fixed on the gun in Doreen's hand. A bitter taste filled the back of her mouth, the taste of fear. She knew she couldn't allow it to show. She had to play out her part. She forced her gaze away from the gun, settling it on Doreen's face. Her eyes were cold, her features hard. Doreen Vincent seemed to be devoid of any compassion or caring.

Tara's legs began to quiver as terror coursed through her body. She sat down before her trembling became visible. The last thing she wanted was for her fear to show. She was careful to pick a chair on the opposite side of the living room from the kitchen door and the stairs to the second floor, putting Doreen in a position where her back was to that portion of the cabin. "Why are you doing this? What do you want from me?"

"Haven't you and Brad figured everything out by now? If not, then I'm surprised. Brad is very bright. He had me worried from the moment he got his hands on the John Vincent case file."

Tara scrunched up her face in confusion. "Had you worried? You personally know Brad?"

A sarcastic laugh escaped Doreen's mouth accompanied by a smirk. "I've been working with him for a couple of months now. He never had a clue, never tumbled to the truth."

"You work in the Marshals Service office? How did you manage to get a job there? Don't they do a background check on people?"

"It was easy. I'd been watching the posting of available position openings in the Seattle office and saw that their computer person was retiring and the job was open. I hacked into the employment records and created a file in the name of Shirley Bennett showing that she had been employed in the Miami office, then I simply transferred her to Seattle to fill the vacancy. As far as Seattle was concerned, all the background checks had already been done and it was a routine internal transfer. It was a simple computer task for someone who's proficient in that area. It's a knack of mine, like a natural talent. I never really studied anything about computers, I just sort of fell into it by accident."

"But I don't understand. What do you have against me? We've never even met. It can't be because I testified against your father. I was only one witness and what I knew was small stuff. I had no idea that he was involved in organized crime."

"Hmmph!" Doreen's contemptuous attitude came out in her voice. "You stupid little nobody. You don't have a clue what's going on here. Unfortunately that won't save you."

"Then it won't hurt anything if you satisfy my curiosity and fill me in on what I don't know."

Doreen perched on the edge of the sofa arm, keeping her distance from Tara while continuing to point the gun at her. "No...I suppose it wouldn't hurt anything. We're going to be here together for the rest of this afternoon…at least until Brad returns. I heard what he told you about calling to you through the front door and waiting for you to answer him before he came inside. So, that buys you a couple more hours of time.''

Brad had concocted that plan as a safeguard to make sure no harm came to her while waiting for him to return. It was now up to her to get as much information out of Doreen as possible while she believed she had the upper hand. ''Uh…did you really kill all those people?'' Get her talking. Get her to confess to what happened. It was Tara's single-minded purpose at the moment. In order to succeed she needed to block out the sight of the gun pointed at her and somehow manage to call up the strength to override the combination of fear and panic twisting into knots in the pit of her stomach.

''*All* those people? *All* of which people?''

Smugness covered Doreen's face, matching the condescending tone of her voice. She radiated an attitude of superiority that said she believed she was smarter than everyone else. Tara latched on to that, focusing her efforts along those lines. An ego of that magnitude would have an almost obsessive need to brag about how clever she had been in carrying out her plans, especially when she thought she was in control of the situation.

Tara put a calculated plan of her own into play. She glanced nervously around the room, allowing her gaze to linger on the front door and windows in order to cover her real objective of checking the kitchen door where Brad planned to enter the cabin and the top of the stairs where Ken was stationed just out of sight.

''What are you looking for?'' Doreen's cynical laugh conveyed her contempt. ''You expect the cavalry to come riding over the hill to rescue you?''

A quick look through the door into the kitchen told Tara what she wanted to know. A dish towel had been looped through the handle on the refrigerator door. It hadn't been there when she and Doreen arrived. It was the agreed-upon signal from Brad telling her he was inside. Her panic subsided and a sense of calm settled over her. Doreen had no way of knowing exactly how much she and Brad had already figured out. She would allow Doreen to assume that they didn't know that much about what had *really* happened.

"Did you really kill those witnesses? I mean, did you do it yourself? Everyone thought they were accidents. Even the police thought they were accidents. If they were murders, then they must have been done by a professional killer."

"I planned all of them. Nobody else had the foresight to handle it. Danny wanted to rush in and blow them away, but then he never was known for his subtlety or his brains." Doreen leveled a look of disdain at Tara. "You'd know about that since you used to be engaged to the jerk."

"But I don't understand…why eliminate the witnesses? Were you trying to avenge your father's death? He died of a heart attack, which means he probably would have died whether he was in prison or not. A natural death can't be blamed on those who testified against him at his trial."

A hard, cruel laugh was Doreen's response to Tara. "Avenge his death? Are you serious? He didn't have anything to do with this. It was those two witnesses…they knew about me. It didn't come out in the trial, but it would have eventually."

"You mean you killed all those people—" Tara hesitated for a moment, not sure how to word what she was trying to say "—five witnesses, a contract killer and your own cousin just because of what you thought two people might say at some future time? What could they possibly have known about you that warranted killing them?"

"They knew about what I did…what I *really* did. Not the cover of aerobics instructor, but the smuggling of drugs from South America and the Caribbean. It was only a matter of time before one or both of them would have sold that information to the feds. So I needed to eliminate all the witnesses. If the connection was ever made between the deaths, it had to appear as if someone wanted *all* the witnesses dead. Pat was sloppy, as evidenced by the fact that you're still breathing. He wanted to be paid anyway…so I paid him off for good with a bullet. And Danny…well, he had the ridiculous thought that he would be running things. That was a matter of survival. Either him or me. It was an easy choice to make.''

''There are too many people who know about this now. You'll never get away with more murders.''

''No you don't.'' She stepped in close to Tara and waved the gun in front of her face. ''You're not going to convince me of that. I know better. I've planned everything down to the last detail.''

Doreen paced back and forth across the living room, her manner jittery, her movements growing erratic as she waved the gun back and forth as she talked. And the more she talked the more agitated she became. ''Brad's the only one who suspects. As soon as Brad gets back, I'll take care of both of you, then no one will know.''

''That's not true. He's confided his suspicions to others. He told me so.''

''You're lying. He took his suspicions to Thom, but that's where it stopped because Thom didn't believe any of it. I know…I've been monitoring every move Brad made. He didn't go over Thom's head, he didn't make any kind of report. He didn't go to the FBI. I've been ahead of him every step of the way. As soon as you slipped away from San Juan Island, I had Danny waiting here for you to show up. It was in Brad's personnel records, his sister's name as the one to notify. All I had to do is check to see what she owned and I turned up this place. It was the only logical move for Brad to make, the only place he could go without having his location compromised. So you see, I've been more clever than him from the moment he stumbled across the information about the dead witnesses.''

Tara's panic resurfaced. A sick feeling churned inside her accompanied by the bitter taste of fear. Why hadn't Brad done something. She saw the signal, she knew he was in the kitchen. What was he waiting for? Doreen was obviously on the edge and spiraling out of control. She fought to maintain an outer calm so she wouldn't trigger any type of violent action in Doreen.

''You're a long way from the office, *Shirley*. Or do you prefer to be called Doreen? Drop the gun on the floor and kick it under the couch.'' Brad's voice carried total authority and control.

A wave of relief washed over Tara. Brad would take care of everything. It was as if every tightly stretched muscle and taut nerve ending had suddenly decided to turn to mush. She felt as if she couldn't move even if she wanted to.

Doreen whirled toward the kitchen, her features set in a hard expression, her eyes cold and ruthless. He had his 9mm handgun leveled at her. She hesitated for a moment then dropped the gun, but didn't kick it away.

Brad moved from the kitchen into the living room. He barked out orders, leaving no room for dissension. ''I said to kick it under the couch—now!''

Doreen edged her foot toward the gun. In a lightning-quick move she kicked it directly at Brad. He ducked, dropped to one knee and took aim at her. But not in time.

Doreen grabbed Tara's arm and pulled her in front as a shield. Her arm tightened around Tara's neck and she had her hand against the side of Tara's head. The adrenaline pumped hard through Tara's body, leaving the taste of stark terror in her mouth. She fought off the panic that tried to take over. She had to keep her wits about her and not provoke Doreen into doing anything.

''Back off, Brad, or else I'll snap her neck. I can do it. I'm very strong. How do you think Danny got into Puget

Sound? I lifted him out of the car and carried him over my shoulder…one hundred and seventy-five pounds of dead weight and I still carried him.''

Brad set his gun on the coffee table and stepped back. ''Don't do anything foolish. You don't have any way out of here.''

''Sure I do. I'm going right out the front door as soon as I get your gun.'' She shoved Tara forward, maintaining her as a shield as she moved toward the coffee table. She reached out to pick up the gun while keeping her other arm around Tara's neck.

Tara swallowed down the sick feeling that rose in her throat. *Stay focused… Stay focused.* She fought to shove away the nearly overwhelming terror that threatened to paralyze even her ability to think. Pervasive quiet filled the room, blocking out everything except the intense pounding of her heart. She kept her gaze locked on Brad's face, drawing courage and strength from the intensity she found there.

The noise filled the air, sounding a thousand times louder than it really was as it broke the ominous silence. Tara felt Doreen's body stiffen for a moment, then Doreen turned in the direction the sound had come from.

Ken Walsh stood at the top of the stairs. He had cocked his revolver and aimed it straight at Doreen's head. His voice was low and no-nonsense. ''Turn loose of her and step back.''

Brad instantly sprung into action. He grabbed his gun from the coffee table and in three quick strides had the muzzle pressed against Doreen's temple. ''Do like the man said. Turn loose of Tara and step back. I can pull this trigger quicker than you can do any harm. Save us both the messy results.''

It was a tense moment, everyone waiting to see what Doreen would do. Tara wasn't sure her legs would continue to support her. Then Doreen withdrew her arm from around Tara's neck and stepped back. Tara took two quick steps and collapsed onto the couch. It was the first easy breath she had drawn since leaving the cabin to walk into the village. It was finally over.

BRAD, Tara and Ken stood on the front porch of the cabin and watched as two sheriff's deputies led a handcuffed Doreen Vincent to the car.

Brad turned to Thom Satterly. "I'll take care of the reports tomorrow afternoon."

Thom self-consciously shifted his weight from one foot to the other. "Uh…about this whole matter…"

Brad slowly repeated what he had said, his voice filled with purpose and a finality that said the conversation was over. "I'll take care of the reports tomorrow afternoon."

Ken stepped in to rescue the moment. "Let me walk you to your car, Thom."

As soon as the accumulation of vehicles and people had departed, Brad and Tara went back inside. He pulled her into his arms, stroked her hair, then held her tightly. It had been three hours since Doreen had finally conceded the hopelessness of her situation and given up. Yet he could still taste the adrenaline. "How are you doing? Are you all right?"

She wrapped her arms around his waist and nestled her head against his shoulder. "I think my pulse has finally returned to normal and my heartbeat has quieted down a bit, but I'm not sure my nerves will ever be the same again."

She closed her eyes as a shudder ran through her body. "Oh, Brad…I've never been so frightened in my life. I was so afraid I was going to say something wrong or do the wrong thing." Tara looked up at him. "She's crazy, you know. I don't mean that facetiously, either. I mean she's truly psychotic."

"You may be right, but that territory belongs to someone else. Other than the subsequent trial, we're pretty much finished with it."

She rolled her eyes, trying to make light of his comments and the situation. "Oh, no...*another* trial. This is where I came in." His reassuring hug told her that this time everything would be all right.

They walked upstairs. "Is it really over?"

"Yes—it's really over."

She smiled at him, showing her admiration. "That was very good detective work, Mr. Harrison."

"You were very good, too, Miss Ford. You put yourself out there acting as bait to bring Doreen into the open. You kept her talking so that we could record her entire confession." The vision of Doreen threatening to snap Tara's neck popped into his mind. He vividly recalled all the fear that rushed through him. That had been the most devastating moment of his life. Nothing had frightened him as much as the prospect of her being injured or worse yet...killed.

He drew her body tightly against his as if to confirm that she was there and unharmed. He ran his fingers through the silky strands of her hair, then caressed her shoulders. They stood in the bedroom, arms around each other, silently reveling in the closeness and the emotion it produced. He loved her. No amount of thought or uncertainty could change that. She had allowed him to face up to his past failure and overcome his personal fears. Because of her he had been able to open his heart again and find the love he thought had been lost to him for all time.

He slipped her blouse off her shoulders, down her arms and dropped it to the floor. A minute later they had each removed their clothes and had snuggled into the comfort of the bed. He held her in his arms. He needed the closeness and the warmth. He needed Tara Ford. The emotions that filled him were stronger than anything he had ever experienced. He kissed her on the forehead and continued to hold her.

Tara snuggled close to him. It seemed like such a long time ago when Brad had first approached her, told her she was in danger and said he would protect her. She hadn't trusted him or really believed what he said, but it had proved to be true. It had been a difficult decision to trust him on face value. In fact, it had been the most difficult decision of her life. It had also been the best decision of her life, one she would never regret.

And now the nightmare was finally over. She still felt safe and protected in his arms. It was where she wanted to be, a place she wanted to stay forever. She loved him, but was this where it was going to end? The danger that brought them together no longer existed. They were each free to go back to their own life. She rested her hand against his chest, the feel of his heartbeat providing a warmth and closeness that wrapped around her like a cocoon.

"Brad?"

He kissed her forehead. "Yes?"

"What happens now? Where do we go from here?" Then came the question she feared the most. "Or is this the end of the line? I go back to my job and you go back to yours and life goes back to the way it was before?"

He knew it was a reality he needed to face. "I…" He held her tightly, drawing strength from the love he carried inside him, but not sure how to deal with it. "We've been thrown together in highly unusual circumstances with everything around us moving at top speed. I haven't given much thought to the future beyond resolving this case." He swallowed hard in an attempt to shove down the panic that started to build inside him. "Maybe…uh…maybe we should slow down a little, get to really know each other first then see where things go."

"Oh…I see." The disappointment crashed inside her followed closely by the pain. She loved him and nothing could change that, but obviously it was a one-sided love. She would have to face that reality and get on with her life by herself. She had once wondered what life with Brad Harrison would be like. Now she had to imagine what life with only her memories of Brad Harrison would be like.

He had not made her any promises, had not led her on. She had fallen in love with him with her eyes wide open and fully conscious of the circumstances. A sob caught in her throat. She couldn't allow him to see the depth of her despair. She sat up and reached for her robe. Her world and all her hopes for the future had just crashed around her and she wasn't sure if she was going to recover. Another sob tried to work its way out. She pulled on her robe. She felt so very alone.

The moment she turned away, Brad experienced the most intense sensation, an overwhelming sense of loss that flooded through him harder and faster than anything he had ever known, leaving total devastation in its wake. It was a reality he knew he would never be able to live with. He had to make a commitment or risk losing her. The commitment scared him, but not nearly as much as the thought of losing her.

He raised up on one elbow. "Tara?" She slipped out of bed and tied the robe's sash around her waist. There was no answer from her. His panic started as a small spot deep inside him, but quickly spread until it touched every part of his life.

He reached out and grabbed her arm, pulling her back onto the bed. He wrapped her in his embrace. Her lack of response sent another tremor of panic through his body. He swallowed down his fears and said the words he knew he should have said earlier.

"I love you, Tara. No matter what happens, I love you. I don't want to lose you."

The tears welled in her eyes. They were tears of joy. He loved her. He had said the words and they were the most beautiful thing she had ever heard. "Oh, Brad...I love you, too."

"Do you think you could be happy married to a deputy marshal?"

"Yes...yes, I could be very happy married to a deputy marshal."

"Then let's make it official next week. Is that all right with you?"

"It's more than all right."

"Let's seal that promise with a kiss." Brad captured her mouth with all the passion coursing through his body. His fears and concerns disappeared, to be replaced with a happiness that he knew would last a lifetime.

HARLEQUIN®
INTRIGUE®
and
DEBRA WEBB

invite you for a special consultation at the

For the most
private investigations!

Look for the next installment in this exciting
ongoing series!

PERSONAL PROTECTOR
April 2002

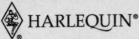

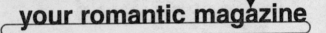

This Mother's Day
Give Your Mom
A Royal Treat

Win a fabulous one-week vacation in
Puerto Rico for you and your mother at
the luxurious Inter-Continental San Juan
Resort & Casino. The prize includes round
trip airfare for two, breakfast daily and a
mother and daughter day of beauty
at the beachfront hotel's spa.

INTER·CONTINENTAL
San Juan
RESORT & CASINO

Here's all you have to do:

Tell us in 100 words or less how your
mother helped with the romance in your
life. It may be a story about your engagement,
wedding or those boyfriends when you were
a teenager or any other romantic advice
from your mother. The entry will be judged
based on its originality, emotionally
compelling nature and sincerity.
See official rules on following page.

Send your entry to:
Mother's Day Contest

In Canada
P.O. Box 637
Fort Erie, Ontario
L2A 5X3

In U.S.A.
P.O. Box 9076
3010 Walden Ave.
Buffalo, NY
14269-9076

Or enter online at www.eHarlequin.com

PRROY